DIMMED LIGHTS

DIMMED LIGHTS

ON STAGE TRILOGY
BOOK THREE

NAMIAR TOPIT

Content Warning

This book, and especially the trilogy as a whole, contains themes that might not be suitable for all audiences. Including and not limited to: profanity, nudity, explicit sex, mental health issues such as PTSD, violence, and substance abuse.

Please proceed with caution.

Copyright © 2022 Namiar Topit
All rights reserved.

ISBN 978-952-94-6491-3

Edited by L. Jo King
Cover design by Fay Lane

Disclaimer: This is a work of fiction. All names, characters, places, businesses, and events are a product of the author's imagination or used in a fictitious manner. Any resemblance to actual persons, living or dead, or actual events is purely coincidental.

For Joe
I swear I named the character before I met you

PROLOGUE: One Man War
Chris's Point of View

Despite the hangover, the sense of freedom while I darted through the front gate and entered the street beside my house for my morning jog, was everything to me. I barely even noticed the footsteps of my bodyguard—Mr. Won—following closely behind. It was a mundane task to him, a thing we had done countless previous mornings, but I loved running.

It cleared my head fairly well—and these days I really needed that.

The road was bordered with a sparse forest. When the area had been put up for sale, I'd bought all the surrounding land, so there weren't any next-door neighbors. Down the road there were some, like the kind old man that had taken care of my house with his wife when I had been in the army, then busy with GRiD. But uphill there were none until the street ended.

That end of the road, and the trail that started there where the forest thickened, was my goal. I took it slow at first, warming up the stiff muscles in my legs. But when I reached the end, I charged ahead full speed. The wind hit my face, and the refreshing smell of the forest after a rain woke up my senses. The rhythm of my footsteps erased the stiffness of my shoulders. The air up in the mountains was just so much clearer than in the polluted city below.

The trail twisted and turned ahead of me, always heading higher and higher. My lungs started to burn after only a short while, but I didn't slow down. If I was weary enough, I wouldn't have the brain capacity to think.

Not thinking was good.

Trees started getting sparser and sparser before I entered a familiar clearing. My feet slowed down at first, then I let myself halt completely when I reached the small, fenced view deck on the cliff. Thoroughly spent, I plopped down to sit, marveling at the sight that opened below me. The view took even the last bits of my breath away, just like it had done the first time I had discovered the place.

From up there, I could practically see the whole of Seoul, at least on a clear day like that one. The countless high-rise buildings on each side of the lazily flowing Han River. The bridges that crossed over it. I could even vaguely spot the area where LBR Entertainment's headquarters stood. And the area where our dorm had been located until, well, *that* night...when everything changed.

Refusing to let my mind wander even close to that black hole of misery in my memories, I focused on evening out my ragged breath. Meanwhile, my eyes scanned my surroundings—a habit that stuck to me from my time in the army. Mr. Won was on his phone, probably texting with his wife. Guilt stabbed my chest as I once again remembered he was away from his family, trapped to be my guard dog up in the mountains...while his wife was due any day now with a new addition to their family. Thankfully it wasn't me who had insisted that he would be here, but all the others that were still freaking out about Min-ho getting away.

Sighing, I stood up and took off—this time taking it a bit slower—following the trail even further up before it started going downhill. Curving back, the trail ended at the brink of my neighborhood. As I'd have to go past a few other houses to round back at mine, I wore a bucket hat and sunglasses as a slight disguise. Not that it mattered, since no-one would've believed it was Chris from GRiD with the awful scars. The news hadn't caught up on that yet since I'd managed to slip out of the hospital unnoticed.

As I jogged leisurely through the narrow, crooked, and curvy roads, the neighborhood was only starting to wake up. Most of the houses seemed quiet and still. I nodded to a man that was picking up his morning paper with a coffee mug in tow. I smiled when he nodded back—it almost seemed like I was already a familiar figure on these roads.

The convenience store owner was just opening his shop at the corner and even waved at me while I passed by. I waved back. Maybe I'd get used to the quiet life around there, in the mountains, away from the hustle and bustle of central Seoul.

Maybe I should just retire once and for all.

I jogged past the last corner to end up back on my street. Not a single one of my closest neighbors were up at this hour, so that was basically it for my social life of the day. For the rest of it, I'd probably spend inside the walls of the prison I had built for myself, away from everything.

Apparently I hadn't tortured myself enough yet; I opened my garage door with the small remote that was attached to my keychain. Mr. Won simply ran past me, straight to the main house. He was probably heading to shower. I stepped in my garage, passing by my most precious belonging—a pitch-black Lamborghini—then straight through the door on the right to my gym. Glugging down the remains of water in my bottle, I tossed the backpack beside the threshold.

I'd become used to taking out my frustrations on my boxing bag over in the corner, and I started throwing some punches at it. The unfortunate thing was that the gym still had one mirror left. It got easier and easier to put more and more power through my fists, as every time the bag moved too much, it revealed a glimpse of the monstrosity that was my face nowadays. And the sight, it just reminded me of what I had become inside too—a monster.

It started a vicious cycle of self-hatred, and sooner than I'd initially thought, I lost control. Kicking the bag with full force, I sent it swinging uncontrollably. Of course, with my incredible luck, the bottom of it landed straight to the one and only remaining mirror in the whole gym, breaking the lower half of it. Miraculously, about half of the mirror survived, and only the bottom fell off to the floor, shattering into a million teeny-tiny pieces.

Closing my eyes, I tried to calm down a bit, fighting back the urge to fall completely apart. When I found the strength, I started sweeping the floor, gathering the pieces of glass to one spot. Good thing I was still wearing my sneakers.

A knock on the door startled me in the midst of it. Mr. Won didn't bother to wait for a response though when he barged in, eyeing the mess around me. He wasn't even the slightest bit surprised. I wished he would've at least pretended to be.

"Another one?" he asked with a nonchalant tone.

"Yeah, I'll handle it," I replied, turning my gaze back to the floor.

"No, let me," he ordered sternly and pried the broom off my hands. "You've got...um...visitors. They're coming up the street as we speak."

I turned to look at the screen on the wall that broadcasted live feed from four different safety cams around my premises. Quickly my eyes found the bottom right corner that showed my front yard and the gate. It didn't take long to see what Mr. Won had already indicated.

Two police cars made their way through the gate that Mr. Won had already let open for them. As soon as the doors opened, four armed-to-their-teeth policemen swiftly took their places in a stiff formation, mostly paying attention to the front door. Only one of them was keeping his eyes on the garage.

"Seems like it's happening today," I stated, my voice as dead as I felt inside.

"It is," Mr. Won confirmed, already focused on his task of cleaning the pieces of the broken mirror from the floor.

"I guess I'm gonna go then. Can you turn on the alarms on your way out?"

"Of course. And you...take care."

I nodded at him and sighed. As unpleasant as it was to admit it, I had known this day would come the whole time. Right from that second when I had lost myself in a senseless one-man war against a lunatic. I wasn't exactly in the position to have the right to complain. Well, if you looked at the bright side, at least it probably meant they had finally caught the bastard.

Presumed Innocent

48 hours.

It was a long time to stare at the white brick wall of my cell in the detention facility. It was even longer time to go in and out of countless interrogations and then meetings with my label's lawyer, Jae-beom. But most importantly, it was a hell of a long time to try to evade small talk with an overly friendly, stinky, and balding ahjussi, who was my cellmate. Eventually he'd resorted to intensely staring at my face.

"Ah!" The old chap stood up abruptly, pointed at me with his index finger, eyes wide. "Now I recognize you!"

I grit my teeth together. "Great."

"You're in that boy band...uh..." He proceeded to shake that index finger of his directly in front of my nose and rub his temple. "Grind?"

My jaw hurt from gritting my teeth together even harder. "GRiD."

"What happened to your face?"

I closed my eyes for a brief few seconds to calm down. At this rate the whole cell-block would know who I was. If they didn't know already. Admittedly this old chap was a little slow. "Ahjussi, can you possibly keep your voice down?"

He jumped a little at my words and glanced around as if he'd only then realized where we were.

"Oh, uh, mianhae," he said, scratching the back of his neck.

He sat down and kept quiet from then on. And just like that, the longest 48 hours of my life continued to trudge forward. At least the interrogations were over.

48 hours was the exact amount of time they would be able to keep me in custody. Not that they didn't try to keep me longer. They even filed a detention warrant on me so they could've kept me locked up until the trial, and I will never forget the exact wording they used to justify it:

Defendant poses a substantial risk of harm to others as manifested by recent behavior causing harm and is likely in the near future to cause physical injury to another person.

And I mean...fair. The police didn't give two shits about Min-ho deliberately having tried to take many lives that night. We had both suffered injuries—and I did beat the guy to the pulp—therefore we were both charged for assault. That was the way around here. And they were right. The only difference between the two of us was purely...money. I at least had Jae-beom. Well, that, and maybe the fact that Min-ho was facing just so many more charges on top of the assault.

I still regretted nothing. Min-ho deserved it. Annoyingly, that didn't make me feel any less disgusted at myself.

Jae-beom made sure I wouldn't be kept in custody until the trial. It was a relief, I admit, even though I wasn't sure I deserved such privileged treatment. The photos of Min-ho's face that they had shown at the first interrogation haunted me. There was no denying that I had beat the guy to the brink of death, and I certainly hadn't expected the...*rage*...that had emerged from within me.

A sigh escaped me. Must've been the hundredth one for that day. It didn't matter that I didn't like myself very much at the moment—regardless I should've been released any minute. The problem was that there were no clocks in the cell so I had zero idea of when those fucking agonizingly long 48 hours would be over.

My eyes were about to involuntarily shut down when one of the guards finally opened the cell and called my name. I don't think I'd ever woken up so fast in my life. I was on my feet in half of a second, hands already stretched out in front of me for the inevitable restraints.

"Eager to get out, huh?" the officer asked, letting me see a glimpse of a half-smile.

I didn't reply. If someone wasn't eager to get out of a place like that, I'd be more worried. As the dude was locking up my wrists and ankles to the chains, I took a last glance around the cell, hoping to never see it from the inside again. Not that there was much to see. A window in the back, all white walls, a TV that only worked from three to five in the afternoon. The smallest bathroom with a hole on the floor and a broken door in the back right corner.

"You're awfully quiet for a guy who's always yapping about something on the telly. Gay rights this, gay rights that…I wonder if you would've found a nice boyfriend here."

Okay now he was downright fucking with me. But as I knew that this was the last time in my entire life to do anything stupid, I somehow managed to stay silent. Apart from a quick "move along," the guard never bothered with any more small talk—thank fuck.

Under Korean law, I was presumed innocent until proven guilty. However, as the guard continued to push me forward, shackles attached to my wrists and ankles, I very much felt like a convicted criminal. Maybe I deserved it, though.

The way out was the same as it was in, through a high fenced corridor across the yard and onto the building in the front.

Once I was inside, unshackled and had gone through the metal detector—why the fuck I had to go through one going *out* of the facility, I had no idea—I was led into a room that I hadn't seen before. It looked like it was some kind of a waiting area. Based on the posters on the walls about the rules of visiting, I assumed it was for visitors. This time there were only two men and a woman sitting on the benches. The woman was, of course, Jiwoo, who winked at me at once when I noticed them. One of the men was Jae-beom, who I had also expected. But the other man…was Joe. Looking as handsome as ever in a pristine suit. Not a hair was out of place, and his mouth was deceivingly set into a stern line that I knew was only a facade, because his golden brown eyes still twinkled that familiar but annoying spark.

As usual, flashbacks from *that night* consumed my entire brain as soon as our eyes met. That night, his hair had definitely not been very neatly combed, and there was not a suit—or any clothing for that matter—in sight.

Yet, the question remained…what the fuck was *he* doing here?

Admittedly, there was also a small sting that hit my chest upon seeing Joe and not…well…GRiD. Was it wrong from me to expect I would've seen one of the guys there, at least? I expected I would've seen Tae. Maybe even Joonie or Minjae. At least Do-hyun would've been curious enough to be there when I was released?

And if it had to be a bodyguard, why wasn't it Mr. Won?

Before I dwelled too far into wondering why my welcome home -party consisted specifically of these people, I was handed a cardboard box where I had left my stuff on the way in, and a bigger bag.

"What's this?" I asked the front office lady, holding up the bag.

"It was delivered to you earlier. Change of clothes and stuff, looked like."

Curious, I tossed the cardboard box to the side and opened the bag to take a look inside. Mr. Won had to have packed it before leaving my place—my phone, wallet and keys were right on top. Seemed like the rest of it was filled with clothes.

It warmed my heart that Mr. Won had gone through such lengths, only to realize it had probably been someone from LBR Entertainment ordering him around. If there was one rule in the world of the Korean music industry, it was that not one idol would be caught red-handed wearing sweaty and ragged workout clothes in public. No, not even after getting himself locked up during morning workout.

I asked the secretary if there was an actual place to change clothes. She pointed me to one of the public restrooms…ugh. I guess I was wearing the scent of urine and shit as a cologne for the day then.

Annoyed, I yanked the door open and stepped inside. Swiftly, I made my way to the cleanest looking stall, trying not to concentrate too hard on my surroundings. The outfit was pretty basic: some black ripped jeans, a plain black t-shirt, and my burgundy leather jacket. Thankfully there was also a beanie to hide my mess of light brown hair, big-ass sunglasses, a selection of underwear—some luxuries not everyone would've thought to pack while in a hurry. One of the reasons I liked Mr. Won so much: he was efficient, didn't invade my personal space, and handled everything with such a level of professionalism that it managed to surprise even me from time to time.

After I was done changing, I jammed the workout clothes—box and all—in the trash bin near the sinks along with the bag. The clothes were shitty anyway, and let's face it, I'd probably ruin them for good anyway when I attempted washing clothes the next time. The wallet I put in my back pocket; the keys found their place in my leather jacket's pocket. I didn't even bother to take a glance at the phone before stuffing it in one of the pockets as well.

I washed my hands and even dared to take a look at my reflection in the mirror. For a moment I was caught up in staring at the bright red scars before I noticed a man standing in the corner behind my back—Joe. My heart beating abnormally fast, I spun around.

"Sweet Jesus don't creep up on people like that," I muttered and clutched the front of my t-shirt. "And can you stop breathing down my neck?"

"Unfortunately not," he said, with a stern, rigidly stiff face and tone that said I was in no place to ask questions.

It pissed me off, but I decided to swallow the annoyance for now and focus on getting the hell out of there. I exited the restrooms after shaking my head slightly. The secretary approached me with a thick paper bundle in her hands. With a smile, she handed them to me, and said, "You're good to go, Mr. Cho. But don't leave the country, and stay out of more trouble, hmm?"

As I nodded politely at the secretary, Jiwoo materialized behind me. Her hand landed on my shoulder, and she squeezed.

"Let's get the fuck out of here," she mouthed in my ear and let one of her arms stay circled around my neck as she started dragging me towards the exit, her heels click-clacking on the linoleum floor.

I rarely ever heard her curse like that, but it certainly fit for the theme of the day. Because "fuck" was what rolled down my tongue too, as soon as we walked around the corner and I saw the absolute *sea* of reporters outside with my own two eyeballs, through the windows beside double doors.

"Now remember, I'll do most of the talking," Jae-beom said as we inexorably approached the door. "Give your statement, the one we went through earlier, but that's it."

"Sure."

I was surprised that my voice didn't shake.
Here we fucking go I guess.

Sharp Dressed

"—First and foremost, our goal is to settle this matter as soon as possible to give the opportunity for our artists to start healing from the tragic events that have affected the group as a whole, but especially Mr. Shin Joon-seok and Mr. Cho Chang-ho here," Jae-beom said and gave me a nod. "For now, we place our trust in the justice system."

Jae-beom pushed me a little forward, and there was a brief, blinding rush of flashes going off when every single camera turned directly to my face and a gazillion mics and other sorts of recording devices were shoved in front of my face. My throat was drier than a desert, but I knew I had to get it working because we needed the media on our side—or that's what Jae-beom told me and I didn't dare to oppose the man, hoping he'd keep me out of prison. So, I gulped, straightened my back, and imagined this was just a regular, perfectly normal interview I'd done countless times before.

"The last few days have not been easy, by any means, and this is still far from over. Nevertheless, I would like to take this opportunity to apologize to my fans—and the GRiD Crew as a whole—for making you worried, but also thank you for all the encouraging messages that have been forwarded to me. I'm also grateful for the support I've received from LBR Entertainment and all our staff during these trying times.

"I will be spending the time until the settlement or possible trial, reflecting on my life and values." I took a deep breath before the last and hardest part of my statement. "For the time being, GRiD will continue participating in the pre-scheduled activities without me. Thank you."

As I performed a nearly 90-degree bow towards the reporters, the most enthusiastic ones already started shouting questions. Each of them felt like a stab in the chest, but I ignored them. I ignored them all. Instead, I straightened my back and started pushing through the crowd with Joe and Jiwoo—the latter shouting "No more comments" towards the reporters.

But ignoring them unfortunately didn't mean I couldn't hear the questions shot my way like arrows through my back.

"Will you leave the entertainment industry?"

"How was it behind bars?"

"Will your face ever see full recovery?"

"Do you think your proven skills in martial arts will weigh against you?"

"Are you quitting GRiD?"

"Do you see yourself as guilty?"

The relief was immense, to say the least, when I finally crashed on the backseat of Joe's black BMW. I saw Jiwoo heading towards Jae-beom's Mercedes, so it was just Joe and me then.

"So, what are you doing here?" I asked.

"Giving you a lift," Joe replied. "Or would you rather have taken a taxi?"

"Nah, thanks. I'm just wondering where Mr. Won is."

"Their new family member arrived yesterday."

"Oh." So it happened. "Have you heard if everything went well?"

"Yes, they're all good. It's a girl."

Joe started driving, skillfully maneuvering the vehicle through the crowd. Once the last of it was behind us and we started inching forward in the busy streets, I finally dared to huff out a long breath of relief.

"You okay back there?" Joe asked and glanced at me in the rearview mirror.

"I guess," I mumbled and rolled my shoulders back, trying to relax. It would take us at least two hours to get to my place.

Both Joe and I fell silent after that.

It seemed like years since we'd last talked to each other anyway—like, really talked. Maybe at the after-party when we were done shooting the latest music videos. But that was ancient history now, from some other time period when everyone was still innocent, and shit had not hit the fan...except for Do and Min. I remembered I had felt invincible, almost like the world was only there for me to take. There was no way it could've gotten downhill more than it had already gone with the Domino scandal, right?

Wrong.

It had gotten so much worse.

In such a short time.

And then I was there. Barely evading jail, *if* I was evading jail. Right on the brink of acquiring an alcoholic status. Sitting in the backseat of a car that was driven by a man that I wasn't the hugest fan of, at the moment. Heading home, to endless boredom, alcohol, nightmares, and self-loathing.

Except we weren't heading towards my house. As far as I knew, we were supposed to be on the highway, not deeper into downtown. Yet we were completely surrounded by even higher high-rise buildings than before. Instead of a highway, my eyes saw malls. Offices. Brand new glass-covered buildings.

With an unsettling feeling hitting the bottom of my stomach, I glanced at Joe. He looked as relaxed and all-business as before. Still, I couldn't stop my heart from starting to pound at an increasingly rapid pace. My palms clammed up and rubbing them against the jeans in hopes of drying them, didn't help all that much. Geez, talk about traumas on riding in the backseat of a car.

"This isn't the way to my place," I said, barely keeping the panic from seeping through to my voice.

Before I went into a full panic mode, Joe assured me. "I know, I just thought you'd want to get some actual food."

The thought of decent food made my stomach rumble. He was not wrong. "Oh. Yeah, that sounds great."

"Sorry. I should've asked."

He should've, yes, but I was more surprised that he had even thought about it. Why did he even care? He was just my lift. It was not like our little one night stand had changed anything between us. He hadn't even been there when I woke up after the deed had been done.

We stopped at my favorite noodle place near our old dorms. Shortly after, Joe came back with a take-out container filled with janchi guksu and some sodas. I practically inhaled the food while Joe played with his phone, and then we continued our drive towards my place. It was a route I had driven a million times myself—from the dorms to my own place.

The only surprise was that I couldn't take my eyes off Joe.

He relaxed around half-way through, taking a more comfortable position and turning on the radio. It was weird to see the transformation, as he had been this distant, all-business, stiff person at the station and during the ride. Quite the opposite of what he had been before all the drama that had happened. The man had changed…then again, so had the rest of us.

I tried to tell myself that watching him like a hawk was only to see if he'd turn mad all of a sudden and maybe drive the car off a cliff or something. Was I being paranoid? Definitely yes. But after all that had happened, could you really blame me?

But then I found my eyes trailing on his sharp jawline, lingering on his hand when he loosened his tie a bit and opened the top button of his pure white dress-shirt. I wanted to mess up his pristine hair. Then his other, veiny, calloused hand landed to rest on the gear stick as we accelerated on the highway, and that was the only thing in the world that I saw.

His hands were huge. I could personally attest that it was true what they said—that the size of a man's hand directly correlated with what they had inside their pants. I'd had to walk sideways for a week after Joe had his way with me.

Momentarily, my mind was filled with lewd images, and I had to avert my gaze. I could still feel his hands even after all this time and drama, those thick fingers tight around my shaft, working wonders. My eyes landed on my own hands that rested in my lap. My hands were average. Reasonably sized, even. Well okay, at least they were not *tiny,* per se…

Sooner than I thought, we turned to my home street, and I had to force my mind to clear up.

"Which one is it?" Joe asked, eyeing the houses beside the road.

"The last one."

He nodded. When we were close enough, I used the remote on my keychain to open the gate and Joe curved the BMW to my small front yard. I shoved the sunglasses further up my nose and opened the door as soon as the car halted, dreaming about a hot shower. However, I didn't get to take one step towards my house, before someone slammed against me full force, almost sending me right back to the backseat of Joe's BMW. Even the air escaped my lungs.

"I missed you," Joonie said and squeezed the living shit out of me. "Even got yourself arrested, fucking brat."

It was like I'd come home. Like *home*-home, where I was supposed to be. I couldn't help but inhale the familiar strawberry scent of Joonie's hair—that was surprisingly blond instead of pink? My eyes fluttered shut for a brief second while my hand circled around his tiny waist. "Now whose fault is that?"

Joonie took a sharp breath through his gritted teeth and let me loose.

"Just kidding," I said and pulled him back into a hug, planting my chin on his shoulder.

Then finally, I registered all the others standing just a little to the side. Tae had hands shoved in his jeans' pockets, a smile beaming on his face—a semi-odd sight. I guessed he and Joonie had resolved things between them. Do and Minjae were holding hands, Minjae looking like he was about to pounce on me as well, while Do held him back. Even Seong-gi was there, leaning against my garage's wall, puffing out a cloud of smoke—now that man never seemed to smile, but his eyes sparkled in the sunshine. At least a little bit.

"What are you guys doing here?"

It was Do-hyun who stepped forward, handing me a green grapefruit soju bottle. "We're celebrating your freedom, obviously."

I took the bottle with the hand that wasn't circled around the waist of Joonie who still clung to me, but grimaced. "I mean...there's still the settlement or maybe even a trial left. It's not over yet."

"Yes, we know. But we're halfway there, right?" Tae said. "Come on, we've all been through a lot lately. We should celebrate the small wins."

I gave it a second of doubt, but it wasn't like Tae was wrong. "Fine but let me shower first."

"Come on, let me make something for us to eat while you shower and then we can all talk," Joonie said and started walking me towards the front door. "It's been a while."

Damn right it'd been a while. I hadn't even realized how much I'd missed the guys.

Guard Dog

"Sweet Jesus, I have not been this full in ages." I leaned back. The urge to open the top button of my jeans was almost getting the better of me after having gobbled down everything there was on the table. Joonie's cooking was superior.

"I'm not sure how you've survived on your own this long. Yes, I found your stash of ruined pans in the cupboard." Joonie said and toyed with his wine glass, an annoying smirk lingering on his lips. "Y'all remember the time he almost burned down the first dorm? It took us weeks to air out the…um…*fine* odor."

While the others laughed their lungs out, I didn't find that memory all that amusing. I had only forgotten the omelet on the stove for a minute, tops. Next thing I knew, there was a pillar of thick black smoke instead of a nicely fried fold of eggs and vegetables.

"While I'm glad you got the memory issues worked out, some things could've stayed forgotten," I muttered.

No one heard me through their cheerful laughter. I didn't mind. But as much as I loved these guys, I had been alone for a while now and having them around was…a lot. And though they did help me forget some of the shit I was wallowing in, it was all always in the back of my mind.

I needed a stronger drink than soju and escaped to the kitchen for a breather. Luckily there was still some whisky left there. I poured some on top of a single rock of ice.

"Pour me one too?" Tae's voice almost made me jump, but I kept my cool.

"Sure…" I grabbed another glass and another piece of ice from the freezer. It was not like Tae to drink that much at all, let alone whisky. But I didn't question him—if anyone understood needing a strong drink after everything we'd been through, it was me. I slid the halfway filled up glass across the kitchen island and watched Tae sit across from me.

"Thanks," he said and took a small sip. "I actually wanted to talk with you."

It wasn't like I hadn't been expecting that. I had, after all, avoided the guys for a while now, and had announced it for the press that I was taking a break from the entertainment industry without even talking it through with Tae.

I nodded. "I know."

"'*GRiD will continue participating in the pre-scheduled activities without me,*'" Tae cited my little statement, raising one of his eyebrows. "Were you serious?"

All of a sudden, I found the subtle pattern of the white marble countertop real interesting. At the very least, I couldn't look Tae in the eyes. I was scared of what I'd find there.

"Yes. Also, Jae-beom thought it would be the best. For now."

Tae stiffened. "You're not planning on quitting for good, are you?"

For a second I completely froze, my chest tightening. When it was the faceless reporters asking that, it had already taken a hit on me…but having Tae ask the same question hit my chest ten times harder. While I didn't have to reply to the reporters, I knew I had to answer Tae. "Honestly? I don't know."

Tae let out a long breath. "Now that's a relief."

"What do you mean?"

"Uncertainty I can work with," he said and took another sip of his whisky.

I followed his example, the strong beverage burning my throat in a very satisfying way. I needed the drink for the conversation. My eyes met Tae's briefly, but I could hold his gaze and instead stared down at the honey colored liquor twirling when I swayed the glass in my hand. "Work with?"

"If you'd wanted to quit for good, I wasn't sure how I could convince you to continue. Come back to work. We've really missed you. Of course until the trial you wouldn't be able to appear publicly with us but once Jae-beom clears your name—"

I had a hard time believing all that, but I also knew Tae wouldn't lie about it. If he'd wanted me out, he'd already said so. But when it came to Jae-beom clearing my name, I couldn't stop myself from cutting Tae off. "And what if he doesn't? Clear my name?"

"He will."

"But Tae, I'm sure you've realized I'm not exactly the perfect idol candidate anymore," I said and touched the edge of my scar with the tips of my fingertips. "And I *did* beat up the guy."

"The scar only gives you character—"

"—I wonder if the label feels the same—"

"—and I would've done the same, or worse, if I'd been in that situation." Tae shuddered. "Honestly I would've just offed Min-ho right then and there."

I grimaced. Now *that* I believed one thousand percent. The image of the complete wreck Tae had been in the hospital when Joonie was still unconscious, was still extremely clear in my head. One moment he had been ready to murder people and the next he was a hysterical, sobbing mess. Or just staring ahead with empty eyes. It had been painful to witness.

"I'm still just not that sure I'm fit to be the teenage dream anymore." I had been categorized as a "substantial risk," after all.

"Well, you don't have to answer now," Tae said and laid his glass on the table. "Just know that you'll always be welcomed back."

I said nothing, as there wasn't much else to say.

"Also," Tae added and picked out a letter of some sort from his jeans' pocket. "I'll leave you this—maybe it'll convince you to get back at it better than I ever could."

Curious, I picked it up and opened it—the first thing I saw being the Billboard logo. "Billboards? Really?"

"Yes, really."

"Crap."

"I'm taking it you haven't read our group chat in a while then?"

Oops. I'd meant to, numerous times, but I'd always failed having the courage to even open the phone after the incident. I hadn't exactly been a people person lately. "Nope."

"You really should sometimes," Tae said and shook his head. "In short, we've been nominated 'Top Social Artist' and 'Top Duo/Group.' Plus, we've been asked to perform."

"No way," I breathed out, my heartbeat accelerating at every syllable Tae had spewed out. "No fucking way."

"Yes fucking way."

"But I'm not even allowed out of the country. How will this change anything?"

"As I said, Jae-beom is on this. Now moving that aside, there's still one more thing..."

"Shoot." I set the invitation letter aside. I had plenty of time to freak out about it later. But I was curious—what was more important than fucking Billboards? "What did you have in mind?"

"Well, since we still don't have a new dorm, I was wondering if Joe could stay here with you."

I froze, then slowly lifted my eyes up to meet Tae's. I couldn't believe my ears. Tae, however, had leaned back in his chair, relaxed, as if he hadn't given me the death sentence only a second ago.

But I also couldn't show Tae how…uneasy…even the mere thought of having Joe here, in my house, having to see him every single day, made me. It wasn't even only the fact that we'd had a one night stand that bothered me, but the fear of repeating it. Not because the sex was bad or anything—quite the opposite. But what if I caught feelings? Or randomly threw myself at him during one of my…bad nights. It was already humiliating that Mr. Won knew about my recent sleeping problems and anger outbursts, let alone the panic attacks, but to have *Joe* here to witness it all too…no way.

I resisted the urge to shudder and simply asked, "Why?"

Tae shrugged. "It would make me sleep better at night if you had someone up here with you, after…well, everything. We also came to a mutual understanding with LBR that we need to keep the security level high even though Min-ho's caught. Better get used to having them around at all times."

"But why Joe?"

"Mr. Won was promoted to be the managing director of their company, as he needs a desk job anyway due to the additional family member having arrived. I don't particularly trust the new ones enough yet to have them here without supervision."

"What, is there something wrong with having my fine self around?" Joe asked, the tiniest hint of glimmer in his warm brown eyes as he leaned against the door frame.

I had not noticed he'd appeared there, and let me tell you just…the way I almost choked on the whisky I was sipping.

Barely managing to hold myself together, I heaved out a "Yes, plenty."

"Too bad, 'cause you're stuck with me, shortie."

Shortie?

"See, you're already getting along just fine," Tae said, sort of snickered and stood up. "It's settled then," he concluded and walked away. Just like that.

"Wait..." I tried to holler at Tae's back, but it was all to no avail.

He was gone. And with a short smirk, so was Joe, having joined the others in the living room.

I shook my head and rubbed my temple. I was too tired for this bullshit at this time in the worst week I'd ever had. It seemed like logic and reasoning had completely abandoned these people, leaving me the only sane person around. I was done handling all these curveballs. And now I was also stuck with Joe?

When I finally gathered myself, plastered a hopefully cheerful expression and walked over to the living room, I noticed that everyone was gathering their things and clearing the dining table.

"You're going?"

"Yeah, it's getting kinda late," Minjae said and handed me a pile of plates. "And since Seong-gi's our only driver now that Joe's staying here, we can't expect him to wait for us the whole night."

I glanced outside and saw the old chap smoking another cigarette, looking incredibly bored.

"Yeah, that might be better," I said and started walking right back to the kitchen with the pile of plates.

"Unless you want us to stay over?" Joonie asked following me to the kitchen with a tray filled with what was left of the food. Which, by the way, wasn't much. It meant I had to cook for myself again the next day forwards. Yuck.

As for Joonie's question, I did actually ponder it for a little. On the one hand, their presence had made my mood ten times better and I had missed them, but on the other I didn't want them to figure out what a mess I had become. And I only had two bedrooms, so it would've been a pain in the ass to figure out a place to sleep for everyone. "Nah, it's okay. I'll survive."

We both dropped the dishes on the island, and Joonie grabbed me into another hug. "Just know that you can always call me."

"Sure," I replied and headed back to fetch more dishes from the living room. I knew he meant that. But I also wasn't about to bother him with all my crap this close after he'd healed enough to get his memories back in the first place. I was usually a bit of a dick, admittedly, but I wasn't *that* inconsiderate.

Once everything was cleaned up, I walked them out and watched them pack into Tae's SUV with a bit of a heavy heart. I wasn't sure when I'd see them the next time, as I still had to decide what to do with the work stuff, and they were every bit like family to me as was my actual family. I was glad they all seemed to be okay. I would've missed living in a dorm with them if it wasn't for my…nightly problems.

I stared at the receding taillights as long as I heard footsteps in the gravel, going towards the main building. And if I wanted this living together thing to work out between Joe and me, I needed to put at least *some* distance between us.

"And where the hell do you think you're going?" I asked.

"Er… inside?" Joe asked, pointing at my front door with his thumb.

I walked a step past him in the stairs before turning to look at him. It slightly threw me off my game, how we were the same height then—our faces on the exact same level. Yes, while he was standing a step lower than me. His eyes were dangerous from that proximity. There was this golden halo near the irises before they faded into such a dark brown it was nearly black.

Damn. His eyes just about managed to distract me from what I was trying to say.

It pissed me off. With what rights was he allowed to be this attractive? I seriously needed to remind my brain that whatever there had been between us weeks back, that had been a mere one night stand and absolutely nothing more.

"Oh no, you've got it all wrong."

"How so?"

"You see, guard dogs stay in the doghouse," I said, forcing as much venom in my voice as humanly possible and clicked the remote again to open the garage door. There were some gym mats in there somewhere that would keep him comfortable enough. The hell he was getting to stay inside.

I threw the remote past a very dumbfounded Joe—I had a spare one inside. It landed in the middle of the front yard. A small victorious smile might've tugged the corners of my lips up as Joe looked even more lost.

"Fetch, Fifi," I said, stepped inside and slammed the door shut.

Recyclable

It completely surprised me how Joe complied with the whole garage thing so easily. Which was why I kept glancing through the windows every time I passed one while getting ready to bed, and jumped at the slightest sound that even remotely resembled someone knocking on the door. Two times I even went to look, but there was nobody behind the door.

Even when I went to bed and started my new nightly routine of either not sleeping at all, immediately waking up to a nightmare, or soaking in my own sweat due to a panic attack, my eyes were constantly drawn to the window. If I pretended to sleep just right, my head slightly turned to my right, I could see the outline of the garage and most of the yard through the sheer curtain. But Joe never appeared. I spent the night startling at every slightest sound on top of the nightmares.

It was nicer to pretend to sleep in my huge comfy bed compared to the cold floor of the correctional facility, so at least I had that going for me.

Eventually I gave up on sleeping altogether around six in the morning and turned to stare straight at the window in hopes of catching even a glimpse of Joe.

Maybe…just *maybe* I had been too harsh on him. I mean, what had he done to deserve such treatment from me? The one night stand had been a mutual agreement, and I wasn't *really* that mad about his disappearance the following morning.

Surely, I could let him sleep in the guestroom—after all, I had let Mr. Won sleep there too. If it came to my nightly problems, I could just tell him to mind his own fucking business.

I grabbed my cellphone and planned to turn the screen on, for the first time in ages, to text Joe to come to breakfast or something. But there was some movement behind the curtains. Naturally, I couldn't resist the urge to look. I pulled the fabric aside an inch, maybe two, to peek through.

Down on the yard, Joe paced back and forth in the space between the garage and the main house, talking on his phone. I had a direct view, but as my bedroom was on the second floor, I thought I'd get away with some stalking and kept looking. It seemed like he was having an argument with someone, a deep frown between his eyebrows as he waved his free hand in a frustrated manner. I leaned closer, wondering what it was about…

The urge to figure it out took the better of me. As silently as I could, I reached over and cracked the ventilation window open a teeny-tiny bit. Leaning back, still having my eyes at Joe, I listened:

"I repeat, you'll have to deal with that yourself," he said to whoever he was speaking to and stopped pacing. He had his back towards me, so I couldn't see his expression, but I bet it hadn't changed much from before. "There's a reason why you're the boss now, so act like it!" he exclaimed after a short pause and resumed walking, this time along the garage wall.

I could only guess he was talking to Mr. Won. Who else would he refer to as the boss, other than himself? It sure didn't sound like he was talking with Tae either, because he was usually a little more formal with him.

"Look, I trust you with the recruitment process. Even more than myself," Joe said, lowering his voice so I really had to get close to the window to hear.

He leaned against the wall and rubbed his temple with a deep frown wrinkling down his forehead. I was taken aback quite a lot from seeing him like that, as he was normally either all business or annoyingly cheerful or flirtatious. This tired and stressed out version of him was a side I had never seen. Maybe he wasn't as unaffected by all the drama surrounding us as I had thought.

"You can keep me posted, but I'm not contributing to the subject any further, and that's the end of it," Joe concluded and ended the call before shoving the phone in his pocket. Then he let out a long sigh, his shoulders dropping as if the weight on them was wearing him down.

That's when his eyes snapped up and found mine. Heart trying to pound out of my chest, I snapped back, let the curtain drop, and rolled further away from the window on the bed, breath hitching.

Fuck. He'd caught me.

The phone buzzed on my hand. Scrunching my eyebrows, I leaned over and turned the screen on. I had to do a double take and rub my eyes once I saw the notifications though.

382 missed calls, 98 texts. Wow. I really should've stopped ignoring my phone earlier.

Once I got through the initial shock, I scrolled past the ones sent way before by my family, then Joonie, Minjae, and Tae, before I finally found the latest one which was from Joe.

Shortie...I know I'm hot and all, but there are simpler ways to stalk me than lurking at the windows...

Another text appeared when I was still reading the first one: *You know, you only have to invite me in if you wanna take a closer look ;) This dog won't bite. Much.*

Hmph. I hopped up from the bed and yanked the heavier light-blocking curtains from the sides to cover the whole window. Then I jumped back to bed, my face hitting the pillow. Hands balled into tight fists, I took some deep breaths through

35

my nose, gritting my teeth together. Embarrassment and anger fought each other within me—I couldn't decide which one irritated me more.

For all I cared, Joe could rot outside for the rest of his life. Or as long as I'd take to get rid of him. Or starve to death. Even the garage started to feel like too much of a luxury for a sly dog such as him.

What. A. Fucking. Self-centered. Douche.

I yanked on some random sweatpants, a t-shirt, and stomped downstairs, straight to the fridge. Quickly, I fished out a can of orange juice, topped over a glass, and took a sip. For a hot minute I contemplated if I should've spiked it with some alcohol or not, to get past the light hangover sooner, but then again, fresh air usually worked even better.

It was only when I sat down on my kitchen island that I spotted the invitation Tae had left me the previous night. At once, my whole irritation towards Joe all but evaporated. As if possessed, I reached for it, and in a dream like haze I opened the envelope and pulled out the two items—a letter and a card. My hands shook and time seemed to stop together with my heartbeat when I picked the card up.

BBMAs x GRiD
MGM Grand Garden Arena | Las Vegas
SUNDAY | MAY 24
Live on NBC

The invitation card was formatted as if it was a concert ticket, but the paper was heavy and one of higher quality. Most of it was matte and incredibly smooth under the touch of my fingertips. Only the iconic black letters that boldly stated "Billboard" in the right margin were glossed and embossed, making the logo stand out in a nice, subtle way.

It was paired with a more formal invitation letter, stating my whole real name and all. Seeing the words "Mr. Cho Chang-ho" so carefully typed out, slightly weirded me out—not because it wasn't written in hanja or even hangul but because I rarely ever used my real name nowadays. I was just Chris, for everyone. Well, except apparently for Billboards.

Below my name, it was stated that GRiD had been nominated for the award categories "Top Social Artist" and "Top Duo/Group." After that, there was a long and eloquent text, just for asking us to perform either "Mad Love" or "Contrast" in the main event.

So, there it was. At last. Our chance to attend and perform at Billboard Music Awards. By no means, were we the first Korean artist ever invited, but it had been our ultimate goal to be there—and maybe even win something—from day one.

To me though, it didn't matter. Now, that fancy invite that I had craved to get for years was just a bittersweet reminder of what I could lose any day now—I still wasn't so sure I could even climb on stage again. But the invitation…it haunted me…I didn't have the guts to throw it away.

It didn't stop me from trying, though. I grabbed the papers along with the envelope, walked over to the trash bin, slammed my foot on the pedal to lift the lid, and…hesitated.

I mean, I was expendable. I knew that. Yes, even though the pounding hangover headache made it hard to focus. I was only a formerly cute face that was very much replaceable.

Sure, I had learned to rap, but I couldn't come up with rhymes quite like Tae's. I could sing, but never in a million years I could hit notes as high or low as Joonie. I learned the choreographies just fine, with a few tips and tricks here and there, but I would never be a beast on stage like Minjae. I had participated in composing a couple of songs but compared to Do-hyun—who produced record-breaking hits after hits—I had nothing.

The end of my career had been written clearly on Jiwoo's face when she first saw what my face had become, already at the hospital. While Tae's words last night, about wanting me back to work had made sense, they started to make less and less sense in the harsh morning light after barely having a few minutes of sleep, when the alcohol had burned from my system leaving my mouth damp and tasting like shit.

But most importantly, I had seen the end of my career in the mirror. Even if LBR Entertainment wouldn't end my career, and the guys would welcome me back with open arms, I couldn't possibly be able to climb on stage any longer. Not with this face, and the mindset that came with it. After all, I had nearly killed a guy. With my bare hands. It was the sole reason why I couldn't sleep without downing a couple of soju bottles before bedtime these days.

So once again, I tried to let go of the papers in my hand. I didn't even understand why it was so goddamn hard to get rid of them. They were just paper. Totally recyclable. Just like me.

But as if they were glued to my hand, I couldn't drop them into the bin. After what felt like a small eternity, I gave up and walked a couple of steps back to the kitchen island. Not even realizing I had held my breath; I sighed and dropped the papers to the same spot where I had picked them up in the first place.

Pathetic.

Leaning against my hands, my palms pressed on the cold marble surface, as I tried to calm down my racing heart. It was like a vein was about to pop in my head as well. I seriously needed coffee—and that's what finally got me moving.

After brewing myself a cup of pitch-black coffee that would most likely wake up the dead, I stared at the phone laying on the counter, reluctant to deal with it yet.

But I had to.

So I turned the screen on.

There were still those same 382 missed calls. No new text messages. As the calls could wait for another short while, I decided I'd take a look at the schedule first.

For the first time in over a month, I opened up the app that held our cloud-based calendar and clicked my name to open up my personal schedule. Sighing, I slumped down on my dark, gigantic couch with the coffee cup in tow and started scrolling.

And sure enough, there it was on tomorrow's task list:

11:15
Task: BBMAs overview
Location: HQ meeting room 4.

The whole note was color-coded red on the calendar, informing me it was added to my schedule by Jiwoo. Maybe they were serious about wanting me back in the game. Maybe it wasn't a bad idea to just go to the meeting and see what was up with the whole Billboard thing. Maybe…I shouldn't give up just yet.

Last Time

I shook my head. I didn't have to decide yet. Tae had also said so. My plan was to go to the meeting and decide later. There was also the possible settlement and trial to think about. Not to even mention Joe—I seriously needed to get rid of him. Maybe I could convince Tae I didn't need anyone staying with me.

When I remembered Joe existed at all, I added a task to the morning. "6:40, morning run."

Let's see if the dog can keep up. I wondered if he had his schedule synced with mine already. I doubted it was. I *wished* it wasn't. I needed some kind of an advantage over him. Especially after this morning. Ugh.

In my sudden productivity spurt, I made an appointment for a haircut and dye as well. As I was on a roll, I might've as well squeezed in a visit to our old dorms to get myself some more clothes too—not that I had ruined half of my current clothes by attempting to use the washing machine or anything—but it was good to have options.

All in all, my schedule, which I had ignored, had been pretty much empty for a month. Now it looked almost as familiarly packed as before, at least for tomorrow. Granted, the tasks weren't usually so miscellaneous, but it was a start. I mean, I still wasn't sure I was doing this whole "getting back to work thing" in the first place, but it couldn't hurt to get myself back in somewhat of a semi-presentable shape.

Then came the most dreaded thing I needed to get done: going through the missed calls. As anticipated, the first half of the 382 calls were mostly from the other GRiD members; particularly from Joonie. The latter half was more varied, and the most persistent of them all had been my mom and Hana— my sister.

Whatever came to Mom and her countless calls, I wasn't in the mood to deal with that early in the morning. Instead, I texted her: *Calm down, I'll call you later.*

Unfortunately, I didn't realize she would be sitting by her phone, but that did come quite clear when the phone started buzzing with "Mom" flashing on the screen almost instantly after I hit "send." Ugh. If there was one thing to be said of her, it was that Cho Da-hee was a force to be reckoned with.

Grunting, I hit the green icon and lifted the phone up to my ear. "Hi Mom."

"Don't you dare to 'Hi Mom' me! First, you're involved in a car crash and then you're *getting arrested!* You're coming home this instant, young man–"

Her high pitched yelling hurt my ear, so I cut her off with a sigh.

"Really, Mom? I don't have time to come home, we're going to the Billboards next—" I slapped my forehead, cutting myself off. Didn't I just conclude I still wasn't sure about this getting back to work business? "Anyway, everything's fine now and—"

"*Fine?* Have you lost it for good? Do you even have the slightest idea how worried…"

I tuned out for the rest of her rant, despite the fact that I totally deserved it. Frankly, I was surprised that she hadn't flown all the way here to nag at me for not picking up the phone and explaining the shit I had gotten myself into.

While Mom continued to yap on and on, my eyes wandered to the window. That's when Joe appeared in the yard wearing a tracksuit and starting to stretch, which took me a little off-guard.

Huh. Looked like he really had his calendar synced with mine already.

"Look, I gotta go," I said to Mom, apparently cutting her off again.

"*Sure*," she huffed, stretching her voice which clearly told me she was annoyed. "But please come visit home as soon as possible."

"Yeah, yeah. Maybe over the next break. Call you later," I mumbled and ended the call, glancing at the clock.

It was 6:35 already.

Jumping up, I gulped the rest of the coffee down before throwing the mug in the dishwasher. Then I darted to the entrance hallway, picked up random sneakers, yanked them on, and briefly stretched inside to avoid any unnecessary socializing with Joe.

I was, after all, on a mission to ignore him completely. Thus, when I was ready, I dashed right past him to the front gate. He hollered "good morning," but I downright refused to reply.

Regardless of how many mornings I had repeated this exact same routine with Mr. Won, I had never been more aware of the footsteps following me as I was now. But when we reached the end of the road, I couldn't stop a wide grin from tugging my lips up—it was time to pick up the speed.

My feet were lighter than ever before when I darted straight into the forest. As I forced my legs to work faster and faster, the adrenaline started to rush in my veins. My mood brightened for the tiniest bit. Well—okay—by a lot.

But like everything else in my life, that didn't last long either. Instead, my annoyance levels rose off the charts soon enough when Joe kept up relatively well. Who knew he had stamina too? Or the agility to keep up through the narrow, zigzagging trail? The fact that he was essentially a full-course meal; the eyes would be the appetizer, the main course was a big pile of muscles with a huge portion of sex appeal on the side and those hands of him promised a sweet dessert, should've worked against him. Who let him be this perfect in everything?

Annoyed at myself and my own thoughts, I pushed my body past all possible limits and ran through the forest as fast as I could force my legs to move, following up the curvy, difficult trail. Somehow, it turned into a race, at least in my mind.

But although I reached the clearing with the view deck first, it didn't feel like a victory. Not when my lungs burned like they were literally on fire. I dropped to sit near the edge of the deck like a sack of potatoes, so spent my legs were shaking.

Joe sat right next to me. I was too exhausted to care.

"Damn you're fast," he huffed, as out of breath as I was.

I was too tired to remember to keep ignoring him.

"You're not too slow either. I'm surprised you can keep up," I panted as a reply. At least he was as winded as me.

"Ha, I'll beat you in a heartbeat next time. Now I know the way," he said, confidence oozing out of him. How unfair. His breath also evened out in a record time and my annoyance made a comeback. Was I getting out of shape? Leaning back on his hands, he continued, "To be fair, you're such a shortie that you have stepped three steps while I'm still taking the first one."

Hmph. "Keep on dreaming."

"Wanna bet? If I'm back through your gate first, I get the guest room. Mr. Won said there is one so don't try to bullshit me."

"Yeah? Then what's in it for me?" I asked, a grin making its way on my face. There was nothing he could've offered me that I needed. I already had everything one could ever dream of. Money, house, looks if not counting the scar…and that one he couldn't fix. Even the best plastic surgeons in the whole country hadn't given me hope. And that's saying something, we're kind of famous around these parts of the world because the plastic surgeons can work miracles. Apparently my scars were beyond repairing.

"Well...I heard you're not much of a cook, so I believe me cooking breakfast for a week would suffice— hey!" Joe offered, though I was already on my feet and darting back the same way we came in as soon as I heard the word "breakfast."

What? I missed a good breakfast. Hadn't had one after...everything. I was more than sick of the same old half-burned, half-runny eggs that I barely managed to muster up every morning with various levels of success. So, I gave myself a head start and ran down the trail.

Unfortunately, about half-way through, Joe started gaining on me. Rapidly. It might've been playing a bit dirty, but I took a couple of shortcuts through the bushes, the branches scraping my arms. It didn't help much, though, and soon Joe was right behind me. Of course, I panicked and resorted to even dirtier tactics. I knew I didn't have the slightest chance against him on even terrain, because he *was* that much taller than me. Hence, my only solution was to try and trip him.

He guessed it though and hopped over my extended foot like no big deal. Grinning. Damn, he must've wanted that guestroom bad, based on the speed he dashed forward right after.

I darted after him like my ass was on fire, but it wasn't enough. As predicted, when we hit the road I had no chance whatsoever. But damn me if I didn't put up a fight nevertheless. I ended up being only a step behind when he ran through the gate as a winner.

Both breathless, we sat down on the damp, cold, barely spring-green grass. I was so exhausted I didn't even try to sit properly. Instead, I fell down, my back hitting the ground. A light thud beside me told Joe ended up doing the same.

"Would you look at that, this old dog beat your fine ass."

I fisted a bunch of grass and threw it on Joe's annoyingly handsome, grinning face. Instantly he tried to take revenge, but I easily dodged it, the grass flying past my shoulder. Realizing I was too fast for him, he tried to pin me down. He wasn't very serious, I figured, as I easily yielded that too by rolling out of his reach and stood up.

Joe was great at pissing me off, I gave him that.

"Bring it on," I said. "You might've earned the guestroom, but I still want that breakfast."

"*Shortie*, you might be good at fighting, but don't get cocky…have you forgotten I have years of experience on you," he countered, towering over me with an amused expression.

Again, with the fucking Shortie. Ignoring him and his bullshit, I took a swing at him. He countered with ease, grabbing my wrist. As I had seen that coming, I managed to land a hit straight to his abdomen. It was rock hard under the grey t-shirt and Joe barely even flinched.

Only for a split second I was distracted by his firm fucking abs, much to my dismay, and of course Joe took advantage of it. Twisting my wrist, he spun me around and locked me tight against his body, his breath tickling my ear when he whispered, "Remember what happened last time…"

Ah, last time. Heat rushed to my face upon the flashbacks from said last time that took over my mind. Aish, he was good. In both regards—*last time* and throwing me off my game this time. It didn't matter how much I struggled against him, he had me in such a tight hold; my back against his chest and his huge arms locking my arms and basically whole upper body.

I tapped whatever part of him I could reach out to, in a sign of surrender.

"Looks like the old man is also driving the beautiful Lamborghini I found at your garage," Joe stated while letting me go.

As if I'd let him drive my beauty.
"You ain't touching my car," I said and attacked again.

Almost too easily, I had him on the ground instead, my thighs wrapped around his throat, blocking his airways. Even though he had many ways to escape that hold, he tapped the ground. It felt like he let me win. It didn't feel like a victory. Nonetheless, I let him go.

"Okay I'll let you have that one. I'm too tired for this so early in the morning," he said, rubbing the back of his neck.

Yeah. He'd definitely let me win. It left a sour taste in my mouth, but as I was also just as spent as he was, I let it go. "Alright. I've earned at least one breakfast, right?"

"Right," he said, brushing his clothes as we both stood up.

I wasn't taking the risk of not getting edible breakfast, so I led him straight to the guest room upstairs. My plan was to exit as fast as I could, trying not to think about the fact that now he would be staying right beside my bedroom. But as soon as Joe spotted the adjoining bathroom, he discarded his sweaty shirt, right then and there.

My brain stopped working.

He was already heading to the shower when my brain untangled itself, and I scurried off like I was on fire. But it was too late…I had already caught a glimpse of his more than chiseled back muscles, and the large, old, faint scar that reached all the way from his right shoulder to his left hip.

One might think I'd be curious about how he had gotten that scar. But my non-functioning brain had some entirely different views on the matter… I couldn't help but wonder how well it suited his character.

For fuck's sake, why do scars make anyone else hotter, but me? Could that guy be any more perfect? It was already unfair that he had been faster than me this morning, and most likely a better fighter too. Heading to my own bathroom, I made it my goal to beat the guy's ass one of these days.

Job Description

I fell while chasing him. Him? Something. I was chasing something.

Somebody?

Debris flew all around me, as I staggered up from the hard asphalt. Everything spun. There was a black fog, weighing me down and making me drop down to my knees, but I fought against it. It was all in vain. The fog just made me drop down over and over again. The air around me crushed my lungs and made my saliva taste rusty and metallic.

I coughed up blood.

Crawling was the answer. I had to crawl to move forward, but the road was endless. Where was I even going? My right hand knuckles were bloody, raw, and tender. The tangy smell of burnt rubber lingered everywhere. My throat burned.

I just wanted everything to stop. Why was the world spinning?

What was I even chasing? The air around me was heavier and heavier. It became almost impossible to breathe. My arms were next to useless, I managed to move only a centimeter at a time. I couldn't reach it…him…whatever I was chasing.

I stopped and let the heavy fog settle around me. I hoped it would've just ended me painlessly, but of course it had to burn. Every breath was like swallowing a thousand scorching hot needles. Yet, I couldn't fight it. There was no point.

With a heavy sigh, I rolled to my side. But there was something there next to me. Somebody, to be exact. I turned to look and was met with a heavy breathing man, his face all deformed, bruised, and smashed in. It was ruined beyond recognition. Who could've done this to him?

As if reading my mind, the man smiled, blood gushing out of his mouth coloring his teeth crimson. "*You* did this to me."

A manic laugh erupting from his chest, the man reached for my throat.

I jumped up to sit in my bed. Gasping for air, choking, and coughing my lungs out, I tried to scratch the man's hands off my throat, but they weren't there anymore. The man wasn't there anymore. I wasn't even outside anymore; I was in my bedroom. Why I still couldn't fucking breathe, I wasn't sure. It was also way, *way* too hot. Sweat soaked through my clothes, leaving me drenched.

Then the sweat made me extremely cold. So cold my teeth chattered when I rolled off bed and dropped to my knees on the floor. Crawling on all fours, I barely made it to the bathroom and directly under the shower which was basically the only thing that I knew would help. I didn't even bother taking off the t-shirt and boxers that I had slept in before turning on the shower.

There I sat on the floor for a good while, clothes on and hot water pounding my back until I could breathe normally again. Until my teeth stopped clacking against each other. Until my racing heart had calmed down.

Eventually, I did wiggle my way out of the drenched clothes, wrung them as dry as I could, and hung them up. I still let the hot water pound my back some more as I tried to keep my mind off the fact that I'd have to face the whole of LBR Entertainment's headquarters and especially its staff today.

And Joe. Let's not forget Joe. I wondered if I had woken him up during the night. At least I hadn't woken up screaming this time. I had tried to fight sleeping in general tonight because just Joe's mere presence in the room right next to mine had bothered me—I knew I would have nightmares; I did every night these days—but I had lost the fight due to pure exhaustion.

As I had no idea what the time was, I forced myself to turn off the shower and step out. The mirror on top of the sink fogged up as soon as I opened the glass door separating the shower and the rest of the bathroom. Normally, I would've been grateful for that, because I wouldn't have to see my face. That time, however, it wouldn't do—I needed to see what I was doing if I were to make myself look at least a ghost of what I once was.

Sighing, I toweled myself before using the same towel to clear up a corner of the mirror, just enough to see how bad the situation was.

And man, it was bad.

The fact that there were two prominent, bright-red, barely-healed scars crossing each other on the right side of my face, wasn't the only problem. On top of those, my hair had also grown out, revealing a two centimeter of black root growth. The rest, that had once been sparkly light brown, had now faded to a much less vivid color that I couldn't quite put into words, just that it wasn't very good-looking. Whenever shaving practically blind because the mirror always fogged up, I had missed some spots. There were very prominent bags under my eyes that were a telltale sign that I hadn't been sleeping much in the past weeks, if at all.

Ah, yes, and then there were the aforementioned scars. One of them from the corner of my eye and ended right above my mouth. The other, slightly thinner scar started between my eyebrows, went down the side of my nose and crossed over the other one on my cheek before fading to my jawline.

Trying my best to avoid the scars, I shaved. There wasn't really time to be thorough, so it still wasn't perfect when I was done. Not that it mattered, no-one would notice a stubble here and there with the scars getting all the attention.

After rinsing my face, I quickly blow-dried the mess of my hair and walked over to my walk-in closet, glancing at the clock on my nightstand—at least I wasn't late. Yet. But I also didn't have much time to spare.

Only some band t-shirts and some of my simplest black jeans had survived my attempts at doing the laundry. Needless to say, it didn't take me very long to decide on a Guns 'n' Roses t-shirt and some simple, faded black skinny jeans that had lost their elasticity. It was practically the only option left. For a jacket, I grabbed my favorite burgundy faux-leather jacket and headed downstairs.

But once I opened my bedroom door and stepped to the upstairs lounge, an out of this world scent, so delicious, intricate, and warm filled my nostrils. I couldn't help but stop on my tracks and just…breathe it in. Even my eyes closed on their own as I just wallowed in the warm feeling of *home*.

Had Joe made breakfast today as well?

I walked down the stairs in awe, one step at a time, taking in the amazing scent. Why had Joe made breakfast? The deal had only been for yesterday when I had "won" against him during our little fight. I didn't think he'd make breakfast for me like, voluntarily, after how I'd treated him yesterday.

Yet there he was, laying down some pajeon with dip sauce on the dining table when I entered the living room. He wasn't wearing a suit this time, which made him look oddly casual. Plus, the tight black t-shirt accentuated his arms with the way it stretched around his biceps…uh, let's leave it at that.

The smell, which only grew stronger the closer I got, was heavenly to say the least. At last, there was something edible in the house. Joe hadn't been very impressed at my food stock, so we had ended up eating instant noodles yesterday. Looked like he had gone grocery shopping as well.

As I sat down, he handed me a coffee mug, already filled.

"Good morning," he said, and sat across from me.

That's when I noticed his eyes…or rather, the bags under them. I didn't even dare to ask if he had woken up to my nightmares. Instead, I muttered out something that might or might have not resembled a "Good morning" as well, but my main focus was on the coffee. It was just the way I liked it—strong, bitter, and black.

"So, what's up with the breakfast?" I asked once the caffeine hit my system and I felt a little more like a human again.

Joe shrugged, offered me a quick smile, and opened a newspaper. "I woke up early. Plus, yesterday's noodles hardly counted as breakfast."

Fuck. I guessed the reason for him being up early, was my nightmares indeed. I topped my plate with pajeon. Once I cut myself a bite-sized bite, I popped it in my mouth. Instantly, I was in seventh heaven—they were better than Joonie's and Tae's combined. That, or I hadn't had them in ages, and thus they tasted ten times better than normal. It had been over a month since I last tasted anything even remotely resembling a home-made breakfast. One that wasn't a disaster I had tried to make, anyway. Emphasis on the word "tried."

Closing my eyes, I let the taste melt my heart into a puddle. I couldn't help a small moan escaping my lips. It was so unfair that Joe also knew how to cook.

Unfortunately, once I opened my eyes again, I saw the clock on the back wall.

"We should get going," I mentioned, and started to gobble the remains of the pajeon on my plate.

"I know," Joe simply said, folded the newspaper to the side, and yawned.

The second I was done, he snagged my plate away, and I rushed to help him clean out the kitchen. I must say that when we weren't fighting or annoying each other, we were a fairly efficient pair in the kitchen, putting away the leftovers and filling up the dishwasher. I was surprised to see how much I liked it.

The normalcy.

I was like ninety-percent sure that I had woken him up during the night with my nightmares, given how tired he looked, but unlike Mr. Won, he never mentioned it. He never asked if I had slept well—because it was obvious I hadn't. He never asked if I was okay or looked at me with pity in his eyes.

Instead, he had made breakfast.

I appreciated that.

So when he was about to rush out of the kitchen once we were done, I couldn't help but stop him by stepping on his way.

"So, uh," I started, not quite able to meet his eyes. "Thank you."

"For the breakfast? Nah, I figured that since I'm here anyway, I could at least do that much."

"Yeah, for that…" I paused. I could've left it at that. But more than the breakfast, I was grateful for something else. And in the name of having to live with the guy, I needed to get it out. "And also for, uh…"

One of his hands appeared on my shoulder and the other lifted my chin up.

"Don't mention it. You've been through a lot. I get it."

Out of habit, I swatted his hands off me—only GRiD and my family could touch me if I wasn't fighting them—but I did elaborate. "Uh, okay. But also sorry, if…if I woke you up."

Joe first reached out to me again, but then took a step back and shoved his hands in his jeans' pockets, as if to stop them from touching me.

"'S alright," he said. "Don't worry about me. It should be the other way around."

Without another word, he pushed past me, to the hallway. After being stunned for a second, I followed him but couldn't help but wonder what was going on inside his head. I mean...it was him who had left me early in the morning after our hot night way back when, why did it look like he cared so much *now?* It didn't make any sense.

Well, worrying about me was technically his job, though. Maybe I was overthinking this whole thing. It's not like he had asked to be stuck with me up here now had he? I yanked on some spent converses, a huge pair of sunglasses plus a cap, and followed Joe out the door.

Joe's face was unreadable when he opened the passenger side door of my beauty—my black Lamborghini Aventador S—and stepped inside. It was no news we were taking my car—I had insisted on it. But while I had been like a kid in the candy shop when I had first hopped inside of this beauty, Joe didn't show any excitement whatsoever, which was a much more of a surprise. I wondered if he just wasn't a car person.

It was only after I sat down in the driver's seat and pushed the button that made the V12 roar to life that I caught a slight glimpse of a smile on his lips. I couldn't help but rev the engine—moderately—before steering it through the front gate with care.

Too Much

Joe's face sported a greenish tint as I parked the car in one of the deepest, darkest corners of HQ's gigantic parking hall. In his defense, I might have slammed the gas pedal all the way down once we hit the highway. Ever since, he had gripped the door handle as if his life depended on it. It'd amused me.

That amusement only lasted until we had to push through the crowd that surrounded the whole entire HQ. The Lamborghini's windows weren't very darkly tinted, which meant that there would be an entirely new photo-pile of my ruined face everywhere. I knew I should have gotten myself used to it sooner rather than later, now that the scars were a permanent part of myself, but it still stung like a motherfucker.

"I'm driving back," Joe stated, opening his door, and climbing up from his seat.

"In your dreams." I followed his example, but I might've put a little bit more force into slamming my car door shut than strictly necessary.

Admittedly, I wasn't in the best of moods.

Joe ignored my little temper tantrum altogether and headed inside with a short dismissive wave aimed somewhat my way. I guessed he was going to meet the other guards or something—he wasn't really needed here because the HQ had its own security personnel—but I still wondered if he just wanted to get rid of me, as he was so quick to escape.

Whatever. I definitely did *not* want him breathing down my neck the whole day anyway. He was a distraction I didn't need. A way too hot, flirty, and enticing of a distraction, but nonetheless a distraction.

If I were to get back to work—which I wasn't sure I was just yet—I needed to become better. A better performer, a better coworker, a better singer… I could no longer rely on my cute looks—there were no cute looks to rely on anymore. Poof. Gone.

I took a deep breath, shoved my sunglasses to hang by the neckline of my last non-ruined t-shirt (I seriously needed to visit the old dorms to get some undamaged clothes) and stomped through the door.

It was quiet in the hallways near the parking this time of the day, as most of the staff were already at work. But once I reached the common areas, the nerves seriously got to me. I would've been lying if I'd said the looks everyone gave me and my fucking scars didn't affect me…or the fact that a trainee at the lobby even audibly gasped, and the girl beside her didn't even try to hide the fact that her jaw dropped. Ignoring them all the best I could, I strode through the hallways and took the lift.

Once inside, I deflated against the back wall like a balloon, resting the back of my head against the cold mirror. A splitting pain surged up my arm; I had squeezed my goddamn keys so hard that they'd left red dents to my palm. I jammed them in my jeans' pocket just before the lift doors opened.

Our floor was filled to the brim with random HQ staff, and every single pair of eyes turned at me once I stepped out of the lift. The silence that fell in the lobby was deafening. Shrugging off the soul crushing stares aimed my way, I strode straight into meeting room 4, our regular, and sat down on the nearest chair. It was right beside Minjae. He flashed me a friendly smile, and I could finally breathe again.

I glanced around the room. Obviously GRiD and Jiwoo where there, but also some company board folks and almost the whole entire publicity team. To say the meeting room was crowded would've been an understatement. Looked like this Billboard-thing was an even bigger deal than I had originally thought.

"Good," Jiwoo said. "Now that Chris has arrived, I will officially start this meeting by stating that I went ahead and accepted all five invitations to attend and perform at the BBMAs. Including Chris's."

The way my jaw dropped. "You did what?"

At the same time, an elderly big-shot from the company board and the label's director, Hangyeol-nim, stood up. "This is unacceptable."

To which Tae reacted by banging his fist against the table. "GRiD is five."

"It's bad publicity," someone from the publicity team muttered.

"Bad publicity is still publicity," someone else countered.

In a nanosecond, it was a whole zoo condensed in one room, with everyone fighting for their territory. They shouted on top of each other. Papers flew in the air. Jiwoo looked like she was about to throw herself over the table and strangle Hangyeol-nim. Joonie was literally holding Tae back. Do-hyun covered Minjae's ears.

I closed my eyes, let the ringing in my ears cancel out the rest of the room, and started rubbing my temples. What a nightmare. Almost worse of a nightmare than the regular ones. If I had known the LBR wasn't as keen on having me back to work as the rest of GRiD was, I would've never come to the meeting.

Though, truthfully, I should've guessed.

After a while, I snapped.

"SHUT UP!" The room fell silent at once and everyone froze, turning their attention on me. Suddenly, all I wanted to do was to disappear through the floor. "Look, if you all think I'm so detrimental to the team, I might as well just quit."

The chorus of "no" was pretty impressive. The one's from the HQ officials' part definitely took me by surprise. Weren't they just now arguing I shouldn't be allowed at the award show?

"Then what the hell do you want from me?"

"You, quitting, is out of the question," Jiwoo said.

I turned my eyes to Hangyeol-nim.

Following my example, so did everyone else. Hangyeol-nim himself, sat and cleared his throat. "I mean, we don't want you to quit…entirely. It's just that this whole assault-charge happened with a very inconvenient timing. Billboard is going to get us a huge amount of press, but if it's all negative…this can end very badly. For all of us."

"Not if we clear Chris's name before that."

It was an entirely new voice. Jae-beom's voice, to be exact. We all turned to look at him at the entrance to the meeting room. Except Jiwoo, who let out a heavy exhale.

"Finally," she said. "It was time you cared to appear."

"Sorry, I got stuck in traffic."

Hangyeol-nim's lips twitched, and he crossed his arms against his chest. "Are you saying you can win this on trial *on time*? Allow me to doubt."

"Not win if it comes to trial, no. Not before the BBMAs anyway," Jae-beom explained while walking in. He sat beside Jiwoo and leaned back. "But *settle*…before it even comes down to trial…sure."

"How sure?"

"Depending on how much you are willing to invest," Jae-beom said. "But considering the possible payoff for attending the award show with *all* members present, I'm sure we can reach a mutual conclusion."

I nearly bursted into a hysterical laughing fit. I had no hopes in LBR Entertainment's willingness in throwing any money at my wrecked ass. But to my complete astonishment, it looked like Hangyeol-nim actually considered it. At one point, he even stood up and walked over to the window to stare into the distance. The silence dragged on, and the air turned heavy in the room as we all waited for the director's say in the matter, every single stare directed at his back.

It was some of my life's longest minutes, waiting for the director to turn around and open his goddamn mouth. When he finally did, I was already lightheaded for holding my breath.

"Fine," he said, and the collective exhale of every set of lungs in the room was audible. "But this better be the last scandal I'm going through with you all. One more hint of a drama and I'm terminating *all* your contracts, whether you sell well or not."

And with that, he was out the door, followed closely by his assistant whose name I could never remember. The publicity team exchanged a few words with Jiwoo and set up their own meeting of how to handle this, but then they were out the door too. While I still had a hard time wrapping my head around whatever had just gone down, everyone left, leaving behind only the rest of GRiD, Jiwoo and Jae-beom.

Jiwoo was the first one to break out a small smile and end the stunned stillness. "Well, looks like we're going, then."

I finally snapped out of the haze. "So no one asked if I even *want* to attend the fucking show."

"Please…" Joonie let out a ringing laugh, standing up and starting to gather his things. "If you didn't want to go, or get back to work overall for that matter, you wouldn't have attended this meeting."

I mean…fair. Maybe at this point it was time to admit to myself that I wanted to get back to work. Back to music.

Especially if it involved living out our biggest aspiration. Sigh. "Y'all are not letting me quit are you?"

"Nope," Tae said and stood up as well. I guess that marked the end of the meeting.

"In your dreams," Jiwoo added. "Which reminds me, you should all check your new schedules tomorrow. I'm updating them tonight. We're seriously getting back to work now. No more of this slacking-off business."

With a choir of approving noises from us, we all headed out. I was the first one to reach the door, but I was stopped by someone grabbing my wrist. Luckily for Do-hyun, I saw it was him from the corner of my eye or I would've broken his wrist.

"Want to grab lunch?" he asked, Minjae attached to his side like they were glued together.

Me glancing at my wristwatch, and Joe appearing to my peripheral vision as he stepped out of the lift, confirmed that this thing had taken longer than scheduled—I was supposed to be headed to the hair salon already. "Sorry guys, but I need to go. Gotta get this disaster of a hair style fixed."

Do-hyun nodded, a smirk plastered to his lips, and Minjae eyed my hair.

"Good idea," Minjae said, the tone of mocking clear in his voice.

Around two hours later, I was grumpy, hungry, and walking out of the salon with slightly shorter, dark red hair. Apparently, that's what you get if you request a haircut and dye called; "Whatever man. Use your imagination."

When I reached the car parked to the side of the road, Joe's glance snapped to my new hair. His eyes started to sparkle as he let out a low whistle. "Nice."

"Not your business," I stated, about to change the topic before it turned into more flirting on Joe's part. "You wanted to drive, right?"

I tossed the car keys. Much to my dismay, Joe caught them with no difficulty whatsoever, despite the surprise.

"Sure, but what's the catch?"

"No catch," I said and rushed to the passenger seat.

Obviously, there was a catch, and that was me not trusting myself to drive to the old dorm—way too many triggers on the way.

But it took me maybe five minutes to regret letting Joe drive, and I promised myself I'd never let him drive again; he drove like a hundred year old grandma. My beauty didn't deserve that kind of treatment, and our journey to the dorm ended up painfully slow. I didn't say anything, though, because I hardly even dared to keep my eyes open when we started approaching the place. And at least Joe had brought me some take-away lunch while I was at the salon.

As the day had been exhausting already, I appreciated that Joe didn't try to spark up any further flirting or conversation. We were in total silence until Joe pulled into the underground garage.

"Mind if I get some stuff from our floor as well?" he asked.

Maybe taking the Lambo wasn't the best call. There wasn't exactly much space in the thing. "Sure, but nothing big."

Joe looked at me under his brows with a smug smile dancing on his lips.

This dirty-minded douche. "You know what I meant."

"I didn't say anything."

"Your stupid face told me enough."

I guess the look on my face convinced him I wasn't in the mood for his shit, because he didn't mutter out another word on our way to the lift. But once the lift door closed behind us, something unexpected happened: my brain got entirely consumed by flashbacks, and my eyes closed. They were flashbacks from one *very* particular night in our past, which was not even the night when I lost my one man war against a lunatic, but before… When my face and sanity had still been intact… When Joe's lips had found all the most delicate spots on my neck, in this very same lift… When my hands had freely roamed on his waist and chest under his unbuttoned shirt the heat of his naked skin under my fingertips sending butterflies to the pit of my stomach and—

Joe cleared his throat, which was a cruel but welcome wake up call. I didn't even dare to glance at him but based on the awkwardness in the air it seemed like Joe was as uncomfortable as I was. I rolled my weight from one foot to the other in hopes of getting some distance between us in the small space, but it didn't help at all—the air still seemed to buzz around us. Heat started creeping up my neck, faster by the second. I hoped Joe wouldn't notice. I still had trouble controlling my wildly inappropriate thoughts.

Thankfully the lift door opened, and Joe stepped out, muttering something about 30 minutes. I only managed to nod to that, not finding my voice through my restricted throat.

It was only when the lift started its ascend to the top floor, that I dared to breathe properly, and could adjust my jeans that had turned very…um…tight…all of a sudden. Once on the top floor, I walked straight to my old room, banged the door shut behind me and threw myself on the black cotton sheets of my bed, back first. A good five minutes were spent staring at the ceiling, my mind completely blank.

What an exhausting day. Way too many turning points. Too much everything.

I wasn't a people person to start with, but the day had affected me more than I cared to admit. Even though I had been used to the spotlight, I had always been in the shadows of the older members of GRiD. Yet today, every single person at HQ had only noticed me.

And after giving it a good thought, I realized something else—something far scarier. Joe, of all people, was the only damn person apart from GRiD who hadn't reacted upon seeing my scars. He didn't even seem to care, like he didn't even see them at all. Not to mention he hadn't blinked twice at my night terrors.

It freaked me out how much I appreciated that.

That realization terrified me maybe even more than the insane pull that rippled between us from time to time. Chemistry, lust, attraction—those things I could handle...but actual empathy and companionship...those I wasn't so sure about. If he continued to be like that, how was I supposed to not catch *actual* feelings? And based on the fact that Joe had disappeared after our one night of pure passion, before I even woke up, he wasn't really the committing kind of guy.

Our thing was just one night, and that was it. I needed to keep that firmly in mind during Joe's stay at my place. Maybe it had been a little too cruel to have him stay at the garage for the first night...but ultimately I shouldn't let him get too close to me. Whatever relationship we had was to stay strictly a business relationship. Nothing more, nothing less.

But that was a problem for later. As much as I would've loved to, I couldn't stay in the old dorms for forever, so I grabbed as many clothes I thought would fit inside the small frunk of my Lambo, plus my acoustic guitar, and headed out.

Almost

The only downside to not living downtown was the super long commute.

Oddly enough, one of the many upsides to not living downtown turned out to be the long commute as well. Let me explain: Because we had so much catching up to do after all the drama, Jiwoo had packed our calendars extremely tight, and on top of that it took like two hours to drive up to my home. It led to me crashing to bed, thoroughly exhausted, well after midnight, only to wake up at 5 or 6 am to head right back to work.

The pure exhaustion…it meant no nightmares. No waking up in the middle of the night covered in a cold sweat, screaming. No staring at the alarm clock too afraid to go back to sleep until it was morning enough to get up. No getting myself drunk to be able to have a couple of hours of decent sleep.

I slept like a log. For the first time in ages.

It also meant that I barely saw Joe.

A few days passed, following the same pattern.

I'd get up early in the morning, well-rested for once. Then I'd head to my regular morning jog. Maybe got pissed at Joe and his more or less flirtatious remarks. Which, in turn, would turn into races or mock fights, much like the first morning Joe had been up here with me. With running, I had the advantage now that I wasn't as fatigued as before, but the fighting... let's just say he won.

Every. Damn. Time.

On the positive side, I had made Joe my housekeeper by winning the races. He did the laundry now. And cooked. Cleaned. Like a good housewife should. Except he wasn't exactly wife material otherwise. More like a huge, flirtatious, and outrageously handsome man. It was perfect.

Except...

In turn, when Joe won the fights, Joe gained access to a new part of my house. Too fast for my liking, he had earned his way to my whole property. Well, apart from my bedroom. That's where my boundaries lay. Not that he didn't try to, though. And he was persistent, I'll give him that. But even if it was seemingly only one of his flirty jokes, I wasn't taking the risk and letting him anywhere near my bed. Nope.

Not that the idea wasn't enticing.

Work started going...better. Most people at the HQ had gotten used to seeing my face. Maybe it helped that I didn't sport those prominent under-eye bags and that sleep-deprived grumpy attitude. Of course, the tabloids were having a field day, spreading new pictures of my ruined face everywhere—but that also earned me sympathy points in the eyes of the public. Or that's what the publicity team told me. Apparently we needed the media on our side to make the scandal disappear faster after Jae-beom settled the matter.

Besides, it wasn't like I wasn't used to them mustering up news about everything and everyone already.

The late evenings were quiet. Joe lingered around but gave me enough space. For some reason, he didn't feel the need to piss me off every other second in the evenings—compared to mornings—and for that, I was grateful. It was still suspicious, but I decided to enjoy it while it lasted...despite wondering how he always seemed to know the exact moment when everything started to get too much for me to handle.

In other words, he read me like I was an open book. Although I would never admit it out loud, those flirtatious moments in the mornings managed to cheer me up from time to time. Most likely because he also knew when to cut it and shut the fuck up.

Our little routine lasted only for a few days, sadly, and then it was dawning upon me—the first day off. The day that I had dreaded the most after learning the nightmares ceased when I was too busy to think too much; our first day off. I had two in a row ahead of me.

The anxiety crept up on me in the early morning as I headed to my routine morning jog. I tried to ignore it, convinced that working out would distract me enough for now.

At least the weather was nice. Sun warmed up my cheeks, and my feet hitting the gravel on the familiar trail made a strangely pleasing sound. The sound of Joe's footsteps still followed me as every other morning, but it was the fact that I felt his eyes on me the whole way that made me painfully aware of his existence.

He didn't even try to get ahead of me this morning.

"Can you stop staring at my ass?" I said as I turned to jog backwards and face Joe.

He gave me a big lopsided grin. "I would, but it's too gorgeous to ignore."

I missed a step and nearly fell. Joe's grin only widened. In hindsight, I *had* kind of asked for it. Nevertheless, I rolled my eyes and ran the rest of the way to the clearing facing forward. Maybe the cure to this nuisance of a man was simply to ignore him.

The view warmed my heart as it always did. Seoul looked weirdly calm from up here. Slow, even. Breathing in the fresh air one wouldn't find downtown, I leaned against the fence.

It was peaceful.

Until Joe randomly decided to wrap his hands around my waist and lean his chin on my shoulder. I gritted my teeth together.

"Can you like, fuck off?" I asked, completely ignoring my already racing heart and the heat of Joe's body pressing against my back.

"Nope. Shortie fits here perfectly," he muttered, not moving an inch.

"What if I make you?"

"You can try," he said, and I could almost hear the smile in his voice.

Hmph. This was how all our fights started. He would invade my personal space. I'd kick or punch him. He'd have me pinned to the ground in a span of minutes, as I didn't have a chance against him. Why even bother?

For once, I didn't.

Joe didn't like it.

Nope, not one bit.

I figured as much as he yanked me off the fence, lifted me in the air, and started spinning me around. When I gasped at the sudden movement and started hissing an endless stream of curses, vision blurring, Joe only laughed.

Hating myself for letting my guard down, I tried everything to stop him. Scratching his arms, punching his ribs with my elbows, struggling…nothing helped. I had no chance, whatsoever, against him. And my head was getting dizzy, fast.

As a last resort, I used the momentum to swing my leg behind his knee in an attempt to make him lose his balance. Unfortunately, I succeeded and realized how bad of an idea that was a nano-second too late. Because when Joe did lose his balance, we both fell towards the bushes. Rapidly.

Joe landed on his back, right in the middle of the bushes, still cracking up. I landed on top of him. Hard. But he barely even noticed and only started laughing harder. With another swift, skilled move of his, he rolled us around. Suddenly it was me below him, pinned against the ground. It took my head a short while to even realize what'd happened, and by then he was grinning down at me with that annoying twinkle sparkling in his golden-halo eyes.

"Get off me!" I roared, struggling against his hold, with little to no success.

"But I haven't decided my prize for the day yet," he stated calmly.

Despite how badly I wanted to wipe that grin off his face, I could hardly move. His face was a mere inch from mine, his spearmint-gum-smelling breath fanning on my face. It made me feel even dizzier. If possible.

"What's with you bodyguards and chewing gum, huh?! Your breath stinks," I spat, narrowing my eyes at him when I had recovered enough to form coherent thoughts.

"Don't dodge the subject, shortie."

So he was still talking about his reward. Ugh. Whatever.

"Just decide for fuck's sake, I'm crushing under here!"

"But I've run out of prizes I want," he started, faking a wistful expression. Then, his face fell straight. "Except sharing your bed."

"Stay the fuck out of my bedroom," I hissed under my shortened breath. Another adrenaline rush was released within me, and I tried some more struggling, but it was of no use. I could've struggled for hours under him, and he wouldn't have budged. He proved the point by laughing at me.

"Oh relax, can't you take a joke?"

Holding down the urge to spit on his way too close and handsome face, I eased up with trying to wiggle out of his grip. Eventually, I sighed in ultimate defeat and gave up completely.

"Ugh, whatever except my bedroom. Get on with it. I can't breathe."

"Then… how about a kiss?"

I froze, stiff like a statue. I could only look him in the eyes with my own eyes widened. He couldn't be serious…or could he?

Joe propped his whole body up, leaving me plenty of escape routes. But those damn eyes with the weird golden halo around the pupils held me nailed to the spot. I couldn't move at all, though technically he didn't even hold me in place any longer. My heart started thumping so fast I was sure it was going to burst.

He leaned closer and closer, so slowly I should've had plenty of time to react and kick him in his nuts, or something, to escape. But I didn't. Instead, I could only squeeze my eyes shut in hopes of waking up from this spell his eyes had cast on me.

I didn't wake up. My body all but betrayed me: When his chest pressed against mine, my hands automatically grabbed his waist. When his fingertips brushed my hair to the side, I shivered. When his firm thigh pressed against my crotch, all I wanted was to grind…just a little bit to create some friction…

Soon all I could think of, was how bad I wanted him to kiss me.

When he was so close his breath tickled my lips, my racing heart stopped beating altogether. For a moment I was sure I was going to die from the tension. Or at least faint.

But his lips never landed on mine.

As fast as he started it, he ended it. His weight rolled off from on top of me. I found out my body could move again and shuffled up to sit, my body already longing for his touch…his closeness. Head still spinning, I finally dared to open my eyes, only to find Joe was grinning, already standing up and was holding his hand out for me to grab.

I eyed the hand suspiciously. "I thought you wanted a kiss?"

"Oh, I still want that kiss…but I'd rather make you beg for it than take one by force," he said and *fucking winked.*

My blood suddenly boiling, I swatted his hand away and scrambled up. "You'll have to wait for a long time for that to happen."

Joe laughed and started brushing his clothes free from the debris. "We'll see."

Giving Up

I should've known that it was only the beginning...that one little almost-kiss. Obviously Joe couldn't have left it at that. I should've known.

Instead, he took literally any half-assed excuse to rile me up and then win a fight. The worst part was that he knew exactly how to make me go from zero to one hundred in mere seconds. Thus, the whole day ended up being an endless fight, to the point that even the tiniest muscles in my body screamed for help by the nightfall. I knew damn well I didn't have a chance to win any of these fights, but I couldn't stop. He knew me too well to let that happen.

It was exhausting, to say the least.

To make matters worse, he no longer bothered to pretend his antics were merely flirty jokes or that this was merely a business relationship. When he had said he was going to make me beg, he hadn't joked around. Countless times, I found myself under him, his lips almost reaching whatever goal they were aiming for each time—my lips, the nape of my neck, my cheek.

He was a fucking tease and a half.

My body betrayed me. There wasn't a cell in me that wanted to cooperate with my mind and do the right thing; to say this needed to stop. Then my mind developed a habit to cease to exist and get dizzy every time my eyes met his beautiful ones.

Aish, even my heart stopped beating every damn time I thought it was finally about to happen.

And for fuck's sake, how many times can a guy get his heart stopped before dropping down dead?!

At the end of the day, I was so exhausted I'd face-planted on my bed, fully clothed, and fell asleep. At least I didn't have to worry about the nightmares for another day. Positive thinking and all that jazz.

That was how and where I woke up the next morning. My t-shirt was glued to my sweaty skin, and I had tried to get rid of the jeans as they were hanging low on my hips. The waistband pressed against my morning wood somewhat uncomfortably, so I wiggled them off and made my way under the sheets.

The alarm clock on my nightstand informed me it was already nine in the morning, with bold red digital numbers. Squeezing my eyes shut, I tried to ignore it and continue sleeping, but of course, I wasn't successful. I had to get up.

To do what, I had no idea. It was my second day off and it was a very tempting option to stay in bed all day, but my stomach protested. Loudly. And then there was Joe behind my bedroom door, mumbling something about the breakfast.

Oh well.

Giving up, I scrambled up and yanked on a ruined, formerly white t-shirt that had somehow turned light pink the last time I attempted doing the laundry. And some plain black sweatpants. It was a day off, after all, so I'd have to save the non-ruined clothes for workdays.

A wonderful smell reached my nose as soon as I walked downstairs. Apparently we were having those awesome pancakes for breakfast again, which Joe had made me the first morning. It seemed such a distant day, though it had been only a little over a week since. Eagerly, I sat down at the dining table and started piling them up on my plate.

"You like them, hmm?" Joe asked, glancing at me over his newspaper before taking a sip from his coffee mug.

"They're okay," I said and shrugged, right before dipping a huge piece in the garlic sauce and stuffing it in my mouth. What? I wasn't going to admit I practically drooled over them.

Joe seemed to sense I liked them even without me saying it out loud, as he let me see a slight smile before he focused back on his newspaper. I, however, was done with the whole pile of pajeon in a matter of minutes.

Positively stuffed, I leaned back on the chair, huffing.

Joe lifted his eyes from the newspaper again. "No morning jog today?"

"Are you kidding? I'm not running with my stomach full. Ugh."

"Figured. I thought I'd ask since it seems like a routine."

"Nah, gotta rest sometime too," I said, rubbing my belly.

Though the weather was nice. Maybe I could've gone for a walk or something. Get some little fresh air. It was not like I could just loiter around either, because that only meant nightmares and panic attacks.

But thinking about a walk for mere leisure made me hyper-aware of the fact that Joe wouldn't get days off while trapped up here in the mountains with me. It wasn't like he could call someone to cover him to take a walk... I guess I could at least *ask* if he'd be up for it before deciding on my own.

"We could go for a walk, later. If you want to?" I said, and okay, that didn't exactly come out as a proper question.

Joe didn't seem to mind, though.

"Why not?" he said and started to fold the newspaper away. That usual twinkle in his eyes looked even more sparkly today if possible. "I mean, we could spend the entire day in your bed, too, but as you wish..."

I snatched the newspaper from his hand and aimed to hit him in the head with it. Joe dodged it in a relaxed manner, apparently not in the mood to start an actual fight. He could've, very easily, as he now knew what would get me going. But I guess he wanted to flex his ability to make me walk right into his traps by letting it go.

Not long after we were heading up on the familiar path. I took it super slow, enjoying another bright day. Some of the sun rays made it past the forest to us, making the path look almost magical. It had rained at night and the rays bounced off the leftover water drops on the trees and the ground.

It took us way longer than normal, to reach the view deck. Once again, I stopped to marvel at the sight that spread below us, leaning against the fence. There were only a couple of white clouds drifting in the bright blue sky, the glass-covered skyscrapers glimmered in the distance.

The fence gave in the teeniest bit when Joe leaned against it as well, right next to me. Normally, I would've moved somewhere else or flipped him off... but I was way too exhausted for that. Besides, it was too beautiful a day to ruin by letting my mind turn sour.

"Would you look at that, the view's almost as beautiful as the company," Joe said out of the blue.

Sigh. Of course, he couldn't have let me spend the day in peace. What was I even thinking?

"Why do you keep teasing me?" I asked, staring ahead to the distance, completely worn out. It wasn't even midday.

From the corner of my eye, I saw Joe shrug.

"Maybe I enjoy it. Maybe I genuinely like you. Maybe both. Take your pick. It's not like you're gonna believe me either way," Joe stated.

It simultaneously made my skin itch in an annoying way and tingle in a very different, softer way. Maybe, or maybe not, it had something to do with the fact that he was annoyingly right.

Before I could recover, he continued, "Why do you hate me so much these days? I thought we had a wonderful time before…"

Another sigh escaped me as I momentarily let the memories of *that night* wash over my consciousness. He wasn't wrong, we did have a wonderful time, if not counting the fact that he had disappeared before I even woke up.

"Hate is a strong word… I don't think I really *hate* you. I don't particularly like you either, but that's not about you. I'm just not a people person in general."

"Says the one that has a few million fans across the globe," Joe said, turning his face towards me. His stare burned a hole in my face, but I chose to keep on ignoring it. Instead, I stubbornly continued staring at the skyscrapers in the distance. They looked oddly tiny from this far away.

"That's different."

"Fair enough…" he said, trailing off. "Though you do seem to get along with Do-hyun and the others well enough. How'd that happen?"

"Over time. Living in a tiny-ass apartment with only two bedrooms for a year, tends to do that to people. I learned to respect them."

"Wait, that doesn't make any sense. You only use honorifics in a sarcastic way. You barely listen to your hyungs. You argue with them all the time. Hardly seems like respect to me."

Rolling my eyes at him, I finally turned to face him. Surprisingly, he didn't look like he was scolding me, only genuinely curious. So I decided to humor him. Only this one time.

"Everyone who lives together argues. And there are other ways to show respect than an age-old system based on people's age. I don't get why anyone would be a better person just because they managed to crawl out of the womb before me."

"You know honorifics are not exactly about that. It's more like... showing people you respect their life-experience and expertise."

I shrugged again, turning my eyes back towards the view. Being old hadn't stopped my father leaving Mom to raise four children on her own. Being old didn't stop our first manager from scamming half the money we would've made from our first tour and album. Being old hadn't made Min-ho any less of a fucking creep.

"Yeah, maybe older folks might have more experience and stuff. It doesn't mean they know how to use that knowledge right. A scumbag is still a scumbag, however old."

"True," Joe said, finally letting go of the dumb subject.

We were silent like that for a while, both having our eyes fixed on the city below. Content with not letting him get me riled up, I made a promise to myself I'd stay calm and collected. But there was one thing I wanted to get off my chest, when we were finally talking like normal human beings and not flirting to make it all more complicated.

"You left. The morning after."

I guess I took Joe by a bit of a surprise, as he didn't reply right away.

When he did, he still hesitated. "Ah, that..."

"Yeah, that."

"Well, for what it's worth, I didn't mean to. It was just...um, there was a lot going on at the time."

I had heard enough. "I don't need an explanation. I was just wondering, what's with the change? I know it was just a one night stand, and it can stay that way."

Joe stepped behind me and wrapped his arms around my waist. He pulled me flush against his chest—softly yet decisively—and I couldn't resist. Once again my feet turned into total jelly, my eyes fluttered close as my heart hammered in my chest, full speed.

"It doesn't have to stay that way if you don't want it to," Joe whispered, his breath tickling my ear in the most pleasurable way imaginable.

Even though this was the moment I should've gotten pissed at him and cursed him to the next century, hoping to start a fight just to get some distance between us, I didn't. I completely gave up. Every damn muscle in my body, including the tiny ones, were still sore. I knew I couldn't beat him anyway. At this point it was time to admit that something was going to happen between Joe and me whether it was healthy for me or not.

Maybe it was better to get my heart broken sooner rather than later. Maybe just getting this thing over and done with between us was the key to dealing with fuckboys like Joe. Maybe there was even a slight chance that Joe might've told the truth—that he didn't mean to abandon me after our last time together—but I was not about to count on that.

So, calmly, I turned around in his embrace and glared him straight in the eyes. Well, as convincingly as I could considering the fact that I had to tilt my head so much to even see his face. How can a human be that tall?

"Then let's get it over and done with," I said, opening my arms wide.

The surprise was very evident on his face. He even let go of me completely and took a step back... if only I'd known I'd get rid of him this easily earlier.

Raising his eyebrows, he asked, "What's going on?"

"What, now that I'm practically throwing myself at you, you're backing off? Pathetic," I said and took a step closer to him. "Didn't you want me to beg? Well, here I fucking am. I'm tired of fighting you, fighting against this...thing between us. Just fuck me out of your system. Let's get this over and done with."

He stared me down like I had gone insane. Wasn't even that far from the truth, to be honest. "You do realize I'm going to do just that if you keep insisting?"

"Then what exactly are you waiting for?" I exclaimed, stepping even closer so our bodies were a mere centimeter apart.

Joe hesitated for maybe half a second, before letting out a growl and pushing me back against the fence. He pinned me there, leaving no way to escape. Not that it mattered. I wasn't going anywhere. Rather, I dared him with my eyes, challenging him. Surely, I could've handled whatever was coming my way.

Let's just say I hadn't been more wrong in my entire life.

When Joe cupped my cheek and leaned closer, my eyes fluttered close. I anticipated that my heart would skip a beat like it had done every time until now… but it started racing instead. I had this assumption that he'd be rough, like last time… but instead, he was very gentle as he softly pressed his lips against mine.

It sent a surge of shivers down my entire body. It became seriously hard to resist the urge to smash my entire body against his, let him do whatever the fuck he wanted with me. Deciding that it was merely some kind of a carnal instinct, I still tried my best to not let my body lean against his… Let my lips move with his… Let my hands wander on his body.

My walls of resistance started to crumble down every passing second he tried his very best to coax out a response from me. He nibbled my lips, let his tongue brush softly over them, caressed my waist with his hand…to the point that my lips started to tremble from the raw intensity I was holding back.

When his kissing started to slow down, I tasted disappointment. And I wasn't even sure if it was mine or his. Even then, I stayed still like a statue. It was only when he let his hands drop and stepped back, leaving my overheated body feeling cold and lonely before my mind finally went, "Fuck it."

As every mental rope that was holding me back got cut off at once, I literally threw myself at him. I jumped into his arms which reflexively caught me, wrapping my hands around his neck. I clung to him with all the strength I had in me, before smashing my lips against his in a heated haze.

His reply was instant, as he started moving his lips in as urgent a manner as I'd come at him. Gripping my ass, he straight up lifted me up before laying me down to sit on top of the fence. If he would've let go, I certainly would've met my end by tumbling down the steep slope, but at that moment I trusted him completely.

It wasn't until his hands made their way under my t-shirt and to my back when my mind finally cleared. All the defense walls around my heart were rebuilt at once. And I was more scared than I had been ever in my life before that precise second.

My own body had betrayed me. My heart was opening way too fast to make room for this weird man who was basically just an overgrown fuckboy. Who I had decided to not let near my heart. Who was my goddamn employee for fuck's sake.

Hastily, I slid down from the fence. Once my feet touched the solid ground, I bit his lip so hard I tasted blood. He jerked away as every sane person would, but it wasn't enough distance for me—I pushed him even further away.

And I ran.

Strictly Business

When I said I ran, I meant I fucking bulldozed my way down the hill. I found my limits, then exceeded them tenfold, charging straight through the bushes. The branches scraped my arms, but I barely even noticed.

Soon enough, Joe's footsteps were reaching me at the same time his voice did, begging me to stop. But I couldn't. And wouldn't. One part of me wanted nothing more than to get rid of Joe and especially the way he made me feel. The other half... still wanted to throw myself at him once again and let nature do its thing.

I was not going to let the latter happen.

Joe caught me when we hit the road. Nevertheless, I managed to charge through the gate first, but that's where my luck ended, and I came to a sudden halt when Joe grabbed my wrist. I almost fell.

"Fuck off!" I yelled, way too worked up to calm down to actually think what I was saying.

Joe stopped. Everything stopped. That wasn't what I'd wanted to say at all. Even then, I twisted my wrist out of his grip, sped through the door, all the way up the stairs, to my bedroom, and slammed the door shut. My lungs finally realized what I had made my body go through and started burning as I locked the door and leaned my back against it. It didn't take long before my shaking knees gave up, and I slid to sit on the floor, thoroughly spent.

There was a knock on the very same door I was leaning on. But instead of saying anything, I closed my eyes and made no effort to get up. What was even the point?

There was another knock. "Hey, Chris... what happened? I'm confused."

So was I. But I couldn't make myself say that out loud. Only the sound of me trying to hold down my ragged breath remained, until Joe knocked again.

"Are you still there?" he asked. "Just tell me what I did wrong, so it won't happen again."

But the problem wasn't him doing anything wrong. It was him doing *everything* right. I wasn't exactly mad at him—I was mad at myself for letting things go so far. For letting him affect me so deeply. I had literally thrown myself at him, before coming back down to my senses.

My heart started to ache and tried to convince my brain that it was okay to say "sorry" and that I didn't really mind. And that it wasn't him who did something wrong but me. But the words stuck to my throat and my vocal cords downright refused to produce a single sound.

All I wanted was to get up, open the door, and continue where we left off before I ran away. But that's what scared me the most. And that's why I couldn't force my body to move or my voice to work.

There was a loud sigh on the other side of the door. "Tell you what, I'm gonna make us some lunch, hmm? Come down whenever you feel like it and we'll talk."

He still waited for a couple of minutes for my reply—which never came—before I heard his footsteps receding.

It took me a solid ten minutes to gather my scattered thoughts and some strength to get up from the floor. And even then it was only because of the discomfort of sweat drying that got me going. On my way to the bathroom, I tore all my clothes away, not caring one bit of where they landed on the floor. Once I reached the shower, I turned it to scorching hot and stepped in.

Letting the warm water pour over me and rubbing my skin with shower gel, I hoped it would wash away all these weird feelings Joe had awoken inside me. I hoped it would melt down the guilt of the fact I had made him think the problem was him while in reality, it was me. I hoped…I wasn't sure what I hoped for. A miracle? Untangling my brain? A happily ever after?

But no matter how long I stood in the shower and rubbed my skin until it turned red, it didn't work. Did it ever? I wallowed in the memory of the kiss, repeating it over and over again in my head.

Which made me realize it hadn't even been Joe who had made me challenge him daily, rather than my own desire to be close to the guy. It hadn't only been Joe with all the flirting, I had made all the opportunities for him to do so myself. And based on how many times I had picked up a fight with him, I had been as obsessed, if not even more obsessed than him.

It hadn't been Joe's disappointment in my lack of response that made me throw myself at him earlier. It was my own disappointment over the loss of his touch that had made me lose it.

It was never Joe; it was all me.

It felt like all the rational thoughts in my head had taken a vacation, and I only now realized all the important stuff when I was forced to. For once, I understood why Min, Do, Joon, and Tae had been so fucking clueless all the time. I didn't have the slightest idea of how this worked until I got a glimpse of the experience firsthand.

And honestly, it would've probably been the best if I ended it before things got even more out of hand.

But did I really want this to end? I knew I had to figure that out before I talked with Joe. Because it was already a fact that I had made him feel shitty just because I couldn't stop my mouth from speaking things I didn't even mean. And I was sure that if asked him to keep his distance—and actually meant it—he'd do it. No questions asked. Then I could never go back.

On the other hand, I had to keep in mind that there was still a chance that this was a mere joke to him, to pass the time when we'd be trapped up here in the mountains. He had said himself, that *maybe* he just merely enjoyed teasing me. But was there anything wrong with that either? Even if this would get even more out of control? Because let's face it, everyone with a brain knew where all this insane chemistry was going to lead us. I mean…people have casual sex relationships all the time, right? I saw nothing wrong with it. It could even be a fun experience for the short time we'd spend together.

Deep down, I knew I wouldn't be able to leave it at that.

But let's just say I decided right then and there that I wanted nothing more than a strictly business relationship with him. Then what? We'd go back to being… what? Work acquaintances? A celebrity and his bodyguard. *Friends?*

I shook my head. No, we had never been friends. I highly doubted we could *ever* be friends. We had nothing in common, except our competitive nature and the mutual interest in martial arts.

Maybe Joe would go back to leading his company. Maybe I'd get a new guard. Maybe they'd ease up the security levels down to the point where they were before the Min-ho drama happened, although that seemed highly unlikely. Time would go by, we'd both forget what happened once upon a time, up in the mountains, on one beautiful spring day.

As my heart clenched at the mere idea of this actually being over, I knew I had my answers to every single one of these questions.

I don't think I've ever gotten out of the shower and toweled myself dry as fast as I did then. I didn't even look at which clothes I yanked on before hopping the stairs down, two at a time. Joe wasn't in the kitchen, though—there was only some kind of a salad in a bowl covered with clingfilm. I strode directly to the hallway, put on the first pair of sneakers I found, and rushed out. I was across the yard in seconds and impatiently waiting for the garage door to open—there weren't really many more places he could've gone to except the gym in the garage. Once the door was half-way up, I crouched under it, passed the Lambo, and… froze at the threshold to the gym.

Joe didn't even notice me entering the room, and I had a hunch why. His whole face was distorted as he threw punch after punch at the poor boxing bag in the corner. I froze. The sight reminded me so much of myself.

He clearly wasn't in a very bright place, something I recognized. But I hadn't had a single one of those really bad days since Joe had started staying here. I had seen only one lonely nightmare. Though I highly doubted the anxiety attacks and the nightmares wouldn't make a triumphant comeback at some point, I was still in a much better place mentally. I hadn't even touched alcohol apart from the occasional glass of wine with dinner.

And now I had driven Joe so far in the corner he was the one punching the living shit out of the poor bag. But I knew better than to try to stop him, so I leaned against the threshold and watched him work the frustrations out of his system.

Eventually, he ran out of stamina and dropped to sit on the floor with one last half-hearted punch, looking defeated. His breath was dragging, and he didn't even lift his glassy-eyed gaze from the floor when I dropped down to sit beside him. Leaning back on my arms, I cleared my throat.

"Do tell, what did the punching bag ever do to you for you to treat it that harshly?"

Barely, I was able to catch a small glimpse of a smile on his lips before it disappeared. "I dunno. It looked annoying. What's with the half-broken mirror?"

"I dunno. It looked annoying," I mimicked, causing a slight skeptical chuckle to break through Joe's stoic demeanor. "Okay, I might've kicked the bag against it. I'll replace it sometime."

He gave me a doubting glance, but ultimately let the subject drop. Instead, he rubbed the back of his head before turning to look at me. "Look, I'm sorry. About earlier. It's strictly business from now on—"

"Nah, it's okay. I overreacted. I was...confused."

"And now? Are you still confused?"

"No. And for the record, I'm sorry too." I glanced at his lip. It was still a little swollen.

"But–"

"But nothing. Look, after the crash and everything that happened with Min-ho, I haven't been in a really good place." It was only half of an excuse. I was a mess on top of being confused about me and Joe, there was no denying it.

"Yeah, I heard about that," he said, dropping his eyes back to the floor. Shit. "That's all on me. I'm beating myself over it every goddamn day, to be honest—"

"Aish," I cursed, cutting him off. This was not where I wanted my lousy little excuse to lead us. "I didn't mean it like that. It was *not* your fault. It's all on Min-ho."

"I could've done a better background check or something," Joe said, his voice breaking a little at the end. "At the time, we were understaffed—which is not an excuse—but I was settling for anyone that came to me with a decent looking CV. I should've been more careful...I—"

Sigh. To think *I* had to be the one explaining this to *Joe*, of all people.

"We could continue this the whole day. Yeah, you could've done a better background check. I shouldn't have gotten myself distracted that night," I said, touching the scars on my cheek. "All of that doesn't change any goddamn thing."

"Yeah," he said, still refusing to look at me. "I'm still sorry, though."

"I know," I huffed and bumped his shoulder with mine. Maybe I could cheer him up with a little sparring. "But enough with this deep bullshit. Get up, let's see if I can beat you this time."

That finally made him smile, but it was somewhat of a letdown since the smile didn't reach his normally so sparkly eyes. Nonetheless, he heaved himself up at the same time I did, and we started circling each other, both trying to find the other's weak spot.

Coffee Incident

The fight turned out to be a huge letdown. Joe's moves were sluggish. I suspected that he didn't even try. And as hard as I tried to coax something out of him, even a teeny-tiny sparkle of annoyance, he never lost his temper. Ever. Nor did he toss around any suggestive and disturbing comments like he usually did. The bigger surprise, though, was that I was even more annoyed by the lack of flirting than the actual flirting. It drove me nuts.

The only enjoyment I got out of the fight, was Joe's scent. It engulfed me. It was amazing. Like a forest after a rain, woody but with a little spice…he hadn't showered after our walk that turned into a bulldozing down the hill, yet he still managed to maintain a fresh aura.

But scent or no scent, I had him on the floor, sitting on top of his chest. He had so many options to get up, but he laid there like a limp dick. When he tapped the floor in a sign of surrender, that too was…lazy.

"You're not even trying," I spat, still irked that he kept evading my eyes.

"I'm tired. You won. Now get off. I already tapped out," he stated, with that annoying fake-disinterested voice and a nonchalant tone that drove me up the walls.

"Ugh, snap out of it and fight me!" I said, grabbing his collar.

He stopped me by grabbing my wrists. "I– I don't think we should do this any longer. I promised you we'd keep this strictly business…"

Ah, shibal—do I really have to do this?

A moment of self-doubt about my recent resolution flashed through my mind, but only briefly. Then I forced my wrists off his grip and pinned his hands to the floor on top of his head. Ignoring the look of surprise on Joe's face, I smashed my lips against his.

He totally froze under me when our lips touched. Solid. Much like I had at first when we kissed earlier…I wondered if he had felt as weird then. But refusing to give up, I kept kissing him. First on his lips but soon moved on to his stubbed jawline, his neck…none of it had any effect.

Frustrated, I sucked his lower lip and bit it. Hard. That finally caused some kind of reaction—letting out a growl, he spun us around and pinned me below him so suddenly that I gasped, and my head was a little wobbly for a moment. Then, when I recovered enough to notice what happened, a grin tugged my lips up. There was a smirk on Joe's lips as well as he loomed over me, those weird dark golden eyes studying me.

Finally, he looked like himself.

"Fucking tease," Joe said, before burying his face to the nook of my neck.

My quiet reminder of not leaving any marks was ignored completely, and I couldn't focus for shit anyway since his whole body pressed against mine. His short stubble scratched my collarbone as his slick lips roamed on my neck. It was a sensory overload. One that made my heart race and pants too tight.

I savored every shiver that he caused to run down my spine. Because who knew how long this was going to last? Not long, that's for sure. This much desire was going to burn to its end sooner rather than later. There was no way this magnitude of passion would survive even a hint of an actual relationship.

So I made a wavering deal with myself to let me enjoy it while it lasted, right when his lips finally found back to mine. Eagerly, I answered his kiss with matching enthusiasm, pulling him even tighter against me. His impressive bulge pressed against my equally aroused but not even nearly as notable length through the layers of sweatpants.

A breathless whine escaped my lips when his tongue brushed against them.

Letting out that sound, however, was a mistake. Because right at that exact second, Joe decided he had had enough and retreated. The sudden loss of his warm body on top of me, made my whole body shiver uncontrollably. This time, that shiver wasn't a pleasant feeling…at all.

I heaved myself to a half-sitting position, leaning against my arms. Joe was now on his knees, not that far away from me…yet it felt like there was an invisible wall built between us in a nanosecond.

"If we go any further than this, I'm gonna end up fucking you senseless right here on the gross gym floor. No one wants that."

"As if I'd even put out for you," I muttered out of habit, though my entire thought process was more in line with, *"Maybe I want that."*

Joe only let out a dry laugh and flashed me a cocky grin as he stood up. "Trust me, shortie, at this rate I'm gonna find myself in your bedroom sooner rather than later."

"Hmph, keep on dreaming," I said, although a bit relieved that he seemed to have gotten his usual spirit back.

I stood up, brushed my clothes to straighten them and headed to the main house. Joe jogged past me, smacking my ass on his way. For the first time, I found it more amusing than irritating, so I only raised one eyebrow at him. He flashed me another grin before disappearing upstairs. Shortly after, I heard the shower turn on.

An annoying smile, that I couldn't erase from my face however hard I tried, lit up my whole face when I brewed us some coffee and munched the salad Joe had left me. I blame the stupid grin on the relief over the fact that Joe was back to his usual annoying self. Mostly because that annoying Joe was way easier to handle than the brooding one.

Everything else went back to normal too, or to this thing that was our normal. Eventually Joe came down the stairs, wearing one of those too-tight t-shirts emphasizing his…arms…and some jeans. He started preparing dinner. Looked like it was going to take a while to get done too.

Occasionally, he tried to disturb me with his comments, but it was way easier to ignore them now that I had gotten used to them. Instead of giving in and letting myself get agitated over his comments, I decided to go through the schedule for the next couple of days. With the coffee mug in tow, I hopped on the couch with the phone.

Looked like our schedule was going to be packed. We were starting out preparations for the Billboards as well as the world tour. Jiwoo had announced all the dates and venues had been successfully arranged. Some of the arenas we were supposed to tour had been upgraded to stadiums. Wildly enough, we were more popular than ever. That, or people just wanted to witness the scandal-ridden group with their own two eyes instead of only reading about it on the gossip pages on the internet.

I was immersed in my phone, reserving some time slots for my own things—like doing social media and stuff now that Minjae was no longer in charge of that—when the phone buzzed in my hand and nearly made me spill the coffee all over myself. It was a text from Hana—my sister.

My sister the cop. To think that out of the offsprings of Mrs. Cho Da-hee, the two of us ended up on the opposite sides of the law. To see what on earth she wanted to talk about with me, I tapped the text open.

I'm so gonna kill you, little shit. Be warned.

Ah, it was Hana indeed. I guessed this had something to do with her hunk of a work partner who might or might've not let into the secret a while back, that Hana had the hots for him. I chuckled.

Surely I'm innocent, but continue, I typed and hit send, an amused smile lingering on my lips as I waited for the reply. This was going to be golden. I was sure it had something to do with the hunk. And suddenly, I was dying to know.

Sang-cheol asked me out on a date. Now it's all awkward and weird at work. It's your fault.

How is it weird? You said yes, right? Or was she an utter moron?

Obvs I said no, you idiot! We work together! she replied, almost instantly.

So? I see no problem. Now be a good little wifey to him and say yes.

AARRGGHH how are you so dense? I'm so done with you playing a fucking cupid!

I'm not– I started to type, but something warm and wet touched the side of my neck.

I jumped up, startled. Not to even mention the fact that I spilled the coffee all over my crotch and the phone flew out of my hand. Joe laughed hysterically behind me. The fucker had *licked* my neck. Could one be any more dog-like? I could practically see his imaginary tail wagging.

"What are you doing," I asked, glad my coffee had already cooled off—otherwise it would have burned my dick off or something. And I still liked my dick, thank you very much.

"I'm bored," Joe managed to say through his chuckles before he lost it completely. He could hardly look in my direction without doubling over and laughing so hard his eyes watered. Taking a deep breath, I ignored him. Instead, I picked up the phone from the floor and set it on the side table before circling the couch calmly.

I proceeded to toss the rest of the coffee that was left in my mug directly at Joe as a revenge. He gasped, and I turned around as nonchalantly as I could. My aim was to get the mug to the dishwasher before heading upstairs to take another fucking shower for the day.

Unfortunately, Joe had other ideas. He tossed his now wet t-shirt aside and grabbed my waist before I managed to take two steps in the kitchen's direction. Then, he dragged me back to the couch, ignoring my struggling completely. I stood no chance whatsoever against him, so he sat on the couch and pulled me down to sit on his lap. Though I was struggling the whole time, boy I did not miss the fact that my back touched his hot—and very naked—chest.

In a flash, both Hana and the coffee incident were completely forgotten. My heart stopped once again when his slick and skillful lips found the nook of my neck from behind.

Whatever this man did to me…particularly my heart… it couldn't be healthy.

Joe played me like…like…I don't know. A fucking guitar or something. And he had certainly mastered the art. I was so gone.

With the second kiss that landed on my nape, my heart got electrocuted back to life. As Joe's hands sneaked under my shirt, my body no longer jerked around because I struggled to get away…rather it was this warm jolt of pleasure that surged through my body.

The rest of my defenses crumbled down if they ever even existed in the first place. As he continued where he had left off with his lips on my neck, his fingers also brushed across my chest, before settling on my waist.

It was unfair, really. The fact that he had this sixth sense of figuring out my weak spots when even I didn't have the slightest clue myself. I didn't stand a chance against the guy, and most likely never had.

To make matters worse, my writhing in his grip had another rather disturbing effect too. Apparently the friction of my behind rubbing against his crotch, caused his dick to start bulging. The pure size of it even terrified me—despite the fact that it had once been inside me. Or maybe it was because of that fact that I was a little hesitant…

I couldn't focus on the size of his dick for long though, as his hands still roamed under my shirt. I couldn't help but let out a shaky breath as his skillful touches slid on my skin and his lips still worked the magic spot on the side of my neck that drove me absolutely crazy.

"You got me thinking…" Joe muttered against my neck at the same as he distracted me by circling his fingertip around my navel.

My reply was practically a moan, as it seemed to be the only thing my vocal cords were able to compose at that point.

"…that even if you won't let me in your bedroom, yet, we could do other things…" he continued, making my body jerk again while his other hand slid down and started toying with the string of my sweatpants.

I was so out of it, only being able to focus on his hands and especially his cock pressing against my ass, that I could only breathe out a soft, "hmm?"

"I mean, it's a total waste if we both are left with blue balls, right?" he asked breathily, making a point by grabbing my hips and swaying me against his rock hard bulge. As if I wasn't aware of the level of arousal around here already.

"Well, I could do something about yours at least, if you let me," he continued, clearly asking for permission of some sort, and explaining what he was after by moving his other hand closer to the waistband of my pants.

Wanting his hands to move faster, I took whatever little control I had over the whole situation and rolled my ass harder against his bulge. He let out a muffled groan against my neck, but otherwise the effect was the opposite of what I wanted—as his hands stopped completely.

"You have to say you want it. I need to know you're ready for this. I'm not taking any chances after...whatever happened earlier today," he said with a strained but firm tone.

He couldn't be serious, right? As if I'd ever asked him to jerk me off for fuck's sake. So instead of opening my mouth and risking saying something completely wrong again, I grabbed his wrists and tried to move his hands further. He didn't even budge.

"Out loud, Chris. Please," he begged, muffling another groan against the nape of my neck.

Deeply blushed, horny as fuck, dick aching against the coffee-stained, and unnecessary clothing, I swallowed my pride and cleared my throat. If he wanted a proper consent, he'd get proper consent. Asshole.

"Can you please just get to it," I muttered, the harshness of my voice surprising even myself.

Luckily even though my words weren't exactly the thing he probably wanted to hear; it was consent. His lips curved into a slight smile against my nape. And finally, after what felt like years, his hands unfroze and found their way back to my waistband.

Agonizingly slowly, Joe pulled one of the strings to loosen up my pants, toying with it for a whole hot minute, driving me even further into insanity. Fortunately, it only took another squirm to rub my ass against his dick, that got him to aim further. My back arched when his hand finally made it under the waistband to rest on top of my bulge. But then he stopped there, completely ignoring my aching dick.

Realizing this fucker clearly teased me for his own pleasure, I tested the theory by grinding my ass against his shaft once more. I was quickly proved right as he gasped almost inaudibly before stroking my dick through the underwear.

Only moving if I did, he kept teasing me to the point I was going to explode and was already leaking pre-cum inside my already coffee-stained boxer briefs. I was a whole, moaning, literal mess. Though a too distracted one to give a single fuck about my reputation at that moment.

One too sudden movement later, Joe's hands had all but disappeared. I almost growled from frustration. Thankfully, I stopped myself before that by realizing what Joe was after when his hands started to slide my pants down. I raised my hips to help him with the task, and at last, my dick was freed from the prison of the damp clothing.

Joe's large hand draped around it, covering most of its length all the way from the base to the edge of the glans. He took it extremely slowly as he stroked me, before his thumb circled over the sensitive tip, spreading the leaked precum. My heart beating faster than ever before, I didn't even try to stay upright on my own and leaned against his chest.

His bulge pressing my ass, paired with his hand working on my cock drove me absolutely mad. In no time, I could already feel the orgasm building, my body squirming in his embrace.

"Fuck, keep rubbing that ass against my cock and I'll cum too," Joe groaned to my ear, making me freeze in a sudden shame. Was I a total wanton?

The embarrassment lasted only a second, as his thumb brushed over my slit ever so gently again. It was all it took for me to get back to the world of ultimate bliss. Deciding to worry about the consequences later, I started to chase my orgasm by grinding against him in some kind of a frenzy.

With my every move, his hand tightened around my shaft as he pumped it up and down. At some point, I could sense he was getting close to his own release as his movements became erratic. The realization that I could cause these same sensations for him too, was so hot that my balls tightened, and the first wave of the most intense orgasm I'd had in a *while* nearly knocked me out.

I squirted what must've been at least a week's worth of load on my already ruined t-shirt, as well as on Joe's hand. As I slumped against him, he grabbed my hips, rocked me back and forth a couple of times before he unloaded between us, further ruining my clothes.

It took me maybe a couple of minutes, but eventually, I came down from the high. And yes, my brain finally started working. Unfortunately. It meant things like wondering how and when the hell had he managed to open his own pants and when, appeared to my conscience. I was basically sitting on top of his bare, now slowly softening dick.

But it wasn't until Joe lifted his hand that was covered in my spunk and licked it to taste my juices when the ultimate devastation of what I had done, hit me like a wave. I hurried to stand up, pulling my pants back up at the same time. I didn't even glance towards Joe who still slouched on the couch, in his euphoric state as I grabbed my phone and ran a hand through my hair.

"I– I'm gonna head to the shower," I muttered, before darting to the stairs.

Joe tried to stop me by saying something, but in my need to get out of the situation, I didn't listen. I practically ran away from him all over again. Yes, even while I knew it wasn't a very bright idea based on what happened last time I ran away.

Once I reached my bedroom, I slammed the door shut and finally breathed.

What the fuck just happened? How did I end up being jerked off by Joe on my couch when I had been supposed to end things with him? Was I losing my mind once and for all?

The phone buzzed in my hand, effectively distracting me before I totally lost it. But that relief didn't last long; I had been texting with Hana. Of all people.

Sighing, I opened the messages.

AARRGGHH how are you so dense??
But okay yes. I said yes. We're going next Friday.
What the hell am I supposed to do now?!
Hello?!?!!? Are you there???
Chris.
You got me into this mess, so you'll have to help me.
...
Answer me you little shit!
What do I even wear?

Whoa, that was a lot of texts for like a half an hour tops. Also looked like Hana hadn't changed much from our teenage years. Letting out another long sigh, I backspaced the previous text that had been...err...*cut short*...before I managed to send it. Then I started typing something along the lines of "calm the fuck down," but didn't get very far before the phone buzzed again with another text from Hana.

How do relationships even work?

How the fuck was I supposed to know that? Yes, I might've meddled in other people's business before. But the deal was that I'd get the right people together, and that's it. I wasn't a fucking couples' therapist. Hell, I didn't even know what to do with Joe for fuck's sake.

Annoyed, I tossed the phone on top of the bed before yanking the spunk covered t-shirt off and pulled down my beyond-ruined jeans. On my way, stomping towards the shower, I shoved the clothes to the laundry bin so hard it knocked over.

Great. Just great.

Wide Awake

After one particularly fucked up workday a few days later, I curved the Lambo down to the highway and slammed the gas pedal down. One of the world's most famous guitar riff intros started blasting my eardrums at the top volume at the same time, effectively making me grin like a maniac over the good timing. James Hetfield's rough baritone almost managed to drown the roars of the V12 engine that was giving its all behind my back as I whipped it to higher and deadlier speeds, but not quite.

It felt good to be in control, for once. Joe had had some errands to run, so he had to take his own BMW today, which meant I didn't even have to listen to him whine on the passenger seat about my "insane driving." How that bastard ever managed to keep up with me and the Lambo was beyond me. Yet, every time I glanced at the rearview mirror the familiar BMW was there. My knuckles turned white when I took a better grip on the steering wheel, before forcing the car to go even faster. My beyond-pissed-off state of mind still wanted to shake him off, even though I knew our destination was the exact same—my house.

The workday had been a hellish experience, to say the least. I had been forced to sit still for three hours straight when the make-up artists had tried to figure out how to fix—their words—the "ultimate mess that is your face." Testing out countless concealers, color correctors, and even fucking glue, they had eventually settled to using this FX sculpture *clay* that was normally used to *create* scars. Not to hide actual scars.

Had the heavy paste managed to make my skin look perfect again? Yes. Well, from a certain distance. A long distance. But I also couldn't move half of my face in it. It got to the point that they started to wonder if I'd have to use a pre-recorded backup track on the Billboard's stage and lip-sync. The struggle was real—it was surprisingly hard to sing if you couldn't move your face properly.

On top of that, Joe had avoided me, like I was a highly contagious disease, ever since the—um—let's call it the "coffee incident." There were no longer any highly disturbing comments about fucking me senseless, no flirty comments about my admittedly perky ass...nothing. He had plainly followed me to work every day and then back to my home. He still made me dinner and stuff due to our previous bets, but it wasn't the same when I hadn't had to fight for those luxuries.

In fact, I was pretty sure he hadn't even touched me—with ulterior motives or otherwise—after that day. Yes, I knew I was the one to blame for that as I had, once again, ran away. But Joe hadn't even tried to catch me either, this time, so I guess he was already over me.

I had no mercy over the BMW or Joe driving it, as I sped up the roads towards my home on the mountains. It wasn't until I reversed my Lambo inside the garage when the adrenaline rush started to fade. I collected myself, heaved myself up from the car and slammed the door shut, and started to wonder what we'd have for dinner that night.

But when I stepped out of the garage, Joe steered the BMW to my yard and cut off my path, halting the car directly in front of me. After killing the engine, he hopped out looking pretty damn pissed.

So much for getting dinner anytime soon, then.

"What the fuck Chris! Are you suicidal?" he yelled at me over his car. "And if you are, can't you do it somewhere where other people aren't in danger?!"

Apparently, the adrenaline hadn't fully exited my system yet, since my blood started boiling in a record time.

"And how's that any of your business?" I shouted back. "Actually, do me a favor: fuck off and leave me alone!"

While Joe slammed the door shut before heading my way, my plan was to ignore him and continue my way to the main house as I was going to before all this yelling.

Of course, Joe wasn't having it. Instead, he stepped on my way, grabbed my shoulders. With eyes blazing fire, he started shaking me.

"Fuck off? *Again?* How much more can I fuck off, considering I *am* your guard? I get paid to keep you safe. Which, by the way, makes it exactly my business," he spat, before finally letting go of me. "I have no idea what's with you today, but I highly recommend you snap out of it."

My entire body started shaking from pure rage. Trying my hardest to not lose it completely, my hands curled into tight fists as I glared him straight in the eyes.

"Why do you even care? I never once asked you to do this. I never asked you to be here. Yet, you waltzed into my life uninvited, turned it upside down, and when you got what you wanted, you fucking stopped—"

"Oh, so you're pissed at me?" Joe growled, cutting me off. "Thanks for clearing that up. Now, I can show you how to let out that frustration in a tad healthier way."

And with that, he grabbed my waist and threw me on his shoulder like a sack of potatoes. I banged his back, legs kicking the air, but it had absolutely no effect whatsoever. No matter how much I struggled, he easily carried me through the garage, to the gym and threw me on the mat. As I tried to figure out what the fuck was happening, he tossed his suit jacket to the corner together with his earpiece and radiophone before loosening his tie.

Stuffing his hands in his pockets, he glared at me with dark eyes.

"Hit me," he stated with a challenging tone.

"What the fuck? No," I said. This was getting ridiculous. I didn't want to fight him at all, especially not when he was actually being serious. It could end badly for either of us. I mean, I would've been glad to beat the shit out of him, but I'd had enough of violence. The last time still haunted me in my dreams for fuck's sake. Besides, how would hitting him make me any less angry at him?

"Come on. Let that steam out or something. I know you want to."

Fine.

I stood up. Cracked my neck and knuckles. Then I charged at him. But he rolled out of the way, almost leisurely so, then yanked me back by the collar of my leather jacket. I landed on my ass in the exact same spot on the mat where I had started.

"Pathetic," he said with a deadpan and stuffed his hands back into his pockets.

Now that got me riled up properly. Who did he think he was? This ain't some fucking karate kid. I could beat the shit out of him if I'd really put in some effort. So I got up and leaped at him.

Again, I landed back on the same gym mat I had started from. Swallowing my annoyance, knowing it wouldn't help me one bit, I attacked him again and again. But the bastard clearly wanted to humiliate me, showing off how he had only been playing with me the past week or so. My every muscle went rigid when I finally shrugged the jacket off and tossed it on top of Joe's stuff over at the corner.

I leaped at him with everything I had in me.

Still, Joe didn't even produce one bead of sweat while he danced out of my reach every damn time. He showed little to no interest in the fight whatsoever, despite having me fall flat on my ass on top of the gym mat over and over and over again.

Yet, I couldn't stop. Not even when I was drenched in sweat in no time, and my breath hitched to my throat. Not when my legs started to shake.

When my stamina was reaching all possible limits, Joe grabbed my shoulders again and shook me. "I know you can do better than this. Stop playing around and just do it!"

I fell, ass first, on the mat once again. What the fuck did he want from me, I had no idea. But what he got was a surge of some new adrenaline provided energy. And this time as I attacked him, the edges of my vision had this strange red hue, and my ears rang.

Instead of charging at him directly, I took a different route and went for his legs. I was trying to aim for his knees with my kick to make him lose his balance, but as he was so fast I couldn't hit him there, and the kick landed on his calf. A strange, muffled sound of intense pain escaped his lips before he staggered out of my reach.

I finally found his weak spot.

Perhaps it was a fairly recent injury.

I didn't get to wallow in the small victory for long though before I found myself sitting on the mat again. But even that slightest win against him, made a tiny spark of hope ignite in my spirit and I lunged at him again. This time targeting his legs. Again. And again.

With every win, I gained more momentum. Every time I managed to get ahead of him, my vision became more focused. Soon, the only thing I could see was him. The world around us disappeared. He got tired, and I gained more power for every small win. Eventually, I managed to trip him, causing him to fall on the very same gym mat that had become so damn familiar for my own ass only a few moments ago.

With a triumphant grin, I hopped on top of him. Pinning his whole upper body down with my legs so he couldn't move, I grabbed his now drenched in sweat dress shirt's collar. I pulled my fist back, ready to land a punch square on his face.

But then, I hesitated. As he held still, not even trying to get up anymore, something held me back. A sweat bead that formed on my forehead, somehow managed to run down on my eye. I tried to blink it away with no success. It burned.

Soon, Joe's face distorted. Then, it wasn't him I was staring at...

Instead, it was Min-ho's blood-covered and deformed face. A wicked smile lingered on his lips as he glared at me with dark eyes, urging me to kill him. It was like I was seeing my regular nightmare where I became a killer...

But this time, I was wide awake.

I blinked again and as soon as Min-ho appeared, he was gone. Thank fuck. The face that was glaring at me once again belonged to Joe.

The hallucination had lasted only a second, but it was enough. I couldn't move a muscle. Seemed like I was more fucked up in the head than I had originally thought.

So, even though Joe kept looking me straight in the eyes, challenging me, I couldn't do it. I couldn't hit him. And I wouldn't. No matter how much he'd urge me to do it. Reminding myself that I was in control of my own actions and my own body, I unclenched my fingers, one by one, in order to let go of his collar.

Sitting upright, I let both of my hands drop to my sides. On the verge of collapsing from pure exhaustion, my head also dropped.

"Do it, Chris. Hit me," Joe said with a cold and calm tone.

A single tear I couldn't hold back rolled down my cheek when I blinked. My voice shaking, I muttered a broken, "I can't."

Joe's eyes softened, while mine started burning as more tears were waiting for their chance to break free behind my eyelids.

"I know," he murmured softly. "It's okay."

With the last bits of my strength, I half-heartedly banged his chest with my fist. "Then why did you make me, huh?" I sobbed, an endless stream of burning, salty tears flooding down my face. "I can't fucking do it! I won't!"

Joe crawled up and wrapped his hands around me, pulling me close. My whole body shook as I tried to not lose control, but as I was exhausted, I couldn't help but let the built-up feeling of mostly anger, shame and exhaustion overpower me.

"Shh, it's okay," he whispered to my ear, stroking my back softly. I laid my chin on his shoulder, losing the last bits of strength and spirit. I let the dams in my eyes crack wide open.

It was like I couldn't breathe. My throat was blocked and the salty stream on my face made the skin burn. Joe, however, didn't care one bit as I hung on his arms, limp. I decided to let the episode run through its course. I couldn't stop it either way, now that I had let it break free.

Through the fatigue that weighed me down and the crying, I barely even noticed that Joe picked me up and started carrying me towards the main house. I didn't give a single fuck. I was fairly certain I wouldn't have been able to walk myself anyway. He carried me straight upstairs, to my bedroom and all the way to the en-suite bathroom. After dropping me down to sit on the toilet seat's lid, he kneeled in front of me.

"Let's get this shit off your face, hmm?" he asked with a soft, soothing tone. Cupping my cheek with his hand, he wiped a few tears off with his thumb. Probably further ruining the already fucked up pile of clay combined with a ton of makeup.

Only gesture I managed was to nod. Staring ahead, practically seeing nothing, I could only focus on trying to not fall to the floor when Joe let go of me to hunt down some products. He went through the drawers, pulling out every bottle he thought would help with the cause. Poor guy didn't realize that the clay wouldn't suddenly melt away with any cleanser whatsoever. It would have to be removed manually before all that. Nevertheless, I made no effort to move and help him whatsoever. I was too damn tired.

Eventually he had like seven different cleansers in his hands as he looked at me questioningly. "Which one should I use?"

Not having energy to even roll my eyes though I very much wanted to, I grabbed the jar from the counter that held the makeup remover wipes. Yanking one out, I started rubbing my face with it violently. Joe stopped me by grabbing my wrist and pulling the cloth out of my grip after dropping all the other products to the sink. He tossed it to the trash, took a new one from the jar, and started to sort of scrape the clay off from my face with way gentler manners than I had.

As I was still a bit out of it, an occasional tear or two still managed to escape my eyes. I let Joe clean my face and he did with extremely careful motions. The clay was stubborn, so he had to use some actual force to get rid of it. I barely noticed.

After that, he wet a towel with some warm water and rubbed the rest of it off. Once he was done with that, he pulled my shirt off, continuing to towel me, most likely to get rid of the sweat. For once, I didn't protest. His touch was very welcoming; it ground me to reality. Maybe it had something to do with the fact that he had avoided me for a few days. Or with the fact that his presence was somehow comforting. Soothing, even.

When he was done cleaning me, Joe pulled me up. I tried to walk but wasn't very successful, so I heavily leaned against him when we slowly moved towards the bed. With a grunt from deep inside my chest, I crashed on top of the bed, face hitting the pillow.

I guess Joe covered me with the comforter, as a warm weight landed on me. Somehow I was still cold and started shivering uncontrollably. I rolled to my side, wrapping myself tighter inside the blanket.

Shortly after, Joe started to leave and suddenly I wanted nothing more than to ask him to stay. But I couldn't speak, my teeth clattering from the cold. So after one brush through my hair to get them out of my face, placing a gentle kiss on my forehead, he walked to the door. Just like that, he was about to leave me here alone, and I had never in my life felt more lonely.

If only he could've read my mind.

As he unfortunately didn't possess any supernatural abilities, he whispered a soft "good night" instead from the threshold, before simply stepping out. The door closed behind him, and a last lonely tear escaped the inner corner of my eye, rolling down the side of my nose before landing on the pillow.

The darkness wrapped me in its tight embrace. Being painfully aware of the fact that I was going to spend the whole night alone with only the nightmares keeping me company, my throat tightened again. I tried to keep my eyes open, but as I was so fucking tired, I couldn't fight it for long…I slowly drifted off to a restless slumber.

The nightmares…so realistic they left me gasping for air most nights. In some form, they always repeated the evening of the car crash. Sometimes in vivid detail. Other times in fog. But in the worst ones, I never lost focus after my face was slashed open. I never became tired. My strength didn't run out.

In the nightmares, I almost always kept going. To the point I ended up beating Min-ho to death. Thankfully in reality, I had lost consciousness and never really turned into a killer…but it had been too damn close.

This night, however, there was a slight difference in the dream, compared to previous nights. One that followed the day's theme of hallucinations somewhat disturbingly.

My knuckles crack as I land my fist, again and again at the face that starts to deform. Blood from my many wounds drips down on his equally bloody face, but I don't care. A growl erupts from somewhere deep inside me, the rage burning every single one of the remaining sane thoughts, more and more adrenaline pumping to my bloodstream as I keep hitting his face.

Over and over and over again.

I don't think I can stop. I don't think I will.

Somewhere deep down, I realize that this will end badly if I don't stop. I still don't. I can't.

Even when he stops struggling, I keep going. Even though his body goes limp under me, I keep going. Even if he loses consciousness at some point, I keep going.

My hands ache, a hot flash of pain jolts up my arm every time my fist meets the flesh and bones. My lungs burn from the lack of oxygen because I barely know how to breathe at this point of insanity. My vision is stained by the blood that gushed from my wounds.

But when sanity slowly seeps back when I lose stamina I drop my hands to my sides defeated... the crushed, deformed, dead face isn't Min-ho's.

It's Joe's.

Blissful Oblivion

Sharp pain hit my cheek as I stared down at Joe. Who—miraculously enough—was not dead any longer? Very much alive, he shook my shoulders and slapped my face. Not very hard. Just enough for me to feel a noticeable sting. How could a dead man move? And yell. He was doing that. Loudly. The words, though, I couldn't understand at first.

"Wake up Chris! It was just a dream," was the first thing I understood. Then when he repeated it again, I realized that was all he had been saying.

It took my eyes a while to focus. And even more time for my brain to register, that we weren't in front of the dorm on hard asphalt. Instead, we were in my room, on my bed, at my home in the mountains. The lights were on, and they started to hurt my eyes as a headache hit my head like a wrecking ball.

Also, my lungs didn't work. I took a deep breath, trying to coax them to function. Oddly aware of the breathing motion that was normally automatic, I sucked in air between my still clenched teeth. Shaky breath in, slow breath out. Long deep breath in, then huffed it out. Another breath in…and so on.

The salty tears that dampened my face started to dry. It tightened my skin—a mild inconvenience. But what became a different, but more noticeable inconvenience, was the fact that I was absolutely drenched in a cold sweat. From head to toe.

How had I straddled Joe in my sleep, I had no idea. Yet there he was, under me, trying to wake me up, as I slowly gained back my consciousness. There was a deep wrinkle between his eyebrows, and those eyes were begging me to get back to reality. The shaking irritated me, so I forced my eyes to focus on his, before grabbing his wrists.

"I'm awake," I stated through my clenched teeth, still not quite being able to unlock my jaw.

At once, his hands dropped, and he inhaled deeply. "Fucking finally."

The realization that I was still sitting on top of him hit me, and I crawled off quickly. I sat next to him and sighed, my back resting against the headboard. Trying to wipe the rest of the tears and sweat off my face with the backs of my hands, I glanced at the digital clock on my bedside table. It was only four in the morning. Fuck. All that trouble for only a few hours of sleep.

Joe also sat upright beside me. "Are you alright?" he asked softly, curling his hand around my shoulders, and pulling me closer. "You woke me up, screaming in your sleep. I came to see what was up, and you…you attacked me."

Beyond tired, and still slightly trapped in the nightmare, I could only lean against him and nod. I closed my eyes and took another deep breath, inhaling the natural, already familiar soothing scent of Eau de Joe. He had showered; his nice, natural scent was slightly diluted with some cheap-ass shower gel. I made a mental note to buy him something better sometime soon.

"I heard about the nightmares from Mr. Won, but I thought they had passed," he continued after a while. "And I know you're not supposed to wake up a person seeing nightmares but…you know. I didn't have much of a choice."

"Honestly, I'm glad you woke me up," I said. "And I'm sorry for attacking you."

"It's okay. Do you want to talk about it?"

I did, too exhausted to be prideful. And maybe still slightly vulnerable from the latest nightmare and barely awake. For the first time after it all happened that made me this mess, I spilled everything. How the events unfolded time and time again in my mind upon nightfall. How the anxiety attack that occurred after the dreams often kept me awake for the rest of the night. How I sometimes was too afraid to sleep in the first place. Or how I couldn't bring myself to sleep, knowing full well I'd only wake up alone and shaking, breaking a cold sweat.

Joe was a good listener. Great, actually. He didn't interrupt me once. Instead, he held me tightly in his embrace and drew random patterns on my shoulder softly with the tips of his fingers.

"I think I've been too exhausted to dream at all these past days," I finally concluded, shrugging. "Maybe that's why they stopped for a while."

"Have you considered seeking professional help? Because to me, that sounds like it could be PTSD. I've seen it before, and untreated, it can turn ugly. Fast," he stated with his voice so silent it was almost a whisper.

I shrugged again. It wasn't like the thought hadn't crossed my mind because it had. They had been warning me about this all the way back when they released me from the hospital. These past days though, I had started to think it was passing on its own. Apparently, I was wrong.

"I'll think about it," I replied to Joe after a long and heavy silence when I thought it through. It seemed to be enough for him, as he only nodded, and the silence fell upon us again.

It wasn't one of those awkward silences—rather, it was the kind when no-one had anything to say but it still wasn't uncomfortable. I had never been much of a small-talker anyway, so it suited me just fine. Trying to forget the nightmare, I let my mind start to wander.

Gazing at the night sky through the huge window beside the bed, Joonie and the others came to mind, and I wondered how they were coping.

Was Joonie suffering through a similar nightmare every night? Probably not. He told me he still didn't remember the crash at all, despite remembering almost everything else. But then again, dealing with not remembering shit had most likely been a lot to handle on its own, so I was glad he didn't remember the crash as well. I wondered how Tae was doing—back at the hospital he had been a total wreck. Which was no surprise, given that he had lost his grandma who had been like a mother to him earlier in the same week, and he almost lost Joonie right after they finally started dating. Even Minjae and Do crossed my mind, but I couldn't even begin to imagine what was it like to know they basically had a sex tape forever circling on the internet.

For the first time since all the drama, I realized how much of a selfish prick I had become after getting out of the hospital. It wasn't like the other guys weren't dealing with their own shit as much as I was. It wasn't like they had abandoned me, more like I had isolated myself up here, as far as possible without exiting Seoul.

They were like brothers to me, all of them. I was honestly closer to them than my own sister. I missed living in a dorm with them. I missed having the simple choice to knock on any of their doors to have a chat. Getting drunk with Joon. Dancing with Minjae. Learning about making music with Do. Having vocal lessons with Tae… And the most, I missed being a carefree maknae who had nothing better to do with his free time than to tease his hyungs.

My absentminded wandering inside my own little bubble of missing the guys was almost violently interrupted when Joe unwrapped himself from around me and started retreating. I shot him a panicked look, which he didn't even see as he was already facing the door.

"Where are you going?" I asked, before I could stop myself.

Joe froze and glanced at me over his shoulder with his eyebrows knitted together. "To the guest room, obviously?"

"Right," I mumbled, my chest clenching and breath hitching to my throat.

I hugged my knees, reminding myself again of how to breathe…while also trying to figure out why the fuck and how the fuck had I gotten myself this attached to Joe in such a short time.

"I mean…you've banned me from your bedroom, remember? Besides, you should sleep," he said.

"Well, I'm not gonna get any more sleep, so you might as well stay for a bit… like, only for tonight," I muttered, embarrassed that I couldn't bring myself to actually ask him to stay. Then I realized that maybe he was tired and thought I was being weird for an entirely different reason. "I mean if you're not sleepy…or you could sleep here too, I won't mind. Or we could get up–" I rambled, cutting myself off before it got even worse.

He shook his head slightly, an amused smile lingering on his lips. "Are you sure?"

I couldn't do anything but nod and avoid his gaze. Then I felt the other side of the bed dip down as Joe crawled under the comforter.

I should've known better than to let him in there willingly though.

Because while he made himself comfortable, he also muttered, "I knew it wouldn't take me long to gain access to your bedroom."

Already regretting ever letting him stay, I smacked his shoulder. But I couldn't help a slight smile tug the corners of my lips up. Joe smashed the lights off chuckling, while I looked at the night sky that had already started to lighten from the horizon.

"So, what now?" Joe asked eventually, probably getting bored with the silence.

He looked oddly relaxed, laying on his side, leaning against his elbow. He was wearing a loose tank top and old sweatpants. Glancing down my naked torso, I realized I was wearing only the same pair of boxers he had left on me when he had tucked me in bed for the night. For the life of me, I couldn't bring myself to be bothered about it—I mean, he had jerked me off the other day on my fucking couch in the bright daylight. I cut off that train of thought short, though, as the flashbacks set my insides on fire.

I shrugged. "Suit yourself. Sleeping is pretty much ruled out for me for tonight though."

"Then I'll stay awake with you."

A shiver ran down my spine, so I scrambled under the sheets as well. Even though I shot Joe the death glare as a warning, he didn't give a shit. Instead, he grabbed my waist and wrapped his whole huge body around me.

I gave up.

Relaxing in his embrace, I wondered if this thing we had would last after our time up in the mountains would end. Probably not. But I refused to think about it yet and inhaled the intoxicating scent his body emitted to the air around me. I could worry about everything else later.

I let his even breathing lull me into blissful oblivion.

Addiction

It was weird—waking up after having a completely normal dream, after a night of terror. Normally I couldn't have gotten any sleep, yet here we were. Waking up to the alarm clock. Even somewhat well-rested.

The dream hadn't even been vivid or anything, just something about me and Joonie getting drunk at our old dorms. As soon as I opened my eyes, I hardly remembered any of it. By the time my brain woke up completely, it was already a distant, fading memory.

Maybe it wasn't that bad, after all, to let Joe inside my bedroom. At least that was my mindset before I started suffocating under the weight and immense heat of Joe's heavily sleeping body that was still wrapped around me.

I tried to get up to absolutely no avail. In his deep slumber, Joe only tightened his grip the more I struggled. There was no choice but to surrender and relax—or that's what I told my brain to shut it up. After glancing at his surprisingly peaceful sleeping face, I rolled around in his grip to face the window and watched the day start on the other side.

It was going to be a sunny day. Not that it mattered since I would be trapped at one of the LBR Entertainment's dance studios the whole day. We had added another dance break after the bridge part of "Mad Love," specifically for the Billboards performance. For once, it wasn't only Tae who was struggling with it—Minjae had gone completely batshit nuts with the choreography.

Reluctant to get up, still weirded out by waking up like a normal person, I lay there and watched the few white clouds move sluggishly ahead on the bright blue sky, even though the clock ticked forward at an alarming speed. If I stayed in bed a minute longer, I would have to skip my morning jog. Somehow, I didn't even care.

That was until Joe's dick woke up before he did. And by waking up, I mean the monster pressed against my back, rock hard. When Joe let out an almost silent groan and pulled me even tighter against him, I'd had enough. My temples hurt as blood pounded inside my skull, and I elbowed him straight between his ribs as hard as I possibly could.

At once, he let go of me and jumped up to a sitting position. He looked hilarious, totally out of it, his eyes unfocused and bouncing all over the room. I couldn't hold in a snort at his expression. He narrowed his eyes at me upon noticing it.

"For fuck's sake why'd you do that?" he asked, rubbing his left ribs with a pained expression scrunching his face. "Ouch."

"Oh, come on. You're a big boy, you'll handle a little pain," I said. "Besides, we're gonna be late if we don't get up right now."

Joe glanced at the clock with a bewildered look on his face, before scratching the back of his head. "Wow, I guess we fell asleep then."

"No shit," I said and hopped up.

I left him there to gather himself and went to the bathroom. I took some deep breaths, trying to calm my racing heart. A minute or two passed, before I heard Joe exit my bedroom, and I could breathe normally again.

I lifted my eyes up to the mirror. What a huge mistake. Joe hadn't gotten all the eye make-up off, so the remainders had smudged all over my aching eyelids. I looked like a fucking raccoon. On top of that, my eyeballs were bright red. Not forgetting that the scars were still there, as red as ever.

My last hopes for that morning jog melted away as I dug through the drawers for the best cleansers. Joe had left a whole mess last night, so it took me a while. It was hopeless to even try to erase the disaster on my face by washing it over the sink, so I hopped in the shower with the products in tow.

After a full routine, I finally felt somewhat myself. And looked like it too. Apart from the scars for which I still needed to get used to. Avoiding the mirror, I scurried off the bathroom, already late. I picked out an all-black outfit for the day and finished the look with my favorite burgundy leather jacket and basically ran downstairs.

Joe was already there in his pristine suit, his black hair combed back and eyes focused. Somehow he looked weird like that, compared to the laid back guy I had woken up with. The laid back one from earlier looked more like the real deal. I didn't have time to think about it for too long though, because we were already late as fuck.

After downing a half cup of coffee in one go and hastily munching down some sandwiches for breakfast, I hurried to the hallway. I knew full well that Minjae would eat me alive if I were late to practice. And as I knew that until Billboards were over, he would be grumpy all the time with his insane drive for perfection. I was basically done for.

I yanked on some combat boots, and then realized my car keys were no longer in the jacket's pocket. I started digging through the bowl that usually had them if they weren't in my pocket, only to find out they weren't there either.

"Looking for something?" Joe asked with an annoyingly calm tone from behind me.

I turned on my heels. Joe was holding my keys up, out of my reach, with a cocky grin on his face. Nevertheless, I tried to grab them, not being very successful as he only had to lift them higher for me to not reach them.

Joe laughed at me before stuffing the keys to his own pocket. "Don't even think about it. Did you really think I'd let you drive after that little stunt you pulled on me yesterday?"

I threw him a dark glare and turned back around. Too bad for him, I had my spare keys right there in the top drawer…or not. Fuck.

"Do you think I'm that stupid?" Joe asked, now from my side, holding out another set of keys.

There was a chuckle behind me when I stomped right out through the door. My arms crossed over my chest, lips pursed in a straight line, I watched Joe stroll to the garage and drive out the BMW. But as annoyed I was, I also knew I stood no chance against him. And, as we were supposed to be on the road already, I reluctantly sat in the passenger seat.

However, Joe didn't start to drive. Instead, he looked at me, his hand resting on top of the steering wheel, amused smile twitching his lips and one eyebrow cocked up as if to ask, "What's up?"

I didn't feel like talking, so I only tapped my wristwatch, trying to signal that we were in a hurry, and I definitely did not have time for this.

"I see I'm getting the silent treatment," Joe said, that damn annoying little smile still playing on his lips. But after a slight shrug, he finally did drive the BMW through the gate. I stayed silent, not about to give in anytime soon.

Joe drove way slower than I did. Well, actually he just followed the speed limits, to the teeth. It still lengthened the commute significantly, so when I dashed through the familiar hallways of LBR towards the practice studios, I was already a half an hour late. Cursing under my breath, I ran straight to the locker rooms and changed in an even more of a hurry.

The others had already started the practice, all having their backs towards the entrance. I tried to sneak past them to my place and started dancing like I had been there the whole time. Of course, my sneaky entrance didn't go unnoticed. At once, Minjae stopped the music and glared at me through the mirror.

"You are late," he stated as if I didn't know it myself.

I held down the urge to roll my eyes at him and apologized. It was almost comical how much his self-esteem had skyrocketed after he had gotten together with Do-hyun. Gone was the apologizing, insecure Minjae. I almost regretted ever helping them.

"Joe drives like a grandpa," I explained, shrugging.

While Minjae only narrowed his eyes at me, before turning the music back on, Do leaned towards me. He whispered, "Relatable," before flashing me a short smile.

I snorted. Joe had been Do-hyun's guard before, so he understood better than anyone. But as soon as Tae shot me a dark glance through the mirror, I cut it and at least tried to focus. No one wanted a full-blown lecture from Minjae; I knew that.

The rest of the day went by fast. We only had a half an hour lunch break around one o'clock in the afternoon, with some take-out they delivered to us from the cafeteria downstairs. It was a rough and tiring day, but even Minjae softened up on me when I was the first to get the choreo right. To be fair, I had spent a lot of time trying to memorize the new parts on my own during the past few days—which totally had nothing to do with the fact that Joe had avoided me until yesterday.

Afterward, I took my time changing. Everyone left before me, while I tried to come up with ways to get my keys back from Joe, deep in thought. Imagine my surprise when I caught Tae waiting for me in the hallway by the time I did exit the locker rooms. As soon as the door closed behind me, he lifted his eyes from his phone and glanced at me with a slight, tense smile.

Before I even managed to wonder what was up, he asked me to come to his office with him. I agreed, nodding, though a bit confused. The day was supposed to be over. The others had left already. Nevertheless, I followed him up in total silence.

Just when I sent Joe a text that I would be late, Tae opened the door to his office. And I was taken by a surprise again. Jae-beom, the middle-aged lawyer, was waiting for us inside. He was sitting on Tae's chair, so I sat down on the couch with Tae, an uneasy feeling settling to the pit of my stomach.

After the mandatory greetings, Jae-beom went straight to the point.

"There have been some complications with Chris's case," he stated, the usual calm in his voice slightly faltering.

It shouldn't have come as a surprise to me, but it did. I couldn't mutter out a single word, somehow shocked.

Tae recovered sooner than me, as he had most likely anticipated something like this. He had always been ahead of others, always preparing for the worst-case scenario. "What complications?" he asked.

"The first attempt at settling this directly turned out fruitless today. It's not the end of the world or anything, I'm sure we'll get this settled one way or the other. But I still need you to understand that if the negotiations fail this coming Thursday, we'll be facing a full-blown trial."

"Which means we can't go to the Billboards?" Tae finished for Jae-beom, leaning back on the couch, deep in thought. "It would be too late."

Jae-beom nodded. Tae became visibly more anxious, his eyebrows drawn together and right foot starting to tap against the floor.

"It means *I* can't go to the Billboards."

"Oh, shut up, brat," Tae huffed. "It's not like the rest of us would go if you can't."

"Why not—"

"More importantly…" Tae cut me off. "We can't let others know. Under any circumstances. We both know Minjae will lose it if we add this to his burdens. He's stressing about the Billboards enough as is. Not to even mention Joonie. We'll continue working towards this as normally as possible."

I only nodded. I knew it myself without him saying it.

"No, Chris, you don't understand. You can't even tell Joe about this."

Now that made me scrunch my eyebrows together. "Why?"

"Because he might tell Do-hyun and we both know where that leads," Tae said.

"Right," I muttered. The realization that I actually knew nothing about the man I was falling for at an unnatural speed hit my guts. I even kept forgetting he was basically best friends with Do-hyun. Aish, this all was giving me a severe headache, fast.

"Is there anything we can do to help with the case?" Tae asked Jae-beom.

He leaned back in Tae's chair and started twirling a pen between his fingers. "There is, but you're not going to like it."

Oh, I knew where that was heading. "If you're planning on including my presence in the negotiations, it ain't happening."

"It would earn us sympathy points."

"I don't give a fuck. I can't see his face."

"I mean for once, I agree with Chris," Tae said, much to my surprise. "I'd rather not see him either. Ever. Or I can't be held responsible for the consequences."

Jae-beom sighed. "Well, that pretty much concludes it then. I'll win this thing sooner or later anyway. Just thought I'd throw that option out there."

After that, both Tae and Jae-beom concluded the little meeting with some meaningless comforting blabbering, trying to convince me that this wasn't a major setback and most likely everything would turn out fine in the end. Tae even ruffled my hair and said, "Don't worry, we're gonna get through this too. It's only a few days more."

I excused myself and walked to the parking hall in some kind of haze.

Joe was waiting for me there and the way home was spent in total silence. I tried to wrap my aching head around all this. Not succeeding very well, I might add. Again, I was grateful that Joe appeared to sense my moods somehow, as he didn't try to make any small-talk on the way either.

When we reached home, I was still way out of it and walked inside, Joe following me right after. But I got ripped away from my deep thoughts as soon as the front door closed behind us, because a large, warm body pressed against my back, arms wrapped around my waist and a chin landed on my shoulder.

"What's wrong?" Joe asked, deep concern saturating his voice.

"Nothing, it was just a long day with the choreo and all," I muttered, delivering a hastily put together lie. "What do you want?" I continued right after, trying to put up my usual defence-walls around my heart but failing miserably as Joe nuzzled his cheek against the hollow of my neck.

"I'm recharging. Or trying to cheer you up."

"What the fuck are you talking about?"

He tightened his grip. "My Chris-battery is empty, so I need to recharge."

I slapped his forehead, trying to hold down a chuckle. "Stop it."

"How about some ramen—"

"Don't even try."

Joe completely ignored me and continued, "I'm addicted to a drug called Chris, and I need my daily fix."

"You're *so* cliche."

"I know, and you like it," he said confidently before pressing his lips to the side of my neck. "No, but really, I have a proposition for you. Assuming you want your car keys back, hmm?"

Truth to be told, I had completely forgotten the thing with the car keys. But Joe did catch my interest with that, I admit. "Yeah, I guess."

"You'll let me sleep in your bedroom."

I nearly choked to my own saliva.

"No, really. Think about it. It's a win-win situation. I'll be there to wake you up whenever you have a nightmare. I get to cuddle. Sounds like a pretty sweet deal to me."

I rolled my eyes. "You never give up, don't you?"

"Nope."

"What if I attack you again? In my sleep."

"Oh please, as if I can't defend myself."

Truth to be told, it didn't sound like a *super* bad idea. Just a regularly bad idea. I actually gave it a thought. I didn't exactly enjoy the nightmares and lack of sleep. I was willing to give this thing a try. There was only one but.

"What happened to the 'let's avoid Chris like the plague' thing?" I asked, surprised, but also slightly relieved that he was getting back to being the flirty Joe I both hated and… something else too.

"Screw that. Teasing you is way more entertaining."

Hmph.

Bathroom Incident

The tiniest hairs on my neck stood up and I instantly knew someone was staring at me. A light shiver, or more like a tingle, ran all the way from the nape of my neck to the tip of my tailbone. As if I wasn't antsy enough, considering the fact that tomorrow was Thursday.

Doomsday. Quite literally.

But who else would've crept behind me, other than Joe? All I wanted to do was to turn around and confront him, but I think we all know that would've only led to hearing some highly disturbing and/or suggestive comments that would've driven me up the wall. We had already been sleeping together ever since the night I'd had the nightmare and attacked him. I admit my nights were way easier when he was around...but he didn't need more reasons to further inflate that already very swollen ego of his. I refused to give in.

Hell-bent on resisting the almost unbearable urge, I flat out refused to give him the satisfaction of seeing what kind of effect his mere presence had on me. So, instead of turning around and acknowledging him, I continued wiping off the light make-up that I wore at work, facing the mirror.

But I couldn't resist glancing at him in the mirror when I was sure he wasn't paying attention. He had already changed for the night, now only wearing some loose sweatpants and nothing else. We matched. He leaned against the door frame, an unreadable expression on his face, otherwise relaxed. When he crossed his arms over his chest, the defined muscles on his arms and chest flexed. Wondering if he did it on purpose or not; I couldn't help but admire his physique...which admittedly was... a sight. Just saying.

I continued with a full-blown face-cleansing routine cycling through it like three times with different products for different purposes, hoping Joe would get bored. Joe switched his position loudly a couple of times and cleared his throat, probably hoping to gain my attention.

I wasn't going to give in. Really. But I could sense his every move, which made ignoring him a task and a half. My ears tuned to pick out the slightest sounds of his every move. For example: the sound of his pants shifting as he rolled his weight from one foot to the other. Even the sound of his breathing sent a surge of pleasurable tingles down my neck.

It was like one of those creepy YouTube ASMR videos but on steroids.

For once, I won. Joe gave up first. I had to bite my lower lip to not let the smile of victory spread on my face when I heard the determined footsteps approach me. Forcing my face to a deadpan, I laid the towel I was using to dry my face on the counter and met Joe's eyes in the mirror.

As soon as our eyes met, he placed his hand on my naked waist. The soft touch sent a jolt of warmness through my whole body, starting from the spot where his hand touched my skin and ending at my crotch. It took every bit of self-discipline to keep my face somewhat blank as I stared at him with my eyebrows raised up questioningly.

"You're taking way too long with this." Joe stated. His deep voice startled me with its loudness because I had been so focused on the smaller sounds in life. "Come to bed."

"In a minute." I grabbed the toner and padded a little on my face.

"I wonder. Why bother putting that shit on your face in the first place if it takes ages to clean it off?" Joe placed his other hand on my waist too, sending another shock through my body. It became hard to remain calm. Leaning even closer, he laid his chin on my shoulder and whispered, "I mean, you're beautiful either way."

In an instant, I froze. My every muscle stiffened as I narrowed my eyes at him and studied his face. Surprisingly enough, he looked sincere. Honestly, he hadn't acknowledged my ruined face ever. Not once.

"I'm starting to wonder if you have working eyeballs," I eventually muttered.

"What do you mean?"

"Well, even if you don't count the fact that there's a square inch of skin missing altogether that is now replaced with scar tissue, I'm hardly beautiful. Cute, maybe. Or handsome, with a stretch. But not beautiful."

"I beg to differ," he mumbled and brushed the scars softly with his thumb. A sad-looking glimpse of some emotion flashed in his eyes, right before they darkened to an almost pitch-black shade—that dark flame flickering in his eyes that I had seen one too many times lately. It was the look that flashed on his face every time he was about to mess with me. I froze solid again.

"Want me to show you exactly *how* beautiful you are?" he asked, murmuring it softly to my ear. If eargasm was a thing, that was it. Damn. Now of course he couldn't leave it at that and call it a day…instead, he stood upright before starting to massage my stiff as fuck shoulders before continuing. "Besides, you could use some relaxation; you've been very tense lately."

I barely held down a moan as he hit just the right spot on my shoulders with his thumb. It became increasingly hard to hold back, as he continued kneading, unclenching my stiff muscles. Eventually, I did find my non-moaning voice again. Thank goodness.

"I have no idea what you're planning, but I do know it's probably not going to be a good idea," I said. Although, my voice wasn't as convincing as I would've hoped.

Joe flashed me a wicked grin, staring me straight in the eyes through the mirror, before pushing me against the counter. His hands sneaked a bit lower on my sides before he circled one of them to the front and started trailing the dip between my abs with the tip of his index finger.

"I have nothing but good ideas."

That low, soft voice of his dissolved the last bits of resistance within me. Damn, I was getting soft. My eyes drooped, my mind hazed up and it felt like I was flowing in a different dimension. Sighing, I leaned back in his embrace, totally giving up. Yes. It happened faster every time.

Joe's hands wandered all over my body. His lips found their way to my neck, to my shoulder, to my back. I lost track of time, so it almost felt like he was all over me at once. Brushing his fingertips on my skin here and there in one moment with the uttermost care, then moving on to grabbing my ass with a bit rougher manners, he drove me wild. He didn't even have to try. It was hard to keep up with him, so I didn't, and let myself feel.

"It's amazing how you can turn me on by just existing," Joe murmured in my ear, apparently reading my mind and stealing my thoughts. He rolled his pelvis against my behind, his hardening dick pressing against it as if to prove a point.

Once again, I hoped the mirror would've been fogged, though this time it was for entirely different reasons than ever before. Before, I had wished it so I wouldn't have to look at the scars too closely. This time, it was because I couldn't escape seeing the lewd expression on my face. My eyes drooped and my mouth hung slightly open, and a moan escaped my lips every now and then. And I had to watch it all play out in front of my eyes.

Well, not if I'd squeeze my eyes shut. But every time I tried, Joe stopped completely. And I couldn't deal with that either. I was too horny and frustrated for that. Again, Joe played me, reading me like an open book.

Annoyed, I dropped my eyes down to the sink. I was trying to resist his charms before embarrassment over having to watch myself would get the better of me, but failed. And got pissed at myself for not having any self-control whatsoever. Again, Joe stopped.

"You'll have to look at yourself, shortie, if you want me to do something about this problem down here," he stated, proving his point by brushing my dick through the sweatpants.

My knees nearly gave in when he reached the tip. Obviously I wasn't able to resist the teasing, and I reluctantly lifted my gaze back to the mirror. It sent a whole new wave of bright red blush to my cheeks.

"Good boy," Joe whispered, sending another tingle running down my back.

If my face hadn't been as bright red as my freshly colored hair, it certainly was now. But I couldn't focus on being awkward for long, because Joe laid another kiss on my neck and finally, *finally*, shoved his hand under the waistband of my sweatpants.

Joe's hard-on pressing against my behind, my gaze strictly glued to my own face on the mirror and his hand palming my erection through the underwear, drove my arousal to reach whole new heights. It was like I was on drugs. And I looked like I was just *that* high, too.

My eyes drooped several times as Joe kept teasing me, and every single time, he noticed. As soon as he decided I was too out of it, he reminded me to focus. And I did. I obeyed him every single time. Deciding once again that I'd deal with the consequences later, I allowed myself to forget the fact that I wasn't supposed to be this much under his spell.

Look, I was so out of it that I didn't even realize he had gotten rid of our clothes—well, yanked the sweatpants half-way down—before his way too big and bare dick first pressed against my lower back and then slid down my ass crack. I shot him a panicked look, petrified—he wasn't going to fuck me, was he? I mean...one would think it would take a little more warming up to fit that monstrously large cock anywhere near anyone's asshole. Let alone mine.

"Oh relax, I'm not gonna fuck you against the bathroom sink...however tempting it sounds," he said and winked.

My cheeks heated up again. I was horny as fuck. And seeing him watch me and stroke my dick, didn't help it. Frankly, I was more turned on than I had been in my entire life, a total moaning mess. My dick leaked, dripping some pre-cum to the floor and Joe's hand as he worked me all the way to the very edge.

And then he stopped.

My eyes flashed to his immediately, only to see him smirk against his thumb he was coating with saliva. My eyebrows scrunched at that as I wondered what the fuck was going on but got distracted again as he continued stroking my dick.

I found out what was going on soon enough. Right at the moment when the gigantic dick in my ass-crack got replaced with the previously mentioned saliva-coated thumb. Which suddenly pressed against my hole. Effectively making me suck in a sharp breath through my teeth as I froze, and my heart stopped. Again.

I mean...can a guy just relax every once in a while and enjoy a perfectly good handjob without all these extra surprises?

The shock only lasted for a second though, before I relaxed and realized just how good it felt. The way he started teasing my pucker, sometimes circling it and other times pressing against it slightly, slowly driving me back to the brink of insanity. Soon, he coaxed just the tip of the finger inside, but I barely even noticed because he stroked my dick at the same time.

And like that, distracting me enough while letting me adjust at my own pace, he had worked the entire finger inside. Oh yes, he was *that* good. It didn't even hurt one bit. If it had an effect, his finger inside my ass only made me grind against him harder, as I found myself wanting more.

So there I was, thoroughly turned on beyond my wildest imaginations, panting heavily while leaning against the sink with my arms, barely keeping myself standing. I was still staring at my own heated face in the mirror, Joe's one hand wrapped around my dick while his other hand was busy with my asshole.

And as I was staring at my face, no longer intimidated by it, I realized something important, even through the lustful and hazy state of mind. It was the fact that the face beyond the scars was still mine. I was still me. With or without the scars.

And I was fucking beautiful.

My legs buckled as I reached the climax and released a huge load on Joe's hand. I could no longer stand. Or keep my eyes open. Didn't matter though, because I fell right into Joe's embrace.

Only barely, I was able to register the sound of the tap running and Joe washing his hands, before he grabbed the towel, dried up his hands before cleaning the mess on me. Throughout the whole ordeal, I could only lean against him just as limp as my dick, hardly even conscious, when he got rid of our remaining clothing.

Joe dragged me to the bed and tucked us both in. I curled against his side and laid my head against his chest. I accidentally touched his still rock-hard dick, but even the guilt of leaving him hanging on edge like that couldn't pull me up from the pure exhaustion.

Seemed like Joe surely knew how to effectively distract me. Not that I'd complain. I'd take a nice handjob a thousand times rather than agonizing about tomorrow's outcome.

Or the usual nightmares.

Love Song

Now, who was the idiot that decided that day had to be a day off? It must've been Minjae or Do-hyun. Yes, definitely it had been one of them. Or both. Ah, yes, it was Do-hyun who had argued that they needed time to pack their shit, but who the fuck takes a whole-ass day to pack for a few days trip to the US? I bet they were just fucking around in their new and just renovated home. Like rabbits.

I would much rather have tortured myself at some last-minute rehearsals or something, instead of this 'staring at the phone that never rang or made any kind of noise whatsoever now that I wanted it to' thing. It was mind-numbing, to say the least. It was like waiting for a date to reply to a message but *so much worse*.

Of course, I could've packed, too. But I definitely wasn't going to do that before I'd know for sure I was going to the Billboards in the first place. And Jae-beom was surely taking his time with the negotiations; it was already late in the afternoon.

"So, can you really play that thing?" Joe asked from the doorway to the living room, yanking me back to reality.

Blinking a couple of times, I looked at his questioning face for a second, dumbfounded. Well, until I realized that by "that thing," he meant the acoustic guitar that had been laid on my lap that I had been plucking at earlier. "Yeah, I guess I can play some. Why?"

"Ha, you've only been staring ahead for the past ten minutes. Why don't you actually play something while you're at it?"

I glanced down at the guitar and then back to Joe. "Well, what do you want me to play?"

A smirk flashed by his face. "Free bird. That's what every guitarist has to learn, right?"

Hmph. Of all the things he could've heard me play, he chose freaking "Free Bird?" What a pathetic cliché. Or an attempt to catch me off guard. Too bad he didn't know I had a thing for 70's and 80's rock.

Not even paying much attention, I plucked away the first few bars of the famous guitar solo.

"Happy?"

"Very," he said, flopping down to loiter on the other end of the couch. "Play more."

I played a couple more things off the top of my head, grateful for any kind of distraction. It wasn't the perfect medley by any means, but Joe would've never caught what I played wrong anyway, so it didn't really matter. People who didn't have the slightest idea about playing guitar were so easy to impress.

It didn't serve as a long-term distraction though, unfortunately. Soon, I found myself eyeing the phone all over again. I mean, the meeting between Jae-beom and whoever was representing that stupid fucking Min-ho, should've started like a few hours ago. How long can settling this thing really take? The guy had tried to kill us, for fuck's sake.

Joe noticed something was wrong, too. He always did.

"You're still not going to tell me what's going on?" he asked.

It was the same question he had been tossing around for the last couple of days. Again, he was reading me like I was a newspaper, and it bugged me out. Made it hard to keep secrets too, that's for sure.

"Nope," I replied...eventually.

"Technically, you are required to tell me. According to the contract."

"Only if it's something that might put me in physical danger," I countered, shrugging. "This isn't anything like that."

"Are you sure?" he asked, raising an eyebrow. "Because last time I saw you this antsy, you went on a suicide mission with the Lamborghini."

"Oh, come on, that was *one* time," I huffed. "Besides, weren't you supposed to make us dinner?"

"Yeah, that was before you started serenading me. So please, continue," he said, gently nudging my thigh with his foot.

My blood pressure rose to a whole new level in a record time. Who the hell did he think he was? A douche, that's what he was.

"Hmph, well here's a fucking real serenade for you," I said, thought of the most basic chord progression and started strumming the guitar, shouting the first words that came to mind to his face.

Go away,
I can't stand you anymore, you are an eyesore
There is the door, and furthermore
I don't need no golden retriever or labrador

Strumming the easiest chords known to human history once more for four more bars, I concluded the "song," set the guitar down, and stood up. Unfortunately, I didn't get very far before Joe grabbed my waist and yanked me back to the couch—or rather, to sit on his lap.

"Aww, how cute. You made a song for me."

"Piss off," I said, struggling in his embrace, having little to no success.

I gave up, going limp against his chest and let his enticing scent drug me to complete distraction once again. What was the point of resisting him when I knew I stood no chance anyway? Hoping he'd grow tired of me, I slumped further down.

But instead of getting tired of me, Joe took his opportunity and nuzzled his face against my neck and slid his hands towards my crotch. The irritation was replaced with arousal, and I let out a shaky breath when his warm lips found the magic spot on the nook of my neck.

I was growing extremely tired of not having any control whatsoever over my own body. "What exactly do you want from me, Joe?"

"Oh, you know what I want," Joe muttered against my skin. "The one thing I will want until you give in. It's not like we haven't done it before. I promise you won't regret it this time."

"I didn't regret it last time."

"Then what's the matter? Just let me fuck you. I know we both want it."

I froze. It was the first time he had actually said it out loud, in so many words. And how tempting it sounded, when murmured softly to my ear while his hands were wandering to some highly sensitive places at the same time. I all but melted against him, so damn tempted to give in.

Honestly, it was the hardest thing for me to resist at this point. Let's face it; the ultimate truth was: I would've given up ages ago if I wasn't used to being so stubborn. Or if I didn't know what I did, based on last time—that he was a total fuckboy. A good fuckboy, but a fuckboy, nevertheless. I was only going to burn my fingertips by playing with fire and I *knew* it.

But my time together with Joe up in the mountains was coming to its end, rapidly. If I was lucky, we'd be heading to the Billboards the very next day, and then we'd be on tour throughout the whole summer. Not that I wouldn't see Joe, but we wouldn't be able to spend as much time alone, so I predicted that night might be the last chance if I was going to give in and let him have his way.

If only he'd stop asking for stupid permissions and fuck me already, this would be so much easier. But of course, that wasn't something I would say out loud in a million years. Yet, it was exactly what Joe wanted, and I knew he wouldn't act before getting that damn consent from me.

"That monstrous cock of yours ain't going anywhere near my asshole," I said and regret set in. It was, again, the complete opposite of what I actually thought, but at the same time, I wasn't brave enough to take it back.

Joe, however, laughed. "Good thing you remember I top."

Hmph, was there ever even a chance for other options? Though now that I thought of it, maybe it wouldn't be such a huge deal if it were the other way around.

"Well, now that you said it... it would make a lot more sense if I top. We both know lil Chris is way more reasonably sized—" I started but was cut off by the phone ringing on the table.

My heart stopped. No, scratch that, I think the entire world stopped. Except for the phone that buzzed against the table, Jaebeom's name flashing on the screen, the annoying ringtone piercing my eardrums. For once, I forgot all about my internal struggles about having sex with Joe and scurried up.

But I couldn't bring myself to take the phone in my hand and answer it. Terrified of hearing my sentence, I couldn't move.

"Why's Jae-beom calling you?" Joe asked, having taken a look on the screen, scrunching his eyebrows together. Then the realization hit him, visibly. "Oh is this what you've hidden from me? They still haven't sorted out the charges against you?"

I shook my head, not being able to say it out loud.

Joe grabbed me into a hug. "Fuck, I'm so sorry…If I had known—"

I cleared my throat. "Err, do you mind?" I asked, nodding towards the kitchen. This was one of the discussions I *really* wanted to have in private. Totally alone. Thankfully Joe understood immediately like he always did and walked to the kitchen at once. I grabbed the phone, hands sweaty already, my heart about to jump out of my chest. I swiped the green icon to the side and lifted the phone up to my ear.

"Hello Jae-beom-nim. How did it go?"

Movie Incident

After the phone call, I sat on the couch for a long while, squeezing the device in my hand and staring ahead. What pissed me off the most, was the fact that the call was over in like…two whole seconds. Jae-beom had only said something along the lines of "congrats, you're a free man now" with an extremely exhausted tone and hung up. I'd sweat over the whole thing for nothing. The entire day was wasted on agonizing over an absolutely non-existent threat. I hadn't even packed.

What a fucking anticlimactic event. Not to even mention the fact that we were cockblocked by it.

Wait, what?

It wasn't like I was upset because of that. Nope. It had nothing to do with the fact that this…thing…we had with Joe, was coming to an abrupt end. Even more surely than yesterday. Because it was now 100% sure I was going to the Billboards the next day, and this thing with Joe certainly wouldn't last through that. Or touring. Or the time after that, when we'd be expected to move back to a dorm of some sort.

But none of those things were the reason why I was upset. They couldn't be. Because I wanted to go to the Billboards—it had been my dream from the day I was scouted when I was 16. I wanted to tour. I wanted to get back to living in a dorm with the rest of the guys. I even dared to admit to myself that I missed them, more than anything.

Then why the fuck did my chest suddenly feel so tight as simple of a task as breathing became difficult?

I don't know how long I sat there, trying to remember how to inhale and exhale like a normal person, but eventually, Joe informed me that the dinner was ready. We ate in a heavy silence that didn't feel natural like it normally would've. Only the sound of the cutlery clanking against our plates filled the room.

Afterward, I helped Joe clean the kitchen. It had already become a habit—our own little routine. I'd handle the dishes and Joe would clean the table. I'd put the leftovers away while Joe would take out the trash...so on and so forth.

I had never really been one for these domestic types of things. I had never even considered I would enjoy doing something so simple, let alone the same thing every single day. Look, I had hardly stayed still enough for half of my life to develop habits of my own other than running most mornings, not to even mention forming mutual habits together with another person. Well, with the exception of the habits I had together with the rest of GRiD-dudes that I considered my extended family.

Yet, there I was, on the verge of losing my mind because I wouldn't be able to continue doing this one habit I had accidentally formed with a man I hardly knew.

Pathetic.

What was even more pathetic, though, was the fact that in my weird state of mind, I had actually packed the leftovers to the fridge like any other day. As if we'd be here to eat them tomorrow. Ugh.

I didn't quite manage to start emptying the fridge from stuff that would go bad in the next few days before Joe was already back.

"I'd guess the call didn't go that well?" he said with a questioning tone.

Was it possible that he would be agonizing about our time coming to an end too? "What do you mean?"

"Did Jae-beom lose your case?"

Oh right, I hadn't told him how it went. Of course, he wouldn't want to be trapped with me for longer than absolutely necessary...what was I even thinking?

"No, it went well. We're going to Billboards." I said and offered him a slight smile that didn't quite convince him.

He scrunched his eyebrows together, clearly baffled. "Then why are you upset?"

"I—I'm not. Look, can you empty the fridge?" I asked. "I should go pack."

Trying to look indifferent about the whole thing, I stared at him back when he tried to read me with those almost hypnotizing gold-brown eyes of his. For once, he couldn't figure it out, and I was finally able to breathe when he nodded and turned towards the fridge.

I all but dashed upstairs, then straight to my walk-in closet, closed the door behind me and leaned against it, taking a deep breath. My heart fluttered incredibly fast, and I clutched the front of my t-shirt in my fist tightly as if it would've helped anything.

Had I...caught feelings? When? HOW? Why?

I shook my head—no, that couldn't be it. I was just caught up in the moment. Nothing less, nothing more. No need to overcomplicate things. Besides, I should've focused on the task at hand—packing. Hyping myself up about getting to go to the Billboards, I finally managed to get my shit together and pull out a suitcase.

Now, our stage outfits had already been handled, so I only needed a suit for the gala, workout clothes for the rehearsals, and a few random outfits for the rest of the trip. The suit and the workout clothes were easy to pick, but I got somewhat stuck with the rest of them. My clothes could practically be all put into three piles—one for the ones I had ruined with my attempts at doing laundry, one for my own actual clothes, and one for the clothes that had been pre-approved and hand-picked by the stylists. They were supposed to compliment the image I once had. Basically, apart from the ruined pile, it was either band t-shirts paired with skinny jeans or some pretty disturbing pastel-colored cutesy shit I had worn before in public.

It felt like that cutie-pie person was dead, long-gone, and that life had been lived a thousand years ago. And it hadn't been me in the first place. So, I muttered an almost inaudible "fuck it" and started to pack my normal clothes in the suitcase. The staff would have to suck it or start to style me with more of my own type of fashion.

And you know what, that also applied to the clay-like make-up they had made me wear the other day. There was no way in hell I'd actually put up with that shit. Why had I even considered it in the first place? I slammed the suitcase shut, hauled it to the small upstairs lobby near the stairs and headed to the bathroom for a long, *long,* and steaming hot shower.

By the time I stepped out of the shower, I had calmed down. A bit. But as soon as I stepped into my bedroom, only wearing a towel low on my waist, and rubbing my wet hair with the other, I stopped on my tracks. Because I spotted a wet haired Joe, loitering on my bed flicking his phone, only wearing some loose pants and nothing else. It had completely slipped my mind that he slept here now. How? I had no idea.

"Oh hey," he said as soon as he spotted me, halted at my bathroom door. "Wanna watch a movie or something? I've already packed, and I spotted your suitcase near the stairs, might as well relax for the rest of the night, hmm?"

It took me a couple of blinks and a slight head shake to get back to reality.

"...sure," I mumbled hesitantly, tossed him the remote for the tv, and headed back to my wardrobe. "Your pick."

Once inside, I let out a long, silent sigh. How the hell was I supposed to survive like two hours of cuddling and flirting, now that I was in this weird state of mind already? As if I wasn't close enough to losing it and giving up already, especially considering this was our last night here? Most likely our last night...period.

Then again...I *could* give up. We could go all the way. We were both single, the chemistry was insane and based on anything that had happened so far, I knew Joe was great in bed. There was nothing to lose. Nothing to fear. Nothing would change. Well, except there was a slight chance that I might not be able to walk after having that gigantic cock up my ass again, and the cardiac arrest he was inevitably going to put my heart through might turn out to be lethal this time over.

And right there, pulling some random sweatpants on in my closet, I decided to wing it. No matter the outcome of tonight, tomorrow was going to be bittersweet. Besides, when the hell did I become such a wuss in the first place, hmm? It wasn't like I was a virgin or anything, and me and Joe had gone all the way before.

I took a deep breath, tried to force my racing heart to calm down—obviously not succeeding—and walked out of the closet, then straight to the bed. Joe was still sitting his back against the headboard and turned those mesmerizing eyes of his towards me as soon as I climbed on the bed. For once I didn't feel the need to evade his eyes and sit as far away from him as the bed allowed me to. I crawled right next to him.

Joe froze solid at first, probably surprised, but nevertheless pulled me tight against him when he recovered enough to move.

"I don't have the slightest idea of what's going on, but I'll take it," Joe said, the amusement clear in his voice.

"We were supposed to watch a movie, that's what's going on."

Joe stared down at me with a bewildered expression but clicked play on his phone's screen—a random action film started to play on the tv. It looked boring, to be honest. Still, I tried to focus at first, but soon I noticed I was playing with the soft trail of body hair that started from his navel and disappeared somewhere below the waistband of his pants with my fingertips. Then I couldn't help a smirk when Joe's pants started to bulk, ever so slightly.

We'd "watched" the movie for like 20 whole minutes before Joe had had enough of my little teasing and paused it.

"Fuck it!" he exclaimed. "Do you really think I can focus on a movie when you're being this…much...all of a sudden?"

Raising my eyebrows at him, I said, "Well, I can go away too if you'd prefer that," and tried to scoot over to the other side of the bed.

"Don't even try," he said, grabbing my waist and yanking me back.

Somehow, I ended up under him. His semi-hard dick pressed against my thigh as he hovered over me, studying me with his golden-brown eyes. Breathless, I could only stare back at him.

"With all that teasing, one might think you're finally giving up," he said, narrowing his eyes at me. When I didn't reply anything, my voice stuck to my throat, he continued with a question, "Will you make love with me?"

One hundred percent taken aback by his choice of words I gulped, before blinking to rip my eyes off from his hypnotizing ones. It was technically what he had been hinting at ever since "the coffee incident" and especially after "the bathroom incident" and even asked for it earlier today... but the word "love" had never been used before. It simultaneously excited and scared me.

But I had already made my decision about this, and it was not like I didn't want to have sex with him…I think we can all admit that at this point. I closed my eyes for a second and chose my words carefully, before voicing them out loud. After all, I had a habit of saying all the wrong things at all the wrong times, and I wasn't risking it tonight.

"Look, if you ask me... I'll always say 'no'..." I whispered, still evading his eyes. Joe instantly started to pull back, but I held him in place, clinging to him. My cheeks burning hot, I added, "...so don't ask."

Tequila Sunrise

Joe blinked as if it took him some time to decipher what the hell I meant. But eventually, realization lit up his eyes that I saw were still aligned at me from the edge of my vision. Yes, I was still evading his eyes. They were too dangerous to look at, okay, so sue me.

"Are you sure?" he asked, then instantly realized his mistake as I froze. "I mean...uh...if you really want to..."

Holding down the urge to roll my eyes, I pulled him down and smashed my lips against his. It took him a second to pull himself together and respond, but once he did, there was no hesitation left in his actions. Despite having originally initiated the kiss myself, it became very clear who led the race after that.

For sure, it wasn't me.

If there were any boundaries or walls of resistance within me left, I ignored them and let the moment take over. There was no turning back anymore. In an instant, Joe dominated my every thought —my every sense—and I let him.

Why I had anticipated that he'd go straight to business and the whole ordeal would've been over in, like, 5 minutes, I didn't know. Maybe because our last time together had been...somewhat urgent. But that couldn't have been further from the truth this time over. Instead, he savored the kiss. His tongue found an opportunity to slip between my parted lips when I took in a ragged gasp. I found myself leaning in on the kiss, even dared to nibble his lip, which in turn made him groan into my mouth.

That was what a kiss was supposed to feel like. There was no pushing or pulling. No denying the mutual attraction. Joe's hard body was pressed against mine, his burning hot lips claiming my own, both of us trapped in the heated moment. It felt somehow…liberating. Maybe because I didn't have to agonize over this any longer, it was already happening. The decision had already been made, and now I only had to go through with the actions.

When Joe pulled back, I blinked up at him. He looked down at me with a strange look on his face, those weird warm brown eyes with a golden halo around the pupils, filled with something I couldn't quite put in words. But I blinked when he pushed my hair back, and the look in his eyes was gone. Or maybe I ignored it because his touch made my already heated skin even more ticklish and feverish.

Joe then raised himself from his hovering position, hands tugging at the strings on his sweatpants. I swallowed as he pulled the pants off along with the underwear, leaving him totally naked and his way-too-big-of-a dick in full display. Despite the fact that I was beyond terrified to have it inside me, his rock hard erection made me painfully aware of my own that was straining against my pants.

As I too started fumbling with my pants, Joe glanced down at my crotch, making more heat rise up my cheeks. I guess I struggled with the pants for too long, because he grabbed my wrists and pulled them away. Then his hands quickly released me from the straining clothes as I relaxed against the bed. The sound of the pants landing somewhere to our right made a smile tug the corners of my lips slightly upwards.

Soon, Joe was again laying on top of me. He was heavy and warm, and…very, very hard. A surprised moan made it past my lips as he moved his hips, rubbing our hard-ons together.

After grinning briefly at all the noise, Joe rested against his elbows to kiss me again, before moving on to the side of my neck. Closing my eyes, I turned my head to the side, one hand gripping the sheets and the other finding its way to grip Joe's thick black hair.

I quivered with anticipation as he moved down to my chest. His lips and teeth left faint red marks all over my body when he moved lower and lower until his lips were hovering over my almost aching dick. He looked up at me through his dark lashes, eyes hungry and darkened. I found myself nodding and raising my hips at his unspoken question.

Joe thankfully didn't need more than that for final consent. Instantly, his lips pressed a soft kiss on the underside of my glans, sending a jolt of pleasure straight to my balls. Though I barely registered that before his slick and warm mouth enclosed half of my hard length.

"Aish, fuck," I hissed between my gritted teeth, head jerking back as Joe let out a low, rumbling hum. My hand flew down to caress the back of his head and teeth sunk to my bottom lip as I tried to muzzle another groan when his skilled tongue flicked on the underside of my throbbing cock. I wasn't very successful with keeping the volume down though.

The pressure started building up in my lower abdomen, as Joe wrapped his hand against the base of my dick. That feeling wasn't very long-lasting though, because after a couple of pumps his hand found something else to do—as in: they slid past my tightening balls, then his finger starting to press softly against my asshole.

My cock still buried deep in his mouth, one of Joe's saliva covered fingers slowly pushed past the tight ring. My back arched involuntarily as a tune of a continuous whine vibrated from my throat. Joe took it a step further, as always, and once the finger was fully inside me and curled it slightly, putting pressure on that one spot that made my toes curl.

Now, that one finger was easy enough to handle, as it wasn't the first time it had been there. But slowly, Joe worked a second finger inside me, effectively making me wince and suck in a tight breath as my eyes fluttered open. That made him completely pause and release me from his mouth with an impudent pop. Gazing at me, questioning, Joe halted all movement completely.

"I'm fine," I whispered, raising my hips as I spoke, eyes locked with his, too drunk with the need to have any decent thoughts left. With that, Joe moved the two fingers inside slightly and with care, letting me get used to the stretching sensation in my ass. His other hand slid up, over my chest, before landing to rest on my cheek.

Shamelessly I leaned against his palm, closing my eyes again. Bit by bit, my rigid muscles relaxed as he worked his fingers inside my hole. Occasionally, he put more pressure against the sensitive spot, causing waves of pleasure shooting through me.

"I'm sorry shortie, but you're gonna have to take the third finger in before…" he started, trailing off. His thumb brushed over my lower lip as I nodded.

Bit by bit, he inserted a third digit inside me. A strange mix of pain and pleasure overwhelmed all my senses, blocking out everything else. In turns, I whimpered and groaned when his fingers moved in and out, filling me up and stretching. My whole body shook every time the pressure against the highly sensitive bundle of nerves inside me became more prominent. The sheet wrinkled in my tight hold as I let out a moan after moan.

"Still okay?" Joe asked, his voice husky and deep, then moving straight on to kiss me in a rough manner. Yes, before I even managed to reply. Another moan made it past my lips, being the only answer he needed. He smiled against my lips at the same time he pulled his fingers out, making me feel strangely empty.

Barely, I heard a foil of a condom getting ripped open, making me only mildly curious of where the hell had Joe conjured that up, as I mostly focused on praying to gods that it was one of those thickly lubed ones. Soon, I bit my lip as the head of his cock pressed against my entrance, before sliding all the way in.

"Aish, ow, fuck," I hissed, the almost burning sensation of my ass being so stretched out it actually hurt like hell, making my every muscle clench.

Joe let out a deep loud groan as I clamped around his cock, far thicker than his fingers had been. "Fuck, you're still so goddamn tight, shortie," he breathed out when my hand gripped his arm and fingers dug into his flesh.

Slowly but surely, I relaxed around him, even my fingers unclenching one by one on his arm at the same time. Once Joe was content I was okay enough, which I oddly was after a while, he started moving, whispering my name. The sound of it rolling off his tongue so easily made me forget the pain completely. I groaned again, hand sliding up before it reached the back of his neck. Whimpering with growing urgency for a release, I pulled him down to a sloppy kiss. His lips moved with mine, just as, if not more eager and hungrier as I was.

With every thrust and pull, I lost myself more. Tears burned behind my eyelids, as Joe's dick seemed to reach deeper with every movement. Soon, he was trembling, before his arms gave up and his weight pressed against me. My hands gripped at his tense muscles on his back as his panting, hot breaths tickled my ear. My mouth muttered out words that didn't make any sense at all when his movements became erratic, both of our draggy breaths and throaty moans filling up the otherwise silent room.

With one last breathy hum, he released inside me, gripping my cock tight in his fist at the same time. His hand draped over my cock drove me over the edge too, and I practically screamed his name as the hot seed sprayed from my cock between us in thick streaks.

Joe's body collapsed on top of mine, heavy, but I didn't make a single move to push him off. He laid his head on the hollow of my neck. My one hand slowly unclenched the sheet on my left as the other kept resting on his back.

We lay there for a while, too high in the after waves of our orgasms to move. Eventually, Joe pulled his already softened cock from inside me, then wordlessly fetched and dampened a towel. While I lay there, still completely out of it, he proceeded to wash us both up with the warm cloth, before discarding it somewhere on the other side of the room.

Joe pulled me in his embrace as we both snuggled under the duvets. He fell asleep in minutes. His chest rose and fell in tune with his even breathing and his face was completely at peace. Occasionally his lips twitched slightly, his arm that was still curled behind my back tightening its hold.

Despite the fact that I was very tired as well, I also became scared stiff of falling asleep. Not because of the nightmares and not because I knew this would be the first and the last time I'd see him this way, but because of a terrifying fact I only then realized...that I was in love with him.

Somehow, he had paved the way into my heart, almost brutally so. In a relatively short time span, Joe had managed to turn himself from being just a work acquaintance I had drooled over from afar, to a one nights stand, to a person I despised, then to a flirty douche, before finally acquiring the status of being the man I fell for so hard it was difficult to put in words.

But apart from other members of GRiD, people had the tendency to disappear from my life once I became too attached to them. It had started with Dad, who left Mom to raise us by herself. Then our first manager turned out to be a scumbag. Even the rest of GRiD had taken their distance from me for little while when things went south, though I'll admit I might have to blame myself a bit on that.

Tomorrow, it was Joe's turn to make his escape. I could feel it. Sense it.

So I spent the rest of the night watching Joe's strong jawline, perfectly arched eyebrows, and those thin but skilled lips, while I still had the chance. But at the same time, I was mentally preparing myself for tomorrow. Deep down, I was forging a new, improved version of the protective shell around my heart from the wrecked ruins Joe had left behind when he first charged through my defenses with a bulldozer.

When the sun started coloring the sky with an orange hue, I undraped myself from Joe. Careful to not wake him up, I crawled up from the bed, tiptoed to the shower to clean myself up a bit better. Especially from down there, ignoring the stinging pain that tunneled up my ass as soon as I touched the slightly swollen passage.

Then I walked straight to the walk-in closet. I chose some stylish-enough, stretchy skinny jeans and a hoodie to serve as an outfit that would both survive a 12-hour flight and at the same time wouldn't make the headlines of the worst outfit to ever pass the regular sea of reporters swarming at the entrance to Incheon International Airport.

As silently as I could, I continued my way to exit the master bedroom that had once belonged solely to me but now somehow seemed shared. At the door, I cast a final longing glance towards the sleeping man over my shoulder. What a beautiful yet comfortingly domestic sight it was indeed. The orange-red glow of the sunrise peeking through the curtains, casting light on his disheveled hair made it ten times more difficult to leave and not snuggle back on the bed beside him. Knowing I had to, I still did, with my heart already aching.

With ultimate care, I pulled the door closed behind me, before silently walking downstairs. I sat on one of the bar stools beside the kitchen table, gripping the soju bottle I had picked up on my way there in my other hand while the other laid a tall glass on the smooth surface.

Then I mixed myself a tequila sunrise.

Real Smooth

Three tall glasses of tequila sunrise, two bottles of soju and exactly two hours and 37 minutes of staring at the small digital clock on the microwave, I was getting seriously buzzed. Not that being drunk helped even one bit with my inner battle. But as it was the only thing I could think of that had helped me calm down in the past, I tried to use it to my advantage again. This time though, it only made things worse.

Because despite my best efforts to use my sparse brain cells with the help of alcohol, I still had no idea whatsoever of what to do with the information that I had accidentally fallen in love with someone. With Joe, of all people.

He didn't exactly give off the aura of what I wanted in life—stability. Someone who would stay despite all the difficulties that being with me undoubtedly would bring. Which meant that now I was getting my heart broken sooner rather than later and that thought alone made me want to throw up.

Speak of the devil, and the devil shall appear. About an hour before our scheduled leaving time, Joe strolled downstairs, adjusting his earpiece on his way, looking neat and styled in his tailored suit, I might add. He definitely didn't look like the guy I left to sleep in my bedroom a few hours ago. The one with disheveled black hair spread over the pillow, sleeping in such an ideal position to provide the most perfectly sized nook for me to curl up in. Nope, this guy looked stern and cold, somehow distant.

I let out an almost inaudible sigh of relief—I could work with this version of Joe. This one didn't make me feel any type of way. As long as he was distant, boring, business-like, I could buy myself enough time to figure this other—more difficult— shit out.

As he was about to lift his gaze from the floor to me, I hastily turned my attention back to my drink glass and glugged down the last bits of the strong liquor. Standing up, I started making my way towards the coffee maker without even acknowledging Joe but halted in the middle of the kitchen because of two strong arms that wrapped around my waist.

"Good morning, shortie," Joe hummed to my ear, his voice sending a set of all too familiar vibrations down my back, flashes of last night flooding my mind. Even the use of the pet-name no longer felt foreign to me, as somewhere along the way I had accidentally gotten used to it. Fuck. So much for having time to figure things out.

Bile rising up in my throat, I pushed the sudden lewd thoughts that Joe's too close presence brought to my mind to the back of my head and took a deep breath. After swallowing stiffly, I simply stepped away from his embrace and continued my way to the coffee maker, not even bothering to glance at him. I could sense he froze to the spot for a hot second before I heard his footsteps heading towards the fridge.

As I brewed some coffee, Joe arranged some breakfast on the dining table from whatever was left in my almost empty fridge. It was eerily silent, apart from the sounds of our usual morning tasks being completed. I could sense more and more that the end of this thing between me and Joe was lurking right around the corner. He might've even ended it that day. Maybe even before we'd left the house. To be fair, that would most likely be the easiest way to end it. A clean cut of some sort. Just ripping the bandage right off. Classifying the whole thing into the category named "random flings" and filing it away.

Because if it wasn't going to end that day, I imagined it going down like this: we'd be awkward around each other for a while, until there wasn't an ounce of spark left between us. Maybe it would end with words like *"it was fun while it lasted"* or *"it was a one-time deal, Don't start to imagine things that won't happen."* Or better yet, the worst possible option—the one that would be all my own fault. The one that would stem from my inability to speak and act like normal people, even more so after the incident with Min-ho. In that case, I imagined the words being something along the lines of: *"I've grown tired of chasing you."*

Deep in thought, I found myself sitting at the dining table, nibbling the edge of a fried egg. It didn't taste very good, oddly enough. Usually I gobbled down everything Joe made, eagerly even. From time to time, I sipped some coffee too, but somehow even that started tasting too bitter.

Meanwhile, Joe was blabbering about some nonsense. I paid no attention, whatsoever. Well, until: "...so I sucked his hairy balls, nearly gagging–"

"Umm, what?" I asked, shook my head a bit to clear it up and blinked, lifting my eyes from my plate to meet Joe's for the first time for the whole morning.

He was smirking, those annoyingly hypnotizing eyes of his somehow sparkling. "Finally got your attention."

Hmph. He *was* just babbling nonsense. I took another sip of the bitter coffee, before replying. "What do you want?"

"I tried to ask, what's wrong?"

"Nothing's wrong."

"Oh really?" he asked, crossing his arms over his chest while he leaned back in his chair.

I only shrugged, before taking another bite of the fried egg.

Joe studied me for a long time, before opening his mouth again.

"I'm not buying that. First, I woke up alone. Then I come downstairs only to find out you reek like alcohol. You barely even look at me..." he continued, not an ounce of humor left in his voice as he counted the factors that proved his point with his fingers. "Fuck, if I didn't know better, I'd guess last night didn't please you..."

I stopped chewing, heat rising up my neck upon last night's memories once again took up all the headspace possible. "I wouldn't say that..." I mumbled, before managing to stop myself.

Joe only smiled. "I know. If it was even half as great for you that it was for me, I'm fairly certain you weren't left unsatisfied..."

I gulped. How had that been great for him? I hadn't even done anything for him last night. I had barely laid there like a limp dick while he did all the work. No wonder I felt like it was going to be the last time.

"...thus, I would rather guess that you had a nightmare or something, right?" Joe continued, blissfully unaware of my inner battle.

Well, technically, I hadn't slept. But then again, maybe realizing I was in love with him could be counted as a nightmare. Agreeing with him seemed to be an easy way out of this highly awkward conversation. "Right."

At once, Joe's face got serious. "Shortie," he started, making me wince slightly at the all too familiar nickname, "I really think you should seek some help for those nightmares and stuff. *Professional* help."

Ugh, so much for an easy way out of the conversation. Maybe his reason to end things between us wouldn't be any of the above, rather than me being too broken for him to handle.

But all things considered, he wasn't wrong, so I replied with a simple, "I know."

Joe narrowed his eyes at me, most likely finding my sincerity somehow lacking. What a surprise. "Do you?"

"Yes. I'm not dumb," I said, shrugging. "I just want to get this Billboard-thing and maybe the tour over and done with before all that."

Joe pondered my words for quite a while, burning a hole in my face with his way too intense gaze as I still refused to look directly at him. "And then, you're gonna get some help?"

"Yes, yes, fine," I muttered, totally over the topic at hand. I had way more important things in my mind at the moment.

"Promise?" he still insisted.

After closing my eyes for a brief second and taking in a deep breath, I pulled the most convincing face I could muster up at that moment and finally met his gaze. "Promise."

He stared me for a long while before dropping the subject with a simple nod. I turned my eyes back to my half-eaten plate of food. Both of us had run out of words, so the first truly uncomfortable silence to ever fall upon us, fell upon us. I cleared my throat and resumed eating, hoping to fill the silence with practically anything at that point.

I mean, what are you supposed to say in that kind of situation? *Thanks for the sex; it was awesome. By the way, it just so happens that I fell in love with you somewhere along the way. Please don't let me run away even though I'm a mentally damaged creep who can't even decide what I really want.*

Yeah… Nope. A big, fat, hard nope. We only fucked like twice for crying out loud—I was not about to count the fooling around. I was getting way ahead of myself. The way I saw it, there were two choices: a) end things myself before he gets the chance to even bring the subject up, or b) avoid the topic for as long as it would take me to figure out how to keep him.

*Wait...*when the hell had I even started considering keeping him?

Good thing—or bad, as we'd soon come to find out—that Joe decided to cut my a little more than tipsy non-linear thought processing short.

"Chris, I think we also need to talk about us–" he started, but of course I couldn't let him finish wherever that was going. I wasn't anywhere near ready for that conversation. Nope.

I panicked. "Err, shit, I forgot to inform Mr. Yun I'm leaving. He's taking care of the house while we're away," I mumbled and all but dashed to the front door and then all the way across my yard, leaving behind a very confused Joe. Such a confused Joe that he didn't even follow me like he was supposed to as my bodyguard.

Smooth, Chris. Real smooth.

Mile High Club

"Who is she again?" I asked Joonie.

He only chuckled at my question from his seat over the aisle of the private jet we had boarded not five minutes ago, his eyes on the woman I had talked about.

"I mean, why exactly is she here?" I asked again, rephrasing the question. After all, I knew exactly who the woman was. Her name was Meiling. As far as I knew, she was supposed to be a nurse. Now what business a nurse had on our way to the Billboards, I had no idea.

Joonie sighed and stuffed his hands in his jeans' pockets before replying. "She's here to look over me. I'm sure she'll calm down in a bit. Let her have a little fangirling moment."

"But I thought you were supposed to be like…all well now?" I asked, still not quite understanding the purpose of her attending our travels.

"So did I. But then Tae felt the need to disclose our going abroad to Dr. Han," Joonie started to explain, rolling his eyes slightly before a tiny smile made its way on his lips. "The doctor wasn't very pleased with me working so much and traveling this soon after my recovery, so she insisted I at least take a specialized nurse to accompany me. Tae didn't let me object. They still think I'm going to lose it sooner or later…which is fair."

"Right..." I muttered, some weight dropping in the pit of my stomach upon hearing Joonie's explanation. To say all this wasn't making me slightly uncomfortable, would have been an understatement. What I was especially concerned about, was the word *"specialized."*

"And what is her field of specialization?"

"Well, that baffles me too. Turned out she has specialized in psychiatry and mental health. Apparently, she was watching over the development of my mental health at the hospital, yet here I thought she was just well...a normal nurse," Joonie said, scratching the back of his head awkwardly at the end while I gulped, the ball of uneasiness only growing in my stomach.

"I didn't even realize I'd need that kind of monitoring. I went through a brain-damage, not a suicide attempt or anything of the sorts," Joonie concluded.

"She has signed a non-disclosure agreement, right?" I asked.

"Yes."

What Joonie saw was me nodding nonchalantly as a reply. But inside, I was a panicking mess. On top of trying to figure out what the hell I was supposed to do with Joe and trying to keep the rest of GRiD from figuring out exactly how fucking non-functioning pile of mentally damaged trash I had become... I'd have to deal with Meiling too.

There was no doubt she would lock me into a white, cushioned room in a mental institution as soon as she'd pay even the slightest bit of that specialized professional attention to me. And I wouldn't put it beyond Dr. Han, that she might've even issued Meiling to keep an eye on me too, while she was at it anyway.

What a mess. Not that I wasn't in need of professional help—because I certainly was. Even I could see it, considering even now I was barely functioning because of the lack of sleep. A power nap in the back seat of a company Mercedes on the way to the airport, hardly passes as resting time. But as that nap had also served as a nice excuse to not have *the talk* with Joe too, I couldn't really complain.

Speaking of whom, Joe was currently kept busy catching up with Do-hyun. I knew that wouldn't last for long though, and I'd have to start coming up with better ways to avoid Joe. At least until I'd figure out what to do with him. I trusted him enough to know he wouldn't bring up the subject unless we were in private, so for now I was safe on that front.

However, there was the sleeping and having violent nightmares issue I'd have to deal with for the whole flight to the US. Lately, the sleeping problems had been dealt with by Joe. This time, however, I'd have to count on alcohol like I used to before he stormed into my life…but I wasn't exactly looking forward to it. Especially the part with the hangover. Then again I still had the buzz going on from that morning, so I figured I might as well continue with it.

Eventually Jiwoo arrived and the stewardess asked us to keep the window shades and the privacy screens open during take-off and landing, as well as every time the fasten seatbelts sign was on. I tuned out when she started going over the details, I had heard it a million times before. Good thing the minibar in my personal pod had been filled up with booze in advance, because I needed that sleep. Bad. It was, after all, going to be Friday morning all over again due to the time difference when we eventually landed.

It wasn't even that hard to discreetly glug down a couple of more wine glasses than the rest of the guys when we were already up in the air, having lunch in the lounge area. Then a couple of beers when we played cards with the guys to pass the time. When even Meiling had a couple bubbly glasses of champagne, I figured I was still on the safe side. Unfortunately, my tolerance for alcohol had increased so much lately that I knew I'd have to up my game once everyone else was asleep.

Which they were, sooner rather than later. After a super early dinner, everyone retreated to their own pods, one by one, until I was the last one to get back to the seating area. Obviously I tried to get some sleep without the help of more alcohol at first, but sure enough the anxiety started creeping up on me in no time.

Every time I tried to close my eyes, my mind decided to either go over the night of the crash, obsess over Joe, worry about Meiling or the rest of the guys finding out about my alcohol—or anxiety—problems. What annoyed me the most, was the fact that I had always been good at sleeping during long flights, but now I couldn't have a blink of rest despite being more than tired.

Soon, the inside of the pod became more claustrophobic than comfortable. I gave up on trying to sleep for an hour or so and stood up to stretch. My bladder was getting a bit uncomfortable too, so I decided to take a leak before opening up a vodka bottle I had found inside the minifridge—now that would be strong enough to knock me out for a good few hours. Everyone was sound asleep in their own pods as I passed by, including Joe, who had forgotten to close his privacy screen. I couldn't help but stop and secretly stare at his peaceful face for a moment, as it reminded me so much of this morning. It had almost been too easy to avoid him during the flight, which made me wonder if he had already given up on me.

Once I managed to rip my eyes off Joe's face, I practically tiptoed to one of the restrooms at the back. Taking a leak, I avoided the mirror there too, knowing that the reflection would only make me even more miserable. It proved to be a damn hard task though when I washed my hands, as the mirror was placed right above the sink.

But when I stepped out and collided with a broad chest, I learned the hard way that I hadn't been very good at avoiding Joe, rather that he had let me do so. And while my brain had a hard time keeping up what was happening, I was pinned in the narrowest space between the sink and Joe. Who, by the way, towered over so high I was surprised he was able to stand straight in the small room.

"Don't wanna talk today? Fine. But at least let me distract you enough so you can sleep," he whispered, those annoyingly fascinating eyes of his keeping me nailed to the spot. "I can't stand seeing you like this," he then added after a moment of silence, with such a soft tone I couldn't help but melt in his embrace while he caressed my cheek with the back of his hand.

Knowing I wouldn't be able to resist him if he'd continue looking at me with those eyes, I averted my gaze. "The others could catch us."

Joe only raised an eyebrow before turning the lock, the clicking sound nearly drowned by the plane's continuous noise I had almost grown used to.

"They could still hear us…" I mumbled, but knew my excuses were running short.

"Then better keep your voice down," Joe said and smirked, before leaning to plant a soft kiss on the side of my neck. And then another, and another, until I couldn't hold in the smallest whine that escaped my lips. Even my dick knew I didn't stand a chance against this man's charms as it started swelling inside the tight skinny jeans, effectively making my life so very uncomfortable. Joe noticed too—it was evident when his smirk grew wider. His next soft kiss landed on my lips.

Maybe that whole thing wasn't the brightest idea on my part, given the current circumstances, but I couldn't help but reciprocate his kiss by pressing my lips harder against his equally eager ones. Besides, we had already established, time and time again, that being like this with Joe was a good distraction and allowed me to sleep—and boy did I need that precious sleep.

Now, that thought processing took only a second, at best, and shortly thereafter my brain was as empty as it could be. My consciousness was filled with something else, something very precious, when I leaned against him as much as I could in the narrow space and circled my hands around his waist. At once, it was clear to me that kissing Joe was a whole different experience after I had realized my feelings towards him, but it was too late to retreat. It became impossible to not try to hold him as close as possible. I even parted my lips to give him better access and at once his tongue flicked across my bottom lip.

A warm buzz spread over my entire skin, making my heartbeat almost painfully fast on its way down before it reached my dick. As said organ twitched in my pants, the smallest whimper made it past my lips. Thankfully Joe's lips against mine muffled the sound a bit and the plane's noise hopefully drowned the rest.

Soon, I could only focus on Joe. His warm body pressing against mine. His hands roamed under my hoodie. His lips claimed mine. I barely even noticed the slight pain the edge of the counter pressing on my back inflicted as Joe pushed me against it. The one uncomfortable feeling I was aware of was the fact that my erection was becoming increasingly painful inside my pants.

I wanted—no, *needed*—to get rid of the restricting clothing as fast as possible. I only needed to reach for my pants before Joe already swatted my shaking hands away and undid the button. After yanking down the zipper, not even parting our lips once, I almost passed out in relief once my dick gained a bit more breathing room. Then Joe's equally hard erection pressed against my lower abdomen and instantly I knew the release wasn't far for either of us.

Like reading my mind, he parted our lips enough to grab my ass and lifted me up to sit on the counter in the narrow spot between the sink and the wall. For once, I thanked the gods for my ass being so small. Joe made his way between my legs and yanked my briefs down enough to free my dick that instantly sprung up to its full but reasonable length, before continuing our kiss. I was thankful that he did, as he grabbed my dick at the same time, making me moan—at least the kiss muffled the sound.

A sudden need to feel his skin under my hands, made me fumble his shirt buttons open. It was too slow for my likes, but the reward was so worth the trouble because Joe groaned in my mouth as soon as my fingers caressed his hot, naked skin beneath. After that, it didn't take him long to get his own, very impressive, erection freed from his pants.

Not letting our kiss break—probably to muffle the sounds that neither of us could hold down—he conjured up the smallest lube bottle from his pocket. I swear it must've been magic how discreetly he managed to do that, as I barely even noticed. In my defense, his other hand was still stroking my length so I had plenty of other things to focus on.

But I was very aware of the existence of the lube once the first drop of it landed on my dick. Joe smeared the cold liquid all over, before coating his own cock with the same substance. Then when he suddenly grabbed both of our members in his fist and started pumping up and down, rubbing them together, I practically saw stars.

Joe's lips on mine became rougher and rougher, as keeping our voices down became increasingly difficult the closer we got to our respective releases. I was the first to come, my hips jerking involuntarily as I tried desperately to keep my voice down when I moaned against Joe's lips. He reached his peak not long after, a grunt so loud escaping him I was momentarily afraid we'd be heard but then reasoned that they were all asleep and there was a whole lounge between the seating area and us.

When we finally parted, panting, we were a proper fucking mess. Both of our releases glimmered on Joe's abs, which he desperately tried to keep from dripping on his dress pants that hung down on his thighs with a paper towel. Heat rushed to my face upon seeing the mess we caused. I quickly tucked myself back in my jeans and hopped down from the counter before wetting a few more paper towels.

Joe muttered out a quick "thanks," smiling, before wiping the rest of the mess off his abdomen. We shared a short, sweet kiss, before he opened the door ever so slightly, telling me silently that we were in the clear. Joe left first, and I followed him right after, but not before noticing the glow on my face upon catching a glimpse of myself in the mirror. I barely even noticed the scars this time.

Afterwards when I laid on my luxurious, soft and comfortable seat, my mind was still filled only with the memory of our dicks enclosed in Joe's tight hold and other lewd thoughts.

Needless to say, I fell asleep in a heartbeat.

Random Dude

"You sure you don't want to hide them?" one of the make-up artist noonas asked, referring to the scars on my face.

"Yes, I'm sure. Couldn't sing with the damn clay on my face, go figure," I replied, trying to keep my voice from sounding too bitter, except I wasn't very convincing. "If you could get rid of some of the redness though, that would be fantastic," I continued with a slightly softer tone that hopefully made up for some of the earlier rudeness.

Noona nodded, though with a bit of a lag, and got to work. Finally, I could relax. Well, as much as I could considering there was a person messing with my hair and another slapping countless make-up products on my face. With a heavy sigh, I closed my eyes and leaned back, but not before I caught Minjae smiling at me from the next chair over.

We were all gathered to the master suite of the hotel to get our hair and make-up done for the night. I was more than ready for the Billboards. Yesterday's rehearsals went great. We met some awesome people. No one in the US seemed to mind my scars. Meiling had calmed down, and for the most part, left us alone. I had a couple of good night's sleep thanks to my right hand and some very distracting memories of our flight to the US. It all had kept my brain busy enough to not get caught up in the anxiety at night, so I couldn't really complain.

Meanwhile Seong-gi was in charge of our security for the whole of today and tomorrow, together with some new dudes. Joe was having time off so it had been considerably easier to avoid him this morning than it had been the last couple of days. While the part of me that was in love with him was glad he was finally having some downtime after having to deal with my difficult ass for so long, there was this other part of me that wondered if he was actually glad to get rid of me as he hadn't even shown his face the whole morning.

I knew I had accidentally gotten used to him and even fallen in love. But one thing I hadn't anticipated was to feel so goddamn lost once he wasn't around. And it hadn't even been two full days yet.

Pathetic.

But when Joe didn't show up at lunch that day either, it seriously started bothering me. Where had he gone? What was he up to? Why wasn't he here? Was he really that fed up with me that, the moment he got some free-time, seeing me was the last thing on his mind? I kept looking over my shoulder, almost waiting for him to show up any minute and start teasing me. It continued to the point that even Minjae turned to look towards the door one time mimicking me and asked, "What's wrong?"

"Nothing," I mumbled and tried my best to tone it down a bit for the remainder of lunch.

Afterwards, it was time to get dressed in our preselected outfits—basically some boring black suits—and I still hadn't seen a glimpse of Joe. He didn't even show himself when we gathered in the lobby of our floor, heading out. Fuck, I even lingered around to the latest possible second in hopes of getting a glimpse of his sorry ass.

At the very least, I assumed he would've shown up to wish me good luck for the Billboards. Perhaps even wagging that imaginary tail of his and staring down at me with those golden brown eyes, as he waited for my thanks. Maybe he would've even promised to wait for me at his hotel room, hinting at some celebratory horizontal exercises—which I would've pretended to not-so-politely decline before somehow ending up in his bed anyway upon nightfall.

But no, none of that happened. Admitting my defeat, I followed the rest of the guys and the security personnel to a larger than life limousine waiting for us at our hotel's side entrance that we all packed in. Then, on the way to the venue, I kept checking my phone, in hopes of receiving even a short and simple "good luck" text. I nearly jumped when the phone actually did vibrate in my hand, and I got that text message.

Good luck, it said, like I had imagined. But I couldn't help but feel a small sting of disappointment hit my heart when it was from Hana and not from Joe. Not that it wasn't nice to get a text from her, too…but today I would rather have gotten a text from Joe.

I was just about to type her a quick "*thanks"* text, but was cut off by Joonie, who suddenly snapped the phone off my hands.

"Aish, I totally forgot!" he exclaimed—no, shrieked, really—from my right, so high and loud I was momentarily worried my ear was about to fall off.

"Ow fuck, can you not yell? And what are you doing? Give me my phone back," I mumbled, massaging my ear that hopefully hadn't gotten permanently damaged. That would have been the final straw in my career as an idol, for sure.

"Nope," he said and turned his eyes to Minjae and Do-hyun. "The rest of you too. I want your phones."

Minjae, Do-hyun and Tae all handed him their phones instantly, as if they no longer owned free will. But when Joonie added his own phone to the pile, I gave up. Admitting my defeat once again under the peer pressure, I could only watch him hand the pile of phones over to Seong-gi.

Thankfully I had something else to think of for a while, as we prepared for the red carpet. Tae briefed us once again on the reporters we absolutely wanted to score an interview with and the ones we should avoid at all costs. The red carpet of the Billboards turned out to be an even bigger jungle than whatever we had over at Asian music awards. Nevertheless, it wasn't that unfamiliar of a scene for us, so I'd say it went fairly well.

We were also handed the award for the "Social Artist of the Year" unceremoniously right at the red carpet. Now, as that was kind of a given, taking the loyalty of GRiD Crew into account, we weren't really surprised. But it was nice. I just wished it would've been an award delivered at the main stage.

Tae scored us an interview with a couple of very big publishing houses, and that basically concluded our first international award ceremony red carpet experience. Then it was merely some waiting until the show would start. We were—again—one of the first to start the show since there were way bigger names on the set list than us. We didn't even get to enjoy the beginning. Well, if you didn't count watching it from the backstage screen without sound, since the small TV in the corner was muted. Not that you could hear it even if it wasn't silenced. The noise backstage was something else, with a blow dryer getting off over here, and a group of people chatting loudly over the other noises over there.

Getting bored, I wandered around the maze-like backstage area. Without my phone, I was lost and way too alone with my thoughts. And I couldn't afford a freak-out right before our performance. Especially before one of our most important ones to date. What did before-the-incident Chris do to entertain himself in these types of situations?

The answer to that hit me right in the face when I spotted Jiwoo's phone on the side table. It wasn't even locked. And, conveniently enough, I had also seen Min and Do making out in one of the more secluded spots not long ago—I bet they were still at it.

It would've been easy. I would've taken a couple of sneaky pics with Jiwoo's phone, logged into @crewinsidr Twitter, posted them, logged out and put her phone back where it was before anyone noticed anything. I knew I could've pulled it off. I had done it before.

But for once, I didn't act on it. For one, Min and Do had had their fair share of unwanted attention. For two, they were more careful now, so it would've been much harder to pull off. Plus, if I got caught, it would get me in so much trouble I wasn't sure I could handle yet. I wasn't about to jeopardize my already shaky position in this group.

Still, I had to admit the thought alone made me feel somewhat normal. It was almost like nothing bad had ever even happened, and I *was* normal. At least when I managed to forget the scars on my face or my annoyance towards Joe.

When it was almost our time to climb on stage, Tae gathered us together.

"Alright, listen up," he started his pre-stage speech while we all grabbed each other's shoulders. "I know we'll ace it, so I'll just remind you to have fun on stage. It is, after all, the first time we're here, out of hopefully many, many times. It's only one song so give it your all, understood?"

The rest of us nodded as we joined hands in the middle. "For the Crew!"

Joonie, Minjae and Do-hyun scurried at the entrance to the stage right away and I was about to follow them when Tae stopped me.

"You good?" he asked, a concerned frown on his face.

Why the hell did these people have to become so observant today of all days? They had left me alone for such a long time for fuck's sake, why did they start to act like this when I was—

for once—feeling somewhat normal? Nevertheless, I nodded to Tae and even flashed him a small smile. "Yeah, I'm good."

"Good," he replied and tapped my back.

Until we were actually up on stage, it hadn't really hit me how big of a deal this Billboard -thing actually was. But once we heard most of the audience chanting our names on top of their lungs, I realized I had underestimated GRiD Crew. Honestly, I was so blown away that I nearly missed my cue to enter the spotlight.

For four minutes and 48 seconds, the whole duration of "Mad Love" paired with the additional dance break, I was in paradise. My mind was blank, not even a glimpse of my usual ghosts lingered around the edges of my conscience. There was only me, Tae, Do-hyun, Joonie, and Minjae on stage, and the rest of the world consisted only of our Crew at that precise, precious moment. It was almost like I had been woken up from a bad, mushy dream, right into a bright sunlight. Or been drunk without actually drinking at all.

Sadly, it was over all too soon, and we were guided to our designated seats in the audience after a quick change of clothes and a bit of freshening up. While each a bigger star than the other did their best on stage, I tried to be entertained. I really tried. But I couldn't help but let my mind wander back to Joe. He was clearly avoiding me. Then again, he was Joe. And some of the new security staff weren't even that hard to look at. Maybe he already had a new target.

I was so caught up in it, that my mind started playing tricks on me. Once I was so sure I saw Joe in the midst of other security staff lingering around, but when the random dude turned his face towards me, I realized that he was, in fact, just that—a random dude.

Worst Option

Fast forward to our very own after party at the master suite of the hotel we were staying in, and I was drunk, dizzy and extremely pissed off. I'd gotten my phone back, but there hadn't been a single text or phone call from Joe. He didn't even show up to the after party—and he rarely passed up a party, especially when he was off duty.

But Joe wasn't really the main issue. I wasn't the only one who was pissed. This time, Do-hyun kept me company, although he was annoyed for a very different reason than I was.

"I can't believe we didn't win the 'top duo/group' award," he said—for the hundredth time—and slammed his empty beer can on the table.

Ah, yes. It had stung a bit when we had lost it to a popular old American group—who had recently made their own comeback—of all the groups in the world, but hey...this was an American award show after all. What did he expect? That the first time we even attend, we'd win in a major category? Yeah, right.

"Can you shut up already? It's not the end of the world, and I'm sure we'll have other chances to win here," Tae said, getting visibly annoyed by Do-hyun's ranting.

"Well yeah, but this was our main goal from the start..." Joonie said, taking a sip from his wine glass. I took it as an opportunity to glug down the rest of my beer, too, before opening up another one, "...to reach that with a meaningless minor award? Sorry Tae, but I'm with Do on this one."

"Hey, I wouldn't say that an award that was granted to us solely because of GRiD Crew, was meaningless in any way," Minjae countered. "In fact, I'd say it was the best award to win. It means we have the best fans."

"I didn't mean it like that, Min," Joonie said, leaning back in his armchair. "But you do have a point."

"Well, I'm still not over it," Do-hyun huffed. "I mean, what now? We've already reached all our goals. Kind of in a lame way but we did."

Tae shrugged. "We'll figure out new goals."

"Like what?" Do-hyun asked, and a heavy silence fell upon us as they all tried to figure something out.

I, however, already knew the answer to that. It was obvious, when I thought of it. It was the logical next step. So it slipped from my mouth before I had the chance to think it through. "Grammys."

"Wait, what did you say?" Joonie asked, snapping his widened eyes from his glass to my face.

I cleared my throat. "I said, 'Grammys.' Our next goal should be the Grammys."

The rest of them also turned to look at me with wide eyes upon that clarification. Then they started laughing...hard. Their asses off, really. I didn't think it was that silly, to be honest, but I chuckled with them and shifted uncomfortably at my seat before taking another sip of my beer. I had never been quite comfortable being in the spotlight, especially when the other members were involved.

That was until Jiwoo strutted back from the kitchen with a new bottle of wine in tow. "I don't know what y'all are laughing at, I think Chris has a point." She laid a new wine bottle on the table before sitting on the armrest of my chair.

At once, the hysterical laughter died. The first one to recover, was Tae. Wiping the corners of his eyes, he leaned back and said, "No, but for real, I also think Chris has a point."

"Wait, are you serious?" Joonie asked after a while, still having a hard time keeping himself contained.

"Well, yeah. I mean, did we ever think we could *actually* reach our goal of attending Billboards? Nope," Tae said. "Yet, here we fucking are." He raised his glass.

Do-hyun and Minjae glanced at each other before picking up their glasses too. "To the Grammys," they said, almost simultaneously, before turning their eyes to Joonie.

Joonie still looked a bit sceptical, but nevertheless raised his glass after a moment of hesitation. "Y'all are crazy...but whatever. To the Grammys!"

They all turned their eyes back at me expectantly.

Oh what the hell, I thought while picking up my beer. "To the Grammys."

An hour or so later, minding my own business, I walked over to the kitchen part of the huge master suite in hopes of fetching a new beer. The others were trying to figure out how the stereo worked, and I had almost forgotten my issues with this whole Joe thing. At least, it wasn't as constantly on my mind as it had been during the day and evening. Basically, I was just having a great time with the guys for the first time in ages. I had nothing to complain about.

Except that serene calmness and a tiny spark of happiness didn't last long. The end to all those nice things came in the form of Do-hyun sneaking behind my back.

"By the way...where's Joe?" he asked, right when I was about to open the fridge.

Thankfully I had noticed him walking behind me, otherwise I would've dropped down dead due to a heart attack. Not that I didn't have a mini one upon hearing the topic he had in mind, but it wasn't as bad as it could've been. And at least I wasn't the only one who found Joe's absence from this party a little odd.

"And how the hell should I know?" I mumbled as a reply and turned around to face Do-hyun.

He blinked. "I thought you guys had gotten close."

I nearly choked on my beer. To say we had gotten close...yeah, it might've been a bit of an understatement. Or an overstatement, depending on your point of view. Then I shook my head slightly. "He's off-duty."

"Right..." Do-hyun said and scratched the back of his head. "Oh well, I'm gonna call him. Let's see if he's up for a beer or something."

"Nah, maybe he's sleeping. Let him have his freetime–"

Do-hyun cut me off, chuckling, "It's, like, eleven. We both know he ain't sleeping yet."

Then he already had his phone pressed against his ear like not even a second after. Fuck.

I began a downward spiral of a million questions popping into my head. What was I supposed to do now? What if Joe thought I had asked Do-huyn to call him? What if he agreed and appeared here all of a sudden? What if he didn't? Should I have left? Should I have stayed? What would I even say to him if he did come here?

But then when Joe didn't answer Do-hyun's call, I got worried. Why wasn't he answering his phone? What if something had happened to him? I had never seen him not answer when Do-hyun called. Ever.

"Huh..." Do mumbled, looking at his screen a bit weird, frowning. "That's weird."

"Err, like I said, maybe he's sleeping—"

"Bullshit," Do said and turned around.

"Hey Seong-gi," he hollered. "Any idea where Joe is? He's not answering his phone."

175

"I saw him in the hallway like five minutes ago, heading to his room. Why?"

At least he was alive.

"Oh. I was just wondering if he'd be up for a couple of beers and some card games," Do said, walking closer.

"Nah, I don't think so Do. Based on the stink alone he ought to be heading to shower instead. Looked like he had been in the gym for a while."

"Okay-okay. I'm gonna leave him be," Do said, finally giving up.

At that moment music started booming in the master suite at top volume. Seemed like they had finally figured out how to use the stereo system and turned the music so loud it was impossible to have any kind of conversation. Luckily we had the whole floor and the one below this one, otherwise I would've pitied the other residents of the hotel.

Nevertheless, I let out a very relieved sigh and joined the others.

How I ended up behind Joe's door not thirty minutes later… I have no idea. Yet there I was, contemplating if I wanted to confront him or not. Pacing back and forth, I wondered if he had already gone to bed. The faint sound of the shower had stopped a while ago. The door didn't let through any other sounds.

The button-up I was wearing started choking me, so I opened a couple buttons on top. Stopping in front of the door, I ran my hand through my hair and rubbed my temple. What the fuck was I doing here? What would I even say if I were to knock on the door? I wasn't exactly in the position to accuse him of avoiding me; I had done the same. And what if he wanted to talk again? I turned around to leave.

Then again…I knew how to silence him if it came to that. And I wanted—no, needed—his attention. Even one day without his constant teasing and presence had been pure fucking torture. I took a deep breath, spun right back around and raised my hand to knock on the door.

Right at that second, the door swung open, and I nearly collided with Joe.

"Chris?" he asked, blinking. Those golden brown eyes fixated on my face.

I let my hand drop and stuffed both of them to my pockets. "Joe."

He relaxed and crossed his arms while leaning against the door frame. I could smell his cologne. And I had no idea why I noticed it.

"Missed me?" he asked, an annoyingly bright smile playing on his lips.

I rolled my eyes. "No. Not at all." Sarcasm dripped from my voice. Like there was any other reason I'd be right behind his door in the middle of the night while there was a perfectly good party going on not further than three doors down. He damn well knew I was missing him.

"Really? I guess I'll go grab a few beers with Do-hyun then," he said and pushed past me to the hallway.

Maybe it was my annoyance about him avoiding me, the alcohol clouding my judgement, or purely just my missing of him, but I grabbed his wrist and yanked him back.

"You're not going anywhere," I muttered and ushered him further into his room, all the way to his bed and pushed him down to sit on the edge of it. He leaned against his arms and glanced up at me.

As I stared him down, not knowing where to start, a hint of uneasiness flashed on his face. "What do you actually want, Chris?" he asked, lowering his eyes.

An odd yearning to see that amazing color of his eyes overpowered me. I let my body take control and grabbed his chin, forcing him to look at me once again. Once his eyes met mine, I got closer.

"This," I whispered, sitting legs astride on his lap and placing my lips on his.

He gasped and grabbed my waist when I staggered, balancing me in his embrace as he let his lips start moving with mine. I poured all my unspoken feelings into the kiss, hoping it would somehow reach him, but unfortunately I only tasted confusion and hesitation from his lips.

Desperate, I tried even harder, but Joe only dropped his arms from my waist. He didn't exactly push me away, but he didn't encourage me to continue either. And once I moved on to his neck, he took in a shaky breath but didn't return the favor.

"Chris, you're drunk…" he muttered, leaning back.

"And?" I whispered, and nibbled his earlobe in hopes of distracting him.

While it did distract him for a second, it didn't last very long. "We should really talk before we go any further."

"Then talk," I mumbled against the skin on his neck and started fumbling with his shirt's buttons.

Unfortunately I didn't get very far on my quest of getting rid of his shirt before he grabbed my wrists and stopped me. "I don't get you. One minute you're telling me to fuck off and when I do exactly that, you're like this. It fucking hurts, Chris."

"Sorry," I said, shrugging, then tried to kiss him again.

But this time, he downright turned his head away. "Is it too much to ask for you to stop pushing me away and approach me on your own?"

I raised my eyebrows. "Am I not approaching you now?"

"You know what I mean. Sober. And not a minute after avoiding me for days in the first place."

"Look, as I said, I'm sorry. It's just the way I am. And you can't blame me for being confused, either," I said, halfway giving up already. I knew I was a shitty person, no need to rub it on my face. At least I tried to do something about it.

"No, I can't indeed," Joe replied, letting go of my wrists, still casting his eyes down. "But I'm also so fucking tired of chasing you."

At once, my heart stopped like it had been shot and I gasped. Because there it finally was. The words I had feared to hear the most. Of course he would go for the worst option. Did I really even expect any less from him?

Words I couldn't hold back, ice cold and flat, fell out of my mouth before I could stop them.

"Then don't," I spat and stood up hastily, trying to remember how to breathe as I staggered towards the door. Once I reached it, I stopped. "I never once asked you to chase me. In fact, I think I told you the exact opposite. Multiple times."

"So you're running away again, huh?"

I didn't reply. I couldn't.

"If you really go now, I really won't come after you anymore," Joe said.

This was it. My choice. I could've told him how I really felt, and laid my heart bare in front of him. Open up and be vulnerable. Play my cards and hope for the jackpot while exposing myself for an even bigger heartbreak. But I chose not to and opened the door.

"I mean it, Chris," Joe mumbled, his last attempt to stop me. "If you leave now, *without* talking this through, it's over."

"Then so be it," I replied, before slamming the door shut after me.

Reminders

Joe kept his word. He was all uptight and business the whole way back home. He barely even looked at me, even though he was close all the time like a shadow with no personality.

He didn't try to avoid me or anything. He simply ignored me completely and replied only if I asked him a direct question. Other than that, he was dead silent. I would honestly have rather had him avoid me, as it felt like he was even further away from me than ever before.

Me, however…I started noticing some pretty weird details about him. Like the fact that he still slightly limped with his bad leg—the one I had probably injured more during our one and only serious battle. He hid it well, but I noticed. I noticed everything.

At first I was angry. I was angry at Joe for not trying harder. I was angry at myself for being like this. I was angry at Joe for giving up on me. I was angry at myself for not saying out loud the words that really mattered.

Being inside my own head became my worst enemy as I dwelled on everything that had happened in the past few weeks. My thoughts became darker and darker when I couldn't sleep due to the nightmares and flashbacks that still didn't leave me alone. I didn't dare to go to my bedroom when we arrived back at my place, so I locked myself inside my gaming room downstairs.

But all that anger burned up soon. Playing video games became my escape, just like it had been before Joe disturbed my routine a few weeks back. Gaming kept me entirely focused. I almost managed to forget that Joe was in my house, somewhere...but not quite.

My eyes ached from spending all the time watching at the screen at a very close proximity. I barely even blinked. My back hurt like a motherfucker. But I didn't care. Each time a game ended, I ushered the others of my small gaming group to start a new one. I tried to not pause for more than a couple of minutes, as the slightest break was enough to drive me insane.

Repeating the same pattern, I was soon acing it. Shoot, run, jump, shoot again, re-load. Game over. Start a new one. Rinse and repeat, I followed the fast pace of the shooting game until I mastered it, losing myself more and more the longer I continued.

"Again," I mumbled after another game over.

Only this time, there was a sound of a collective sigh on my headphones.

"No, C. It's time for a break. I'm fucking dead," M93's exhausted voice told me.

"Same," replied Jonezzi.

With a huff, I gave up. At least it would give me a chance to down another beer. "Fine. Fifteen minutes max, tho."

"Alright alright, geez. Calm the fuck down man," M93 said while we opened the chat instead.

I tuned out as they started throwing meaningless memes around. For a solid minute I contemplated if I should take off the headphones to not hear it. Fucking pissed me off, to be honest. Now, of course that was when Jonezzi decided he had something to say to me.

"Hey C, my girlfriend is a huge fan of this boy band called—err—Grip, or something like that..." he said, trailing off as I froze.

"And?" I asked, faking a disinterested tone but swallowed heavily at the same time. Trying my hardest to not correct him that he was most likely just saying our group's name wrong. I did not like where this was going.

"Well, I happened to overhear an interview she was watching on YouTube—"

M93's hysterical laughter cut him off. "I bet you're just a huge fan of them yourself—"

"Shut the fuck up, M. Anyway, I've been meaning to ask, why do you sound an awful lot like one of them C? The one called Chris?"

A silence. I had never been in a situation quite like this before. Nobody had ever called me out. And I mean, what the fuck I was supposed to reply to that? *"Well, maybe, because I am one of them."* Yeah, nope.

"Dude, all Asians sound the same," M93 countered eventually, still laughing.

"Hey, that's kinda rude," Jonezzi muttered, but couldn't suppress the small chuckle that escaped from him.

I, however, jumped straight into M93's bandwagon. "Yeah, whatever M said. Look I need to go, beer's running low. Good game."

Hastily, I threw my headset to the table and sighed. Too bad I had grown fond of these faceless guys on the internet, because if they wouldn't drop this subject I'd have to disappear. Change my nickname and make a new friend group. I didn't exactly look forward to that.

I grabbed the nearest bottle in hopes of settling my nerves. The bottle was empty, though, and so were the five others laying around. Unfortunately, it seemed like I was actually running low on beer, the lame excuse suddenly turning into reality.

The tiny clock on the bottom right corner of my screen told me it was nearly ten in the evening. I hadn't had a lick of sleep since the US. Not that it mattered; my internal clock would be fucked up again in a couple of days when we'd head to Europe.

Fucking jet-lag. Fucking Joe. Fucking nightmares. Oh well. New day, new me. Hopefully a new beer too, if I had any left.

Grunting, I stood up, stretching the stiffness away, and headed to the kitchen. Half-way through though, I collided with a wide chest in the hallway, instantly regretting emerging from my gaming cave.

Oddly enough, it wasn't Joe who I collided with.

"Mr. Won?" I asked, eyes widening.

"Oh, hey Chris," he said, taking a step back.

"What are you doing here?"

"Filling in for Joe. He's taking a few days off until you head to Europe. I thought he told you."

He totally didn't.

"Uhh, whatever," I said, my mood sinking even lower than I thought possible at this point. "Good to see you again, though. How's it going with the family?"

Mr. Won cringed, rubbing the back of his head. "Let's just say I won't recommend anyone to have children anytime soon."

"It is what it is. Congrats, pops!" I said, grinning, the gesture somehow hurting my face. I guess I hadn't even smiled in a while.

"Yeah… thanks. Look, I was heading to shower. I just got here, and I'm still covered in baby puke because I had to leave in kind of a hurry. Catch up with you later?"

"Sure," I said, and watched Mr. Won scurry upstairs with his duffel bag in tow.

I went in the kitchen, fetched another bottle from the fridge and hauled my heavy ass in one of the bar stools on the kitchen island. After opening the bottle, I threw my head back and stared at the ceiling. Somehow, the lump in my throat that had bothered me all the way from *that* night, seemed to have grown bigger in the span of a few minutes.

Was Joe really so done with me he couldn't even spend a few days under the same roof? Had to take time off *now* even though he had had no problem staying with me for a few weeks just a moment ago? Was this whole thing even worse than I had initially thought?

Mr. Won appeared at the door. "Ah, beer. An adult beverage I never thought I'd miss so much."

"There's more in the fridge if you want some."

"Mind if I join you?" he asked, already heading towards the fridge.

I shook my head and raised my bottle. "No, go ahead."

He sat on the stool next to mine. "So...how's everything? Still have those nightmares?"

"Yup. Other than that, everything's fine."

"Good, good..." he said and trailed off. I guess he didn't really believe me. I was proven right because he kept asking more questions. "Are you seeing anyone professional...like a therapist or something?"

"Not yet. But I'm planning to."

"And Joe? You get along well?"

Fuck. "Let's just not talk about him."

Mr. Won sighed. "Well, if he gives you a hard time, I can try to talk to him. I mean, he technically does own the company, but I *am* still his boss now, and I know he can be a little much sometimes—"

"No, nothing like that. Thanks for the offer though. I'll keep it in mind." Dammit. Why hadn't I said something? My original plan had been to get rid of Joe, and now I had just blown my first chance to do so. Fuck. Then again...did I really even want to get rid of him? "In any case, I better get back to my games. People are waiting for me."

Mr. Won finally dropped the twenty questions and headed to the living room.

When I got back to my gaming room, I tried to absorb back into the games. Thankfully the guys had already moved on to Jonezzi's relationship problems and no one brought up the subject of me sounding the same as this Chris-person from a Korean pop band named Grip. Somehow I found it hard to focus for shit.

It was like four in the morning when I finally gave up, gave the guys my excuses and turned the machine off.

Planning on trying to get some sleep on the couch, I wandered to the living room. A big mistake: the couch gave me flashbacks of me sitting on Joe's lap, getting one of the hottest hand jobs I'd ever experienced. The guitar that still leaned against it reminded me of my shitty song I sang for him. The coffee stain on the back of the couch that neither of us had noticed when cleaning, now stood out as if it was highlighted.

I went to the kitchen and nibbled on some leftover sandwich that I had bought from the airport earlier. It tasted like shit compared to those heavenly pajeons Joe made me for breakfast a couple of times, so soon I gave up on that too.

Everything around the house reminded me of Joe. Even brushing my teeth in my bathroom made me blush and my heart beat crazy fast. Spotting the running shoes tossed next to the laundry bin reminded me of our kiss on the mountain trail.

The worst of it all, though, was my bedroom. The bed was still exactly as we had left it before heading to the Billboards. The sheets were still wrinkled, an obvious reminder of the best night and the best sex of my life. The image of him sleeping there when I had left the room in the middle of the night haunted me, especially as the dent on the pillow where Joe had laid his head was still somewhat visible.

If I hugged the pillow tight enough, I could almost imagine a faint trace of his scent lingering in the air.

Immediately No

We arrived at our hotel in Rotterdam almost at midnight on Wednesday. To say I was exhausted would've been an understatement. I had barely slept while at home—only a couple of hours here and there in between gaming and packing.

Let's not even start with the flight. It was basically a hell designed just for me. Joining the mile high club was only a memory, and Joe hadn't as much as glanced my way the whole time. He hadn't even bothered to pick me up at my place, and rather met us at the airport. I had no clue what was going on.

The level of awkwardness between us was unreal. I couldn't bear it. But Joe didn't seem bothered at all—as I followed him through the carpeted hallways of our hotel for the night, he didn't even glance at me once. Well, until he stopped in front of a room.

"This is your room," he muttered, handing me my keycard.

I nodded, glancing at the door. The numbers 404 on a plate glared at me like an omen. A bad one at that.

"I'll be in 405 if you need anything," Joe continued, before taking a step towards the next room. As if I was a mere object he'd have to be around out of necessity. Fucking hurt, to be honest. It was almost like I no longer existed.

Before I could stop myself, my hand had involuntarily grabbed Joe's sleeve to stop him. And before I could swallow the words, they fell out of my mouth. "Joe, I can't stand this. It's weird and—"

"I know," Joe huffed, not even turning around to face me. "I talked with Mr. Won and he will find a replacement soon. Until then, we're stuck. You'll have to deal with me for a little while longer."

"That's not what—"

"Save it."

"But—"

"Fuck off, Chris."

My heart stopped as I froze at first, and then let go of his sleeve, taking a step back. Time turned into slow-motion when I watched his hand drop to his side, before he stuffed it into his pocket, glancing over his shoulder while my eyes widened and jaw dropped open.

How did he dare to use my words against me? I wanted to scream, shout, say anything to him but my vocal cords didn't seem to work. I could only watch him walk the few steps to his door, open it and step in.

"Hurts, doesn't it?" he asked, finally glancing at me with all the warmth in his eyes totally gone, before letting the door close behind him.

I don't know how long I stood there, frozen to the spot. Maybe a minute, maybe an hour. In any case, it felt like an eternity. I don't know exactly what I hoped for by staying there, but none of it happened. Joe didn't come back. He didn't apologize. Nothing.

To me, those last few words of his sounded way more final than what he had said back on the night of the Billboards after party, and it was absolutely sickening. Though…I guess I deserved it. Which made it worse.

"Yes, it does hurt," I whispered to the empty hallway. "A lot."

I forced my heavy feet to move, one step at a time, and my arm to raise enough to open the lock. Once it flashed a green light, I all but stumbled inside, my chest so tight it was hard to breathe. My suitcases were already there, but those were not what I was interested in. I rushed straight to the minibar.

The selection inside was sad, to put it mildly. The only strong enough was a mini bottle of vodka which I downed in one go and sat on the edge of the bed. It helped for maybe fifteen minutes max, burning my throat enough for me to not feel the other, more significant pain that was rapidly consuming me entirely.

But that fifteen minutes was enough for me to get my hoodie changed into a semi-sheer button-up, my shoes changed from sneakers to dress shoes and my scars buried under a light layer of color corrective make-up. There was a bar downstairs. It surely had a bit better selection of booze than the minibar in my room.

And booze was what was going to get me through the night.

There was one obstacle between that bar and me though, and that was Seong-gi reading a newspaper in the lobby of our floor. He spotted me at once and folded the newspaper away and glared at me with narrowed eyes, but I ignored him completely. Instead, I smashed the lift's call button.

"Evening, Chris," he said. I nodded at him to let him know I heard and noticed him, so he continued. "Mind sharing where you're going this time of the night?"

It was better to tell the truth or I wasn't going to get rid of him. "There was a bar downstairs."

"I saw. Want me to join you?"

In disbelief, I glanced at the older gentleman and raised my eyebrows.

"I guess that's a no."

"Yeah."

"Should I tell Joe?"

The lift doors opened, and I stepped inside. "I doubt he gives a shit, but if you must, whatever."

Seong-gi's face was completely unreadable when the lift's doors closed. He probably had to tell Joe anyway. I didn't even get why he asked. Hmph.

Whatever. This was me, fucking off like Joe told me to. He could think whatever the fuck he wanted about that. Followed me or not, I had no say in that anyway. But he better have kept his distance—if he wanted a strict business relationship, I'd give him exactly that.

The bar—dimly lit, dark wooden tones everywhere—was mostly empty when I stepped inside. Only a couple of businessmen occupied two tables. Didn't matter; I was here for the alcohol and nothing else. The bartender was polishing glasses when I sat on the barstool directly in front of him.

"What can I get you, sir?" he asked, his voice a little rough on the edges.

"Something strong. Whisky, preferably."

"ID?"

I chuckled in slight amusement but did dig my wallet out of my back pocket and threw my driver's license on the table anyway. It was quite common to get my age checked in the west, but this bartender was very extra about it—he even picked up the card and squinted his eyes when examining it. I had a hard time not rolling my eyes. I mean I was 25—international age—already.

Eventually he did get me a whisky on the rocks. "You know, most people your age are downstairs."

"Downstairs?"

"Yes, there's a club," he said and pointed to a set of stairs on my right that I had not even noticed.

Huh. I suppose I could've checked it out, as I was almost there anyway. I called out a quick thanks to the bartender who

189

had already turned to serve another customer, before heading downstairs.

At the bottom of the stairs, was a door with a round window that looked like a side entrance. The party, however, seemed huge based on the pure amount of people dancing on the inset dancefloor in the middle. The door was opened from the inside by a bouncer to whom I handed the entrance fee of a blue 20€ bill, having no idea whatsoever, if that was a lot or a little for an entrance fee in these parts of the world. It wasn't like I couldn't afford whichever way it was.

And I was already aching for the dancefloor anyway, the bass luring me in, making my heart beat in its rhythm instead of its own, more painful tempo that reminded me of Joe with every single bounce in my chest. I threw the rest of the whisky down my throat, handed the glass to the bouncer and all but rushed in the midst of people dancing together as if in some kind of a trance.

It was exactly what I needed.

In Seoul, I could've done nothing like that. I would've been instantly recognized there. But here, in a random nightclub in Rotterdam, people either didn't recognize me or didn't care. And that was more than fine with me.

I let the music and the crowd be my guide, and the bussers keep me adequately drunk by the cheap, way too sweet shots they sold by circling the midst of the dancing people. Maybe once or twice, I felt a piercing stare on my back—which made me suppose that Joe was probably there too, somewhere. Yet, besides the fact that I was oddly aware of his presence, I decided to ignore it completely.

Because fuck him. He made his decision, and I did mine.

Plus, it was not like there weren't plenty of other options around. Like one of the two businessmen from upstairs, who had followed me down. Let's just say that he was....hovering around. White skin, dark brown short hair styled neatly, green eyes—he was definitely not too sore for the eyes.

I wondered why he never made a move. Like, he was always there but he never approached me directly, just exchanged some glances...or passed by and "accidentally" brushed his front against my back while pushing through the crowd. Maybe he was in the closet or something.

I tested the theory and went to the restroom—my bladder was full of all the shots anyway. I couldn't say I was disappointed that he didn't follow me, but it got me curious; had I read him wrong? I thought I had picked some vibes...

But when I stepped out of the bathroom and spotted the man leaning against the wall in the corridor that led to the restrooms, I there was a small smile tugging up the corner of my mouth. Not because I was particularly interested, but because I was right. My theory was further confirmed when the man grabbed my elbow and said something in Dutch.

"Sorry?" I asked.

He immediately changed to English. "Ah, my bad. What is such a beautiful guy doing in Rotterdam?"

Did they not have hot guys at Rotterdam? Plus, I guess this one also didn't have working eyeballs, considering the state my face was in. But I played along and flashed him a brief smile as I stepped beside him and leaned my side against the wall as well.

"Business trip...more or less." Can a world tour count as a business trip?

He stepped in front of me and trapped me between him and the wall. When I spotted a wedding ring I had all my questions answered—of course he didn't go after me in public, he was taken. What a slime of a man. But when he asked, "How long are you staying?" I played along as a silly little airhead twink that he was clearly after, and grabbed his tie, starting to twirl it in my hands.

"Just a couple of days. Why, are you after some…fun?"

"Are you offering?"

My only answer was pulling his tie until our lips met.

Immediately no. It was all wrong. His breath smelled like an ashtray. His lips, too thin and sloppy, were all over my face at once because he opened his entire mouth like a fish. Too soon, his hands grabbed my ass and he pulled me flush against him. And…just the pure amount of saliva all over me…I soon had a hard time trying to not puke on the man's shirt.

And even if he would've been a better kisser than Joe—which he definitely wasn't—he wasn't *him*. He wasn't even nearly as tall, or firm, or handsome as Joe. He didn't smell like a forest after rain. He didn't know how to make me go from zero to one hundred with merely a few flirtatious words. He didn't have those magic hands that knew how to play me like I was the world's most sacred musical instrument.

In fact, he read my body all wrong, as he mistook my pushing him gently away as enthusiasm and started trying to push his slimy tongue all the way inside my mouth. I was appalled, so much that my stomach lurched. Despite my trying the damn hardest to not use violence ever again, I had no other choice than to kick him in the nuts with my knee just to get rid of him. Trust me—it was the softest move I could've used against him in that state of annoyance and disappointment that excuse of a man had evoked in me.

The man, however, didn't seem to appreciate my holding back the urge to smash his face in, as he grabbed his crotch and writhed in pain a comfortable meter or two away from me.

"Crazy bitch," he muttered between sharp intakes of breaths between his teeth.

I laughed at his face. "Say hi to your wife, fucker."

Holding down the urge to spit on his face, I combed my hair somewhat back in place with my fingers, before turning to walk away. Totally fed with my less than fun little night out, I was about to start brushing my clothes back in place and head to bed but was met with an extremely familiar pair of golden brown eyes when I lifted my eyes up.

Joe.

"Had fun?" he asked as soon as our gazes met.

There was not one single emotion showing on his stoic face despite the fact that I had just let a total stranger suck my face off, apparently directly in front of him. How long had he watched us? Why didn't he react in any fucking way? Not that I expected anything from a fuckboy like himself in the first place, but seeing him so blatantly not care a single shit about me still stung like a motherfucker.

I pushed past him. "As a matter of fact, I did."

Complete Nothingness

The next night, I drank myself into oblivion at my hotel room, alone. And the next. Yes, while there was a full party only two doors down in Joonie's room, celebrating two successful gigs in Rotterdam to start our tour in Europe.

On the third night, we changed cities to Amsterdam. I tried more clubbing. Then drank alone again. One morning I couldn't deal with the hangover, so I started my day with a couple of beers. It was somewhat effective, so it became a habit rather quickly.

I shut myself down in a way. Muted everything. I became a shell of a person who acted and performed on stage on autopilot—but there wasn't even a hint of a spark within me left, of the full-blown fire that used to burn inside me when I was on stage before. Now I felt nothing. Saw nothing. Heard nothing. Even my own voice somehow sounded distant.

The paradise, that being on stage once was for me, had turned into my worst nightmare.

Every concert went by in a haze of some sort. Another city, another concert, another club. Only flashes here and there managed to reach my consciousness every now and then. Moments like when someone smashed an ice-pack on my neck backstage, to cool my overheated body. Or when someone ripped the tightly taped cords off my back after a concert. Or a different man sucking my face off in a different city, a different night club. The faces and the cities started to blur together.

I could never go all the way with them. The men. As much as I tried, they were just never good enough. Never quite right. Never had the right words.

They were never Joe.

I think it was in Italy when I noticed I'd started to sweat like a pig...when someone from the staff removed my suit jacket and the whole white button-up below was so drenched it clung to my skin and turned see-through. But I couldn't be sure as I didn't really pay that much attention to my surroundings.

Of course, I knew I was burning the candle at both ends, barely seeing a sober moment in days while still working my body way over its limits on stage. The rest of the guys tried to reach me, one by one, when they finally noticed something was off, but I shrugged them all off and pushed them away. I guess they thought I was just exhausted, like the rest of them...and getting drunk often during tours wasn't any news for any of us except maybe Tae, so I managed to somewhat keep them off my back. After a few days of dealing with my cold indifference, they stopped trying. I heard them whispering about me from time to time when they thought I wasn't listening. They had nothing nice to say.

In a way...fair. I wasn't listening to them. At least, I didn't care. I didn't care about anything in particular. And the thing I cared about the least was myself. I even welcomed the numbness with open arms, as it was way easier to handle than the panic attacks, anxiety, nightmares... and especially seeing Joe, who was there, every fucking day, but at the same time wasn't. As he was my guard, he was also my driver, my shadow, a ghost that didn't leave me alone, yet didn't even try to communicate with me. At all.

In a way, I was completely, totally and utterly alone while still surrounded by people. People I loved, even. Fans, who practically worshipped me. Still, I was more alone than I had ever been when I had isolated myself up at my home in the mountains. I was lonelier than ever before. Even when I was in jail.

The thing with alcohol, though, was that it never helped for long enough. Eventually, the nightmares made a comeback, and with them came the anxiety. But at that point, I was so hooked on the numbness, I couldn't deal without it.

So I drank more. Worked my body on stage more. Went to more clubs. One way or another, I made myself pass out every night, in order to reach the needed level of not existing to have a couple of hours of sleep per night.

Soon I had no idea where I was every time I dragged my heavy feet on stage. Time became meaningless. The days and nights mixed together and I only slept whenever I passed out either from pure exhaustion or drinking too much.

Yet none of it mattered very much. There was always someone who'd come and get me from my room, drive me to the venues or other promotion activities, so I stopped bothering to check the schedule again. There was always someone who would push me on stage whenever it was my cue. And on stage, it was like I was fighting against a dark, murky water that wanted to drown me.

Every passing day, it became harder and harder to breathe. Too painful to keep my eyes open. Too bothersome to keep my head above the surface.

For who was I even fighting for? Not for myself, that's for sure. Definitely not for Joe—he didn't want me to. Maybe for the rest of GriD? But even that seemed like a stretch. It was like I was trapped in a carousel going round and round and round, faster and faster, without having the ability to hit the brakes to make it stop. Or going 200 kilometers per hour in the wrong lane. Floating on a wrecked ship in the middle of an ocean.

Then it all stopped during one single day.

The first to go was my sense of smell. It was early in the morning, and I legit stared at my coffee mug in my hand for at least fifteen minutes, trying to make myself smell the deliciousness I knew the beverage was emitting to the air. But I got nothing.

"What's wrong?" Minjae asked.

"Uh, nothing," I said, and continued on with my day.

It was about midway through our concert of the night in who knows where when I lost the sense of touch. Something was off, I knew it, but I didn't realize what was wrong until I started wondering where I had put my microphone and found it in my hand. I couldn't even feel the weight of it. For a few seconds, I stared at it, then clenched it harder. I saw that my fingers were still wrapped around it, knuckles white, but I still couldn't feel that I was holding it.

I shrugged it off. Maybe I was imagining it. But then after a few more songs when I ran backstage for an outfit change, one of the noonas came rushing at me.

"Chris! Why are you bleeding?" she asked, a horrified look on her face.

"What, where?" I asked as I sat down, weirded out.

"From your mouth! What happened?"

I laid my fingers where I thought my mouth was and, indeed, they got covered with red liquid in an instant. Great, I hadn't felt I had hurt myself and also couldn't taste the blood.

My reply came out as a mumble. "I must've bit my cheek or something."

"Here, ice it," she said and handed me an ice package. I planted it on my right cheek but didn't even feel the cold. Thankfully the bleeding stopped.

They made me breathe some oxygen, because apparently I looked tired, and then I was good to go again. It was only a few songs left anyway so I was sure I'd make it to the end.

But when I was back on stage the only thing I could hear was loud ringing in my ears. I yanked one of the earpieces off and it was a tiny bit better for a while. If I concentrated enough, I managed to pull through the last song—"Contrast." Pacing myself almost completely based on sight—the audience moving, the rest of GRiD dancing, our stage monitors showing the lyrics…that sort of thing. Though Joonie kept glancing at me with a weird look on his face for the whole duration of the song until I was done with my parts.

Then even the ringing in my ears stopped. All sound stopped.

Desperate, exhausted, and freaking out, I staggered towards the back of the stage, not caring one bit about the choreograph I was still supposed to complete though my singing parts were done. My mind repeating the same broken record of *"please let me hear something, anything,"* I dropped to my knees in front of a floor monitor that was behind one of the larger stage props, near the spot where we entered backstage.

Even though the red dot on the side told me it was on and producing sound, I didn't hear it. I didn't even feel the vibrations. I leaned closer and closer, eventually pressing my right ear against the surface, but there was still nothing. I crawled to the next one over, hoping that this one was just broken, grabbed the sides and pressed my ear against that one too, but I still heard absolutely nothing.

I was about to crawl over the next one in hopes that the second speaker was broken too when someone yanked me away from it so forcibly I slid a few meters backwards. I turned my gaze towards the intruder, ready to push them off, but my vision blurred. I could only see that his mouth was moving as if they were yelling at me.

"I can't hear," I said, or tried to, but I wasn't sure since I couldn't hear myself.

They reached their hand to the right side of my face, and when they pulled it out, there was blood on their fingers. I also pressed my hand somewhere on the right side of my head and that too was soon smeared with blood.

A strange whoosh went through my head upon seeing the blood and everything turned white. As if my eyes were suddenly bleached. As if I was floating in complete nothingness.

On My Own

An eternity passed, while I floated in the white nothingness. Or at least it felt like one. I guess I'd finally lost it for good. Was about time if I were to be honest. It had been inevitable with the way I had lived the past weeks.

But in this world, where I floated disconnected from everything else, even from my own senses...none of it mattered. There was no past, no future for me to worry about. It was almost euphoric, in a way.

For a fleeting, scary moment, I wished I could've stayed there forever.

What made the thought even scarier, was realizing that I had that choice. Everyone does. I'm sure I could've just chosen to stay inside the bubble of nothing, chosen to leave everything behind me, unsolved.

That wouldn't have helped anything, though. In fact, that choice would've made everything worse for everyone else than me. I might've not been a people person, but I wasn't *that* selfish. I wasn't going to give up. However painful it would be to deal with things, I knew I had to do it. If not for myself, then for Tae. Joonie. Do-hyun and Minjae. Even for Jiwoo.

Most importantly, I'd have to deal with things for Joe. Even if he wouldn't let me back in his life, I would try to get better for him. Even if he wouldn't want anything to do with me ever again, I'd do it for him. I had promised him that.

I made a promise to myself.

To get help.

It was time to face the fact that I wasn't going to be able to handle this on my own. If I had learned anything from the past few weeks, it was that. In fact, I was a hazard alone, and it was time to admit that.

Unfortunately getting back to reality was easier said than done.

And fucking painful.

Literally. When I got my hearing back my head almost exploded. It was like someone pointed a microphone directly towards a loudspeaker, and my head echoed an endless loop of audio feedback. The screech of it was all I heard.

Then I lost it again. The white nothingness turned into darkness. But then I got my vision back and the first thing I saw was Joe's face. Those eyes I had missed so much. Except they looked dull and tired this time over. There was no spark. It wasn't the same. Nothing was the same.

"That's right Chris, welcome back. Now keep your eyes open until the paramedics get here," he said, but it sounded like he screamed right into my ear. Loud. Too loud.

At first I was thrilled that I hadn't lost my hearing. Then the screeching started all over again. I couldn't help but gasp, cover my ears and curl up on the backstage room's floor where I had apparently been put to lay down. I could see the worn out couch on my right.

"Make it stop, *please* make it stop," I mumbled almost inaudibly, but it sounded like I was yelling with full volume. Well, inside my head.

But it was even louder when Joe replied which I assumed was his normal voice because it didn't look like he was yelling. "Make what stop?"

"Shh!"

"What?" he asked, scrunching his eyebrows together.

"It's so loud—" but I couldn't find the right words and gave up. "Just shut up."

"Okay, shutting up. But you have to stay with me and keep those eyes open," he mumbled, thankfully getting a bit further away from me so the noise wasn't that bad.

The screeching also eased up a bit after a while. But then my whole body started aching, as if I'd just run a marathon. Which I probably did a moment ago on stage. And I got cold. *Really* cold. So cold my teeth clattered.

Oh, and let's not even mention the *stench*. It was like there were wet, sweaty socks left to rot all around me. It made me nauseous as fuck.

But then the others bulldozed in the room, and I almost lost it again. The screechy sound started circling in my head once again and Joonie's voice sounded like a fire alarm going off right there in my brain when he started yelling some words I couldn't make out through the pounding inside my skull.

Instinctively, I grabbed Joe's arm.

"Please make them stop," I mumbled, hoping he'd hear it through the chaos.

Apparently he did, or maybe the chaos was all in my head. In any case, he ushered everyone out and I was able to breathe and calm down again. The noise stopped.

I guess it was clear to everyone that there wasn't going to be an encore that night, as no one even tried to get me back on stage. The staff paramedics appeared soon too, wrapped me up in a blanket and tossed in the backseat of an SUV. It wasn't a true emergency, and they didn't want to attract attention by calling an ambulance…or that's what they told me. I bet Jiwoo was in on it. Nobody could catch that woman off guard these days, let alone the press.

It was a hustle from then on. Joe even spoke to me occasionally, on the way to the hospital. Well, after the overwhelming noises in my head stopped completely and I gave him the permission to do so. After a while of total silence, it was weird to hear his voice, but I was grateful, nonetheless. Though, it was probably just him trying to keep me conscious on the way to the hospital, and not like he actually cared. Still, I could at least pretend.

The doctor we met barely spoke English, let alone Korean. Sounded like he had a French accent when he spoke English. There wasn't a translator at hand, so we tried to get by somehow.

The verdict was that I got a somewhat ruptured eardrum on my right ear I had pressed against the stage monitor, and that I was physically exhausted. He let us go after giving me a pamphlet of how to deal with a ruptured eardrum and told me to sleep a lot. As if that was something people could easily do. Just sleep. Hmph.

I didn't bother telling him the whole story, but it didn't really matter. My end game was back at the hotel, if I would take an educated guess from the fragments of my memories from the past…weeks? Months?

Her name was Meiling.

Once we hit the streets with the same SUV we came to the hospital with, I even dared to take a glance outside. Seong-gi was driving. When I finally started to actually pay attention to my surroundings, I saw that we sped past some pretty buildings, European style, fancy architecture from the past, but as far as I knew, we could've been anywhere. The signs were in French, though.

"Where are we," I mumbled under my breath, not particularly to anyone.

But Joe still answered from next to me. "Paris. We're in Paris."

Well, sucks to be a French fan, then. Today's show was most likely a whole mess. "Oh, okay."

A shock ran through my entire body when I felt a touch on my hand. I snapped my eyes to Joe, who only grabbed my hand tighter in his hold and turned his attention on his window as if he did nothing. I melted from the inside—maybe he did care after all.

Maybe, I hadn't fucked up too bad. Yet. But I knew I couldn't continue on this road of self-destruction.

"Can you take me to Meiling's room when we get back to the hotel?"

Joe didn't even turn to face me, but I caught a slight, sad smile on his lips. "Are you sure? It's pretty late."

"I don't care. I'm pretty sure she won't mind either." That woman was always lurking around.

"Okay. I'ma give her a heads-up, though," Joe said, dialed a number and pressed the phone against his ear.

I turned my gaze back to the streets of Paris, wondering if this visit in this city of love would've been any different if I wasn't a complete fuck up. If things would've gone differently between Joe and me.

It wasn't a long ride, and soon we were strolling through the carpeted hallways of our hotel. Took a lift to the upper floors. Walked through some more corridors and an endless amount of doors lining each side. To be honest, I wasn't even sure where my room was, but it didn't matter since I wasn't going there anyway.

Joe stopped in front of a door numbered 628.

"Here you go. Good luck."

I took a deep breath and faced the door. "Thanks."

"I'll be at 532 if you need me."

"Okay."

A hand landed on my right shoulder, making me turn my eyes slightly towards Joe. He didn't say anything at first, just smiled at me and squeezed the shoulder lightly.

"You can do it," he eventually said, letting his hand drop and walking away.

I watched his back as he went, until he reached the corner and disappeared behind it. I wanted to ask him to stay, I wanted to run after him, but for once I knew this was something I'd have to do on my own. So I raised my fist and knocked on the door, heart racing.

Instantly, I heard some rustling from the inside, and Meiling came to open the door. She didn't even look surprised to see me there.

"Hello Chris. I've been waiting for you."

Heartbroken

At first, it wasn't a problem to sleep a lot, as per the doctor's orders. I slept, like, 24 hours straight and then some. Well, after our little three hour chat with Meiling in the middle of the night after my—err—let's say "collapse." Practically speaking, I had barely left my bed. My eyes only stayed open for very short times when I stuffed my face with food from room service and maybe used the bathroom...but otherwise I was out like a light.

But one can only sleep so much. Which, in itself, wasn't a huge deal since we were supposed to change the city today. The real problem? My phone's clock informed me it was 4:36 in the morning. I was not about to get up at 4:36 in the morning. Ugh.

The anxiety started kicking in again as I watched the horizon start to lighten up on the edge through the window. Soon, I was covered in sweat, trembling with cold. The sheets clamped on me, and I could've given everything for a hot shower and drowning in booze right after in order to get some peace of mind.

But that was no longer an option. Because I was forbidden to touch alcohol.

Upon that realization, Meiling's voice from the other night echoed in my head. *"I can't prescribe you any sleeping pills, because I'm only a nurse...but what I can do is teach you some coping methods for anxiety which might help with the sleeping problems as well."*

Fine. I could give the "coping methods" (that honestly sounded like a lot of bullshit) a shot.

I rolled on my back, closed my eyes and took a deep breath through my nose, trying to relax. I held it in, then released it slowly through my mouth. But that only made me oddly aware of my breathing and did nothing to the sweating and trembling. Still, I tried keeping up with it for a while, with little to no success.

Then I tried tensing and relaxing my muscles. It did help some for the trembling, but my heart was still beating way too fast for any kind of relaxation, so I gave up on that too in a while. Sighing, I turned to stare at the aromatherapy candle I had on my nightstand, which Meiling had given me, contemplating if I was that desperate.

"What the heck," I mumbled, deciding that desperate times needed desperate measures.

After grabbing the matches that sat on the table beside the candle with trembling hands, I lit the candle and took a deep breath. But the lavender scent only gave me a headache instead of having any calming effects whatsoever.

Leaning my back against the headboard of the comfy hotel bed, I gave a second of my thought for starting a journal. There was a notepad and a pen on the table across my hotel room that practically screamed my name, but ultimately, I knew I would only feel silly writing this stuff up.

"And if all else fails, just give up." Meiling had said. *"Obsessing over sleeping will only make it worse. So don't sleep and do something else instead. Maybe a light exercise. Anything to get your mind off sleeping."*

So I got up, yanked on some sweatpants and a random t-shirt and began my short trek to the private gym on our floor. To be honest, I wasn't really even tired anymore, so maybe some light jogging wouldn't be such a bad idea after all. It made me awfully aware of the fact that I missed my little forest mountain trail back home, though.

But as soon as I reached the gym and pulled the door open, I spotted a man lying on the floor in front of the mirror in the back, headphones on and deep in thought. His dark brown hair sprawled on the floor as he stared at the ceiling with blank eyes.

Minjae.

At once, all the shame over ruining our Paris concert and for being a zombie for the past few weeks washed over me like glowing hot lava. Burning with a sudden wave of anxiety, trembling from fear of facing the man lying on the floor, I gulped.

How could I ever face the rest of GRiD again? Because this time, I had really fucked up, bad. And I had no-one else to blame but myself. Not only had I most likely made a mess of our past few concerts, but I also hadn't even been able to complete the last one here, most likely making the staff and the rest of GRiD so disappointed in me.

On top of that, I hadn't even been a very good friend or brother to Minjae lately. Selfishly wallowing in my own misery, I had brushed them off countless times. I *knew* the rest of them had also had it as bad, if not worse than me, and still never let their problems affect their work or friendships, let alone relationships. Even knowing all that, I had pushed them away every time they tried to help *me*—who didn't even deserve their concern being the brat I am.

All I wanted was to run away and disappear. For a moment, it was all I could think of. Gritting my teeth together, I prepared myself to flee without making a sound to earn the attention of the man on the floor. Like a coward, I was about to choose running away over fighting all over again.

But Meiling's voice returned to me, and I froze.

"...and don't distance yourself from the others. You'll only make it worse for yourself, and the others, the more you avoid them."

I mean...true. To some extent. Maybe it was time to fight instead of taking the usual flight -option I was so fond of.

Thus, I braced myself and walked right next to Minjae and sat down beside him on the floor, startling him so much that he almost jumped up before his eyes cleared up upon the recognition.

"Oh, Chris," he mumbled, pulling the headphones off, and sitting up. "Good, um, morning?"

"Yeah, good morning," I replied, giving him an awkward smile, confirming it was, indeed, morning now. "Couldn't sleep?"

"Nope, not very much."

I nodded. "Me neither."

Minjae sighed and the most awkward silence of my life ensued. Until we both started speaking at the same exact moment.

"Look, I'm sorry–"

"I'm *so* sorry–"

We both chuckled and Minjae scratched the back of his head and evaded my eyes. I leaned back against my arms and smiled. Genuinely so, for the first time in ages.

"You go first," I said.

"I don't even know where to start," Minjae said, shaking his head but at the same time smiling a little. Then he took a deep breath. "I guess I'm just sorry for everything. I'm sorry for not noticing how bad this whole thing wore you down. I'm sorry for not being there. I'm sorry for not knowing how to make it better."

Huh. I guess I wasn't the only one feeling like shit. "It's okay. Wasn't your fault things got... a little out of hand."

"But—"

"No. No buts. It's okay. I get where you're coming from," I said, cutting him off. "And I'm sorry too. For isolating myself. For not even trying to deal with my problems sooner. And, uh, for being so stubborn. And ruining our tour—"

"Nonsense. You ruined nothing. It was only one encore we missed."

"But the concerts before…"

"Went okay… Well, relatively speaking."

"Still. I feel such a fuck up."

"Look, we've all fucked up at some point. I think me and Do-hyun fucked up way worse, career-wise, to be honest. And we literally *fucked* up. You can look it up on the internet," he said and laughed.

Even though I wasn't sure if his laughter was genuine or not, I couldn't help but laugh with him. Plus, he was kind of right. Still, it was odd and at the same time very comforting to notice he could laugh about their scandal these days. It gave me some hope, in some sick way, that I could maybe get over my own shit someday as well.

But while I wallowed in my sudden hopefulness, Minjae's eyes slowly lost a bit of their sparkle as his laughter died down. "What happened to us? We were all so close before…"

"Shit happened," I said and shrugged.

"Yeah…"

Just then, a loud thump startled both of us and we hastily turned to look behind our backs. Found Do-hyun, looking at us with a guilty look on his face, apparently having dropped his bag on the floor.

"Don't let me interrupt your little bonding moment," he said, grinning and throwing his arms up. "I'm just here for a workout."

I glanced at the clock. It was six in the morning already. Whoa.

"Whatever, I should go pack anyway," I mumbled and stood up, then headed to the door after giving Minjae a short smile.

But when I was passing Do, he decided to grab my neck in a chokehold and rubbed the top of my head with his knuckles.

"Ow, that hurts! Stop!"

"As it should. Don't you ever do that to us, ever again. You little shit," he said.

I grabbed his wrist, forced it off me and bent his arm behind his back, pushing him against the wall beside the door. It wasn't as effortless as before though, which either meant I was out of shape or Do had gotten stronger. Either way, it annoyed the hell out of me. If they'd ever find out I could no longer beat them, the teasing would be endless.

Do-hyun, however, continued laughing and said, "I'm glad you're back, though."

I let go of him. "Yeah, me too," I said. "See you around."

He nodded and turned around to try and make my exit again. But I was shortly cut off as I collided with another person right away at the threshold. Stumbling back a step, I closed my eyes annoyed out of my wits—what the fuck was wrong with this morning? It was like the rush hour had moved from the streets to our private gym for fuck's sake.

Rubbing my temple, I lifted my eyes from the floor up to the intruder, only to meet a very familiar set of dark brown eyes with a golden halo around the pupils. Joe's face was as handsome as ever as he made my heart stop with a single glance, only this time he wasn't sporting that signature smirk of his. Nor did his eyes sparkle like they had before, when he had undoubtedly planned whatever mischiefs he had had on his daily list of making me flustered.

Now, if there was one person I did not have the balls to face yet, it was Joe.

"I—uh… morning," I mumbled and pushed past him, hardly able to breathe.

I don't think I've ever walked as fast as I walked then, straight to my room. It was only after I pulled the door close behind me and leaned my back against it that I was able to take a couple of deep breaths.

There had been way too much socializing for the day already, and it was only a little past six. How the hell was I supposed to get used to this all over again? Though, if I were to be completely honest…my chat with Minjae had lifted so much weight from my shoulders that it was almost unreal.

Then Joe had to appear and ruin everything.

Frustrated, I banged the door with my fist and stomped to shower. But even a scorching hot shower did nothing for my anxiety attack. Or to the irritation towards my own inability to figure out what I was supposed to do with the whole Joe-thing. I mean…had he already found a replacement? Was he going to disappear from my life altogether after the tour was over?

Or would I be able to win him back? Hypothetically speaking, of course, in the rare case I decided to try and keep him. He had, after all, basically saved me back at the concert. From myself, to top it off.

Then again, maybe I had no chance to try and keep him anymore. What was even the point? I had fucked everything up, and now I'd have to live the consequences. He hadn't been wrong when basically saying I had told him to fuck off one too many times. Was I even able to change that much that I'd try to not drive him away or run from him myself at the slightest hardship that came our way?

After going over Meiling's relaxation regimes all over again, I was able to calm down and start packing. Ultimately, I was surprised that I had managed to unpack in the first place upon finding my clothes in the closets. I guess I had been a high functioning drunk after all, even though my mind had been in a complete haze.

But in a short while, I was interrupted by a knock on my door. Why did everyone seem to have some business with me today of all fucking days, left me baffled. Nevertheless, I strolled to the door and took a glimpse through the peephole.

It was Do-hyun, grinning right at the peephole from the other side. Wondering what more he could possibly have to talk with me so shortly after our chat this morning, I opened the door.

He walked right in without uttering a word and even closed the door behind him after pushing me further in the room.

"Um, hey?" I muttered. "What's up?"

Do-hyun grinned before narrowing his eyes at me. "Mind explaining why my best friend is acting all heartbroken after seeing only a glimpse of you?"

I frowned. "How the fuck I'm supposed to know how you've pissed Minjae off this time?"

Do-hyun slapped the back of my head.

"Ow, what the fuck?!"

"I'm not talking about Minjae, dumbass! I'm talking about Joe."

"Oh."

"'Oh' indeed. Now start talking."

My Spot

Do-hyun could be one sneaky bastard whenever he was in the mood. I wonder how he did it—especially because he was usually all about minding his own business—but he easily managed to squeeze the whole story of my little fling with Joe out of me. And that's saying something, considering that I'm not really fond of sharing my own stuff.

Hell, I hadn't even told the whole story to Meiling. And Meiling would never tell anyone due to a) being a professional and b) working under a non-disclosure agreement anyway. Now Do-hyun...yeah, there was no guarantee whatsoever, that he'd keep the story to himself. Not that I could blame him, considering my history with DoMino and social media.

In a few days, I was proven right.

Why am I always right?

It was obvious when Tae pulled me to the side right before the after party of our London gigs, and started interrogating me about Joe and I.

"Oh, you know how this goes," he started when I asked how he knew. "Do-hyun told Minjae, Minjae told Joonie, Joonie told me. There ain't secrets within GriD, and you of all people should know that, right?"

I shook my head but couldn't stop a slight smile from lighting up my face. "Right."

Tae only stared me down with a look that said, *"And don't even try to change the subject,"* as a reply.

"Fine," I huffed. "Something might've happened between us. I still don't get how it's your concern in any way."

"It's not. I'm just worried, that's all. We've—err—*you've* been through a lot lately." Tae scratched the back of his neck. "Is it really wise to start something now?"

Hmph. "Just to be clear, are you worried about me or worried that we will cause another scandal and the money suddenly stops flowing in?"

"Both. And you know me too well," he admitted.

"It doesn't matter," I said after shaking my head at him. "It's over anyway."

Tae gave me a skeptical look, one eyebrow raised and everything. "But is it *really* over?"

It was my turn to look at him like he had one brain cell left.

"Okay, let's put it this way: what if there was something going on between you two..." he started again. "Hypothetically speaking, of course."

I rolled my eyes but decided to humor him anyway. "Okay, let's say there is...hypothetically speaking."

Tae paused, choosing his words carefully. "I mean, what do you even know about him?"

"Enough," I said. Joe was awesome in bed. He was good at completing chores, unlike me. I was in love with him. What more was there to know*? Hypothetically speaking.*

"Mhmm, right..." Tae mumbled, still skeptical. "Do you even know his real name?"

Ouch. "Umm... Joe?"

Shaking his head, disappointed, Tae sighed. "You're hopeless," he said. "Don't you think it's a little weird that he's so chill about the fact that he *shot* a person?"

He did what *now?!* "I'm sure he has his reasons."

Tae picked up a pile of paper from his desk and handed them to me. "If you're not going to listen to me, then here. At the very least, read this before you make any rash decisions."

I took a glance. "You pulled a background check on him."

"You bet I pulled a background check on him. I pulled a background check on everyone after the whole Min-ho fiasco. Including you."

My teeth gritted together. It's not like LBR hadn't pulled a background check on me before, but I had preferred to keep some things for myself from the rest of GRiD at the very least. Either way, I had been wrong about Tae being dumb and gullible.

"Well, as you said, it's none of my business. But don't come back to me crying if and when this backfires," Tae said and raised his wine glass.

I chuckled and raised my cola can back at him, clearly not thinking it through. Because Tae went back to the "I'm worried" -zone in a nanosecond.

"Um, about that," he said and pointed at my cola can. "Are you really fine that we're drinking and you're not? No temptations? No underlying angst towards us?"

"As I've said a few times..." I started, holding myself back from rolling my eyes all over again. "I'm *fine*. My drunk ass is my problem, not yours."

"I'm taking your word for it, then."

"Please do. Now excuse me, I've gotta go read this," I said and waved Joe's background check papers, before heading to the door.

Thankfully Tae let me go—finally. Well, after a short nod and a mocking smile.

Thoroughly exhausted by the interrogation—which, mind you, was worse than the one they pulled on me at the police station back at Seoul—I made my tired way down the aisle from Tae's room to my own room. Once inside, I put the cola can down on the desk and sat down on the bed. The papers still nestled in my hand, I let myself fall. My back hit the mattress and I just breathed for a while.

Then Tae's words started getting me. I mean, what *did* I know about Joe? All jokes aside?

Honestly, not much.

The giant scar on his back, for example...there had to be a story to that, right? But he never talked about it. Then again, I didn't talk about my scars either, so I guess we were even. But that thing about him shooting someone? Yeah, that couldn't be counted as normal. I also didn't know anything about his family.

I lifted Tae's papers in front of my nose and stared at them for a long while. I saw the words but couldn't really focus on them enough to decipher what the hell I was looking at. Had I lost the ability to read?

Focus, Chris.

"Lee Joo-hwan."

There. His actual, legal name. And I even said it out loud. I imagined how it would sound like if Joe would call me Chang-ho one day.

I tossed the papers away. Let's face it, I didn't want to read them. I didn't want to know every little detail of him. My heart was already beating uncomfortably fast. It was like I was dying all over again, as I had multiple times back at home. And all this happened from just imagining him saying my real, given name.

This being in love thing...it was no joke, that's for sure.

So instead of focusing on the papers like I had been planning to, I heaved myself up from the bed. It was a good idea to make an actual appearance at the party anyway, at least to avoid the awkward and unnecessary checking-up-on-Chris part of the evening the guys were so fond of these days.

The way to the master suite of this hotel wasn't long. The party was in full swing when I arrived. There were even some of our tour staff present, so the room was unusually packed. And all of the guards were there too. Including Joe who was playing cards with Do-hyun at the dining table. I wondered if they had talked about me. Not that it mattered. Actually, I didn't even want to know.

I ignored them and chatted with Minjae at the seating area instead. He was already wasted and trying to get me to dance. I had no patience for him, so I ushered him towards the tour staff members. Thankfully they were more than happy to join Min on the makeshift dance floor to our right.

Maybe Tae was right, and this trying-not-to-drown-myself-in-alcohol thing was harder when the others weren't in on it. To be honest, I could've given my left hand for an ice-cold beer. Or better yet, for a bottle of soju. Hell, I didn't even like wine that much, but I could've downed a bottle in a heartbeat.

Almost suffocating in the drunken atmosphere, my eyes started to scan the suite for an escape. When I spotted the half-way open door to the balcony, I nearly rubbed my eyes; I was almost convinced it was merely a mirage—an oasis in the middle of a desert.

My feet carried me towards it as if I was in some kind of a trance.

The door led to a balcony, indeed. Well, it was way bigger than your average balcony, had sofas and all, but it wasn't quite big enough to call a roof terrace or anything. I took a breath of some (semi) fresh nighttime London air, and nearly fainted from the absolute bliss. If I closed my eyes and leaned against the half-wall on the edge, I could almost imagine I was back home. If I concentrated hard enough, it was nearly as if I had run up the steep mountain path all the way to the view deck and leaned against its fence instead.

But the last time I had been there seemed like a lifetime ago. Another era of some sort. A happier one, even though I hadn't seen it back then. Too hung up on my own demons, I had missed my own chance at happiness.

Someone cleared their throat behind me, cutting my self-pity party short.

I jumped a few inches, startled as fuck.

When I finally realized it was just Joonie, my shoulder's dropped in relaxation. Joonie had probably even been here before me, based on the fact that he emerged from the shadows of the back of the terrace…balcony…thingy. I really should've started paying more attention to my surroundings.

"Oh, you."

Joon let out a quiet snicker. "Oh, me."

Not knowing what else to say, I turned back to look at the nightly cityscape spread as far as the eye could see below us. Joonie walked next to me, leaning against the edge as well. His now strawberry blond hair had gotten longer again and got caught up in the wind at the top occasionally. It has been a while since I've paid attention to him like this. Seemed like he had chosen to keep the undercuts, though.

I couldn't take the silence for long. Not with Joonie. He always had something up in his sleeve and I knew by experience it would be better to get over it sooner rather than later.

"So, why are you here?" I asked. "I mean, shouldn't you be inside, getting drunk with the rest of them?"

"Do you ever wish you smoked, just so no-one would ask any dumb questions when you only want to have a little alone time?"

"Err…point taken," I muttered. "Do you want me to go, or…?"

Joonie chuckled.

"I wasn't serious, you dummy. And I am getting wasted," he said, lifting up the half-empty wine bottle that I hadn't even noticed he had in tow. "Just not with everyone. At the moment. Want some?"

I raised my eyebrows at him. "I'm not supposed to drink, you know."

"Right…" he mumbled, trailing off. It was almost like he didn't quite believe me and my resolution of staying away from alcohol.

"I just think I should lay off for a while. Just in case."

He nodded and turned his gaze back to the night sky. Him being this chill was a nice confirmation I wasn't fucked up in the head too much, at least beyond repairing. I imagine I would've gotten a lecture if he was really worried.

Unfortunately, all the light pollution didn't allow us to see any stars, so the silence became a bit boring. Thankfully this time it wasn't an awkward one. Still, it ended in a short while when Joonie finally decided to discuss the thing he wanted to. I knew he had something in his sleeve. I should've known.

"So, I heard your little conversation with Tae earlier."

I blinked a couple of times, surprised. "Um, okay? But…you weren't there?"

He smiled at me, almost mockingly, but still sported a slightly worried expression. I had no idea how he did it—be chill one moment and this worrywart the next. It gave me whiplash.

"I was there," he said. "Technically. In the bathroom. And I got curious."

I rolled my eyes. "Let me guess, it's your time to give me a lecture."

"Nah. You're a big boy. You can figure it out yourself."

"Then why are you bringing it up?"

Joon shrugged. "It's just something Tae said that bugs me. But I'm not sure if I should tell you this or not."

"You already started."

"Fair," he said and winced, a slightly nauseous expression flashing on his face briefly. I don't know what it was, but it made me feel sorry for him.

I sighed. Joonie was such a drama queen it was probably nothing. Still, I couldn't help but say, "It's fine, you don't actually have to."

"No... It's just... I *think* I know why Joe's so chill about the shooting incident," he explained, so silently I had a hard time figuring out the actual words. He even evaded my eyes, dropping his shoulders so he looked small and fragile.

"...okay?" I whispered back, and scrunched my eyebrows together. What in the actual fuck had happened to make Joonie this uneasy? He was the most confident guy I knew for crying out loud. This Joonie, small voice, hunched shoulders...was definitely not normal.

Joonie took a couple of deep breaths, and then straightened himself up, offering me a slight smile. "I lost my phone right before the...err, incident. In Yongma Land."

I had absolutely no idea what he was talking about, but I nodded anyway. What? I was curious about this...mostly because it involved Joe.

"When I finally got it back, and went through the photos, I think I regained some memories from that day. You know, as I'm brain damaged and all, they were kinda lost. At least I think I got some of them back. But I'm not exactly sure. It's hard to explain."

"Joonie, no offense but you don't make any sense. I mean, where are you going with this?"

"I don't think it was Joe who shot Min-ho," he said and took a deep breath. "I think it was me."

"Oh." Joe had shot Min-ho. Wait, or Joonie did? Anyway, someone shot that dickwad and if it was Joe, all the more respect to him. Chill or not.

Also…wait, what? Was Joonie even more of a badass than I had thought? My eyes widened as I processed the information.

Joonie let out a long breath, as if he had held it in. "Oh, indeed."

Then the whole thing settled in.

"Well, fuck. That kind of changes… *everything*." I mean, if this were to come out, whether or not Joonie would be found at fault, his career would really be over in a heartbeat. And so would mine. We wouldn't have a lead singer, for fuck's sake, without Joon—

"I know."

Not to even mention what would happen to Joe if Joonie would ever confess. He'd lose his license and the right to work as a bodyguard for sure, as he would've used his privileges wrongly. He wouldn't be allowed to carry a gun ever again. Hell, he'd most likely face prison time.

"Oh, don't worry. I'm not gonna rat out your boyfriend," he said and snickered, apparently reading my mind. "Well, if he doesn't rat me out first."

Now that was a relief.

But I just muttered, "He's not my boyfriend," and turned my gaze back to the cityscape.

"He will be," Joonie countered, winking.

I held down the urge to roll my eyes for the millionth time that night. "Yeah, right."

"I'm serious. That man's whipped. Back in Paris, he didn't let anyone come even *near* you, except the paramedics. I halfway expected him to start barking at us."

I chuckled. It wasn't like I couldn't picture that. Joe was such a Golden Retriever after all. Or a Labrador.

"Well, that's his problem," I still said. "I never said *I* wanted anything to do with him."

"That's so much bullshit and you know it," Joon said and raised his wine bottle at me, winking. "Oh well, I'm gonna head back to the party. Have fun with that *soda* of yours."

"I will," I said, raising my can and watching him go, leaning my back on the concrete edge of the balcony thing.

Contemplating if I should go back inside too, I watched them all through the window. Joonie went straight to the table where some of them were playing cards and joined them. Minjae was still dancing. Do-hyun smacked the back of Joe's head when he lost to him. Do had never been a very good loser. Tae was sitting next to Joonie, softly stroking his back with his fingertips.

There was a chair left empty next to Do, and I just knew that was reserved for Minjae for whenever he'd calm down enough to actually sit. But there was one empty chair right there in between Joe and Tae as well. I daydreamed that it was meant for me. That the guys had left it empty for me. Either way, *I* felt like I belonged in that exact spot. Surrounded by the rest of GRiD...but especially next to Joe.

Right then, Joe said something and Joonie turned to face him, pointing towards the balcony—towards me—with his thumb. I wondered what they were talking about, but then the moment was already over.

My phone buzzed inside my pocket. I frowned—lately the only one who ever texted me was Hana, but it was like nine in the morning in Korea and I knew she had a morning shift today. She never texted me at work. So I dug the phone up and turned the screen on.

There was a text from Joonie. An ultimate surprise. I hadn't even noticed him picking up his phone or anything.

See, he's even asking about you. Now come get your man, the text said.

It became hard to not smile like a goofball. And trust me, that look doesn't suit me. At all.

He's just doing his work, I typed back, and jammed the phone back in my pocket.

But that was the moment when I decided that if Joe showed even the slightest hint that he had even the tiniest sparkle of feelings towards me, I'd have to take my chances, and at least try to win him back.

Of course, that meant I'd have to actually spend time with him. I strolled inside, straight to the table and sat on the chair next to him.

Important Realization

Nothing happened that night. It was the same as all the nights before. Joe barely spoke to me, and if he did it was always business.

Concerts came and went. Days went by. Cities changed... and there were no hints on Joe's part that he had any feelings towards me, whatsoever.

And soon, way too soon, it was time for our last concert in Europe. It was to be held in Helsinki, to be exact. Their Olympic Stadium had gone through a renovation, and we were to be the first foreign musical act to stand on its stage. Seemed like a huge deal to the Finns.

I was starting to panic. Slightly. No, who was I kidding; I was scared shitless. Not about the concert, though. Well, not that much about the concert.

Rather, I was running out of time. Who knew if Joe had already found a replacement for his position as my bodyguard? I mean he didn't exactly talk about these things with me anymore. Surely, there was someone just waiting for us to get back home so they could ruin my life. I couldn't even start to imagine how long it would take me to try and trust a completely new person who would be a huge part of my life.

Not to mention I'd lose the very last one of my chances to try and get my happiness back.

But before all that—concert and getting back home business—we were to have a fan meeting. Two hundred people would soon be packed into an auditorium. And us, having to face the enthusiasm at a close distance, sitting by a long table at the stage of the said auditorium. That's where the fans would be lining up to, to get their two very expensive minutes with each of us.

Yes, it was going to be only two minutes per guest. Still, it would take us the whole, long-ass day, to get through it. At least eight to nine hours, taking the breaks and overall goofing around into account.

Minjae was thrilled and practically bouncing around the still-empty place as we were waiting for the event to start. The rest of us…yeah, we weren't that hyped. Don't get me wrong, meeting the fans up close was always fun, and I was very grateful for them. But they could be exhausting at times too.

"Alright, let's get this done," Joonie hollered.

Everything was set up. The background music—our latest album—was playing at a low volume. Our wireless mics, which we'd use to talk with the fans whenever there was a break in the line, were connected. There were snacks prepared and water at hand.

Joe and the rest of the security personnel were taking their places. A chill went down my spine when I noticed he had taken the position that was directly behind our table. That indicated to me his job for the day was to keep his eyes on us, as well as keeping the fans going forward in an orderly fashion.

Great, just great. Now I'd have to deal with feeling his eyes on me the whole day. As if I wasn't frustrated enough already.

"Now, are there volunteers to take the first seat?" Joonie asked, when we reached him.

No one, not even Minjae, volunteered. It wasn't a surprise by any means. It would have to take an insane person to volunteer for that.

"Rock, paper, scissors?" Tae asked.

Joonie and the rest of us nodded and formed a loose circle.

The first round was a tie. We all chose rock for some fucking reason. Then me, Do-hyun and Minjae lost with paper, while Tae and Joon picked scissors.

"Yuss," Joon cheered, high-fived with Tae and they took the last two seats behind the table.

Minjae won the next round and took the middle seat. Do-hyun and I both became desperate, so we settled for a match for three wins.

Paper vs paper.

Rock vs paper.

Scissors vs rock.

Paper vs rock.

Paper vs scissors.

And I lost. Three to one.

Defeated, I slumped down on the first seat, already exhausted by the mere thought of having to be in this spot the whole day.

It was going to be rough. Still, Jiwoo didn't have any mercy for us, and opened the doors. The pure volume of the fans, screaming as they went to wait in their seats for their turn, was already a lot.

I plastered on a smile, took a deep breath, and glanced at the crowd. Minjae was already chatting with the fans. His voice amplified by the microphone, he skillfully hid some fairly good instructions for the fans, for how we'd all get through this smoothly. I directed a grateful smile towards him. I'm not sure if he caught it or not.

"Alright, that is all! Now remember we're gonna spend the whole day here so keep yourselves hydrated, have some snacks while you wait and enjoy," Minjae concluded and Seong-gi took the lead.

He herded the first batch of fans to come by our table.

It was on.

My head started to hurt in no time. The first seat was always the worst, having to take the peak enthusiasm of the screaming and squealing ladies—and some gents.

But that wasn't the worst part. Joe's eyes burned my neck. I could feel it every time he looked at me. I knew it was most likely only out of duty, I truly did. Still, every time it happened, the tiny hairs on my neck stood up and I had a hard time holding back a shiver.

I regret to admit that I was soon so out of it, I barely even glanced at the guy that stopped in front of me and dropped his copy of the "Contrast" album on the table. He didn't even say a word, only stuffed his hands in his jeans' pockets. It slightly amused me— why the hell had he paid nearly 200€ for the tickets and gone through the hassle of getting GRiD Crew membership to be here when he clearly didn't want to.

I glanced at his name plate. "So, Joonas, what do you want me to write here?" I asked, smiling slightly.

"Just the autograph, or whatever. It's for my girlfriend," he said, pointing his thumb towards a girl that had just passed my spot. She was almost squealing while trying to have a conversation with Do-hyun on the next seat over.

Chuckling under my breath at his disinterested tone of voice, I snapped my gaze up to take a better glance at the guy's face. He had bright blue eyes, sort of sandy blond hair. Very handsome. But his looks weren't what caught my attention. It was the voice. A very familiar one at that.

"Or actually scratch that. You better make it interesting for the absurd price you're taking for this… event," he continued while I was still frozen in place, now one hundred percent sure the guy in front of me was actually Jonezzi, upon hearing that voice again. After all, I already knew he was from Finland and that he had a girlfriend who was a fan.

"You must really love your girlfriend?" I mumbled, toying with the marker on my hand.

Jonezzi—or Joonas—even blushed a bit at that. "Yeah…" he mumbled, stuffing his hands deeper in his pockets while evading my eyes.

"One minute," Joe mumbled behind me, letting us know the time was almost up. And giving me one of those heart attacks he was so good at causing, but we're not talking about that. I turned my attention back to Joonas.

I nodded at him, a smirk tugging the corner of my mouth up as I figured out exactly what I'd write on the album. Hastily, I popped the cap of the marker open, and scribbled: *'Good game, Jonezzi'* and my autograph directly below it.

"Thanks, dude," he said as I handed him the album back.

"You're welcome," I said and winked. "Take care of that girlfriend of yours; clearly she has a good taste in music."

Joonas barely glanced at my signature and started walking over to Do-hyun's spot. Then, the realization hit him hard, and he stopped, snapping his eyes to meet mine with his mouth hanging slightly open. I shushed him discreetly. I wasn't able to hold down a full grin that spread to light up my whole face when I looked at the shock evident on the dude's face.

"Time's up," Joe said behind me with a surprisingly stern voice, signaling the next gal in line that it was her turn. "Move along, *now*," he continued to Joonas, who quickly shook his head, blinking, before dropping the album in front of Do-hyun.

From the corner of my eye, I noticed him getting through the rest of our table, before giving me an odd glance again right before disappearing through the exit. I couldn't stop smiling for the rest of the day. What an odd encounter it was.

Eventually, after what felt like a small eternity, the last fan had collected our autographs and the doors closed. I wasn't the only one who slumped down on their chair. In fact, Do-hyun even sort of collapsed, hitting his forehead against the tabletop, mumbling something incoherent about never doing this again. Well, to be honest, I was also glad that we wouldn't do any more fan signing events for the rest of the tour.

I would've been glad that the European leg of our tour was going to be over after tomorrow's show, if it wasn't for the fact that Joe still hadn't shown me a single hint that there was a chance for us. I was pretty sure I had never seen him act this professional before. Ever. And now this nonchalant indifference towards me had been going on for weeks, with no end in sight.

Quite frankly, I was losing hope. All I needed was the smallest hint of interest from him. Anything, really. I did not have the courage to try and win him back without one, that was for sure.

"Let's head back to the hotel," Joonie huffed, stretching his back still sitting on his seat at the end of the table. "I need a bath and a glass or two of wine."

"Yes, please," I mumbled back.

Everyone turned their eyes directly at me.

Narrowing my eyes at the rest of them, I asked, "What?"

They just continued staring. It honestly creeped me out a little. I frowned, briefly, before the realization hit me. I rolled my eyes.

"Oh, for fuck's sake, chill. I meant the bath, not the wine."

The drive to our hotel was a relatively long one—we didn't want any fans to follow us to the hotel, so we had chosen a venue far away for the fan signing event. I was riding with Joe, though he didn't so much as acknowledge my existence in any way—meaning there wasn't much company to pass the time. Or anything interesting going on outside either.

I grew bored.

I picked up my phone in hopes of passing some time by playing games or something. Strangely enough, there was a notification from the messaging app that I used mainly for gaming purposes. I had told them I might not have time for any gaming for a while, so my curiosity peaked.

Once I tapped the app open, it looked like Joonas had started a private chat with me. I couldn't help but grin when I opened it to see a picture of my own signature.

So you ARE Chris from GRiD?! And no bullshitting allowed this time. Fool me once... Joonas had captioned.

Holding back a chuckle, I snapped a quick selfie, pointing a finger-heart at the cam and all. Thankfully I hadn't wiped the makeup off yet, so the scars didn't look *that* bad. In fact, I looked kind of hot. Not gonna lie, noting that felt pretty damn good after months of self-loathing. I was almost back to my old self. Maybe getting some professional help hadn't been such a bad idea after all.

I sent the pic to Joonas with a caption, *Yeah, it's me. I must say I never imagined you as a blond.*

Seemed like he had been waiting for my reply by his phone, because the reply was immediate. *Fuck me. It really is you.*

Maybe I would if you weren't taken already. And yes, you're right.

Joe cleared his throat beside me.

"We're here," he muttered, his voice so cold it could've frozen hell over as he got up from the backseat next to mine.

I held back an eye-roll to his cold tone, thanked the driver, and got out as well. Joe was already heading inside, his stiff back disappearing through the back entrance. I followed suit, nearly having to jog to keep up with him.

Once inside and walking through the hallways, I picked up my phone again.

Ew, gay. I guess it's not called gay-pop for nothing, Joonas had replied meanwhile.

It became fairly hard to type as I laughed so hard my eyes watered. Didn't matter though, as I was cut short by Joe. As he snatched my phone away.

"Focus, Chris," he snapped, pointing at the door with his thumb. "Your room."

I tried to snatch my phone back. Unsuccessfully, as Joe only needed to hold it slightly higher for me to not reach it without looking dumb as fuck jumping around like a kid.

"Look, I know you hate me these days, but can you fucking chill?" I snapped.

At once when my eyes met his, Joe calmed down and averted his gaze. He looked at me, but also didn't. It was this thing he did these days whenever having to talk to me, looking somewhere not quite at me but just slightly past me.

"I don't hate you," he said, his tone of voice back to that annoying disinterested one. In fact, even the smallest hint of emotion on his demeanor disappeared. But when he was handing my phone back, he made the mistake of glancing at the screen. Something dark and dangerous flashed in his eyes as he frowned his eyebrows upon whatever he saw on my phone's screen.

"You should think a little more about who you give your personal phone number to," he said, scolding me. "I think we've had enough stalkers around lately."

This time I couldn't hold back from rolling my eyes. "Relax, I haven't given my personal information to anyone. It's a relatively anonymous messaging app for gamers. I can delete my account anytime. And even if he managed to fish out some of my information, I can always—"

Why was I even explaining this to him?

"Anyway, what the fuck is wrong with you today—" I started asking, but Joe smashed the phone back on my hand before turning his back on me.

"Nothing's wrong," he muttered, and started walking away.

I didn't believe it.

"Well, clearly *something's* up..." I mumbled.

The whole thing was giving me a severe headache. Not that I could do anything about it except watch him go. When did things between us become so complicated?

Then a realization hit me. Maybe the most important one ever. I couldn't believe I nearly missed it.

"A-are you jealous, by any chance?"

Helsinki Incident

Joe stopped on his tracks. I admit; it ignited the smallest sparkle of hope somewhere deep inside me...until Joe replied, that is.

"It's not like I'm jealous, per se. Just annoyed that you have no problem flirting with others after you constantly pushed me away when I tried to make any advances towards you."

What a disappointment. And I regretted asking. Heat creeped up my neck. Fuck.

Fortunately, I didn't get to wallow in it for long, as Joe opened his mouth again.

"Why do you ask?" he asked, barely glancing towards me over his shoulder.

"Err, I was just wondering. Forget it," I mumbled, flashing my key card on the lock in hopes of escaping to my hotel room.

But right when the lock flashed a green light, Joe's hand appeared on the door handle. Suddenly I got dizzy. I could feel the warmth of his body right beside me—that's how close he was. And I realized I hadn't only gotten addicted to alcohol, but also Joe; it became extremely hard to not throw myself at him and hope for the best.

"Answer me, Chris. Why do you need to know?" he murmured to my ear with that annoyingly eargasmic voice of his that sent a current of warmness running through my whole entire body.

I froze, trying my hardest to not shiver upon that sensation he inflicted within me. I guess this was it. The moment of truth. Unfortunately, it was hard to focus with Joe at such a close proximity.

"I—" I started, but the rest of the words stuck to my throat.

Joe became frustrated. I could tell because he yanked the door open and pushed me inside. Then he followed me in and slammed the door shut behind us.

Soon, he towered over me. I backed off; eyes widened as he stared me down. He was pissed. His eyes had turned dark, or maybe it was the lighting...anyway I became scared shitless. Lips pressed into a thin line, he approached me, step by step, until I had backed off so much my back hit the wall and he was so close I could feel the tingle of his minty-breath on my face.

But then he let out a deep sigh at the same time the light in his eyes dimmed.

"Please Chris," he pleaded, his voice all soft suddenly. "I need to know."

I swear to the gods that my heart picked up the pace so fast it must've been some kind of a world record. I dropped my eyes, balling my fists tight in order to stop them from shaking.

Joe needed to know. He said so. I realized I needed to tell him, even if it was the last thing I'd do.

"I—umm...I was wondering if...if there was a chance you cared..." I said, then gulped. "About me. At all." *Sigh.* "And that's why I asked."

There. I said it.

A silence occurred, so deep I could hear my own heartbeat and the sound of my blood rushing straight to my face. Fuck I hated blushing. And speaking. And feelings. Why was this so goddamn hard?

The warmest, softest sensation on my cheek interrupted the chaos inside me. As soon as I realized it was Joe's hand, cupping my jawline, my heart stopped. At once, I flashed my eyes up at him in wonder and almost melted under his intense but still somehow soft gaze.

"Of course, I care about you," he said, a small smile tugging up one corner of his mouth. His thumb brushed my skin, leaving behind a tingling trail. I almost melted to the spot.

"No, but...I mean, like, *that* way."

The smile on his lips got wider. "Chris, everything I've done after the day I picked you up at the police station...I've done for you."

At first I nearly melted upon hearing that statement. I mean...it definitely meant he cared about me, right? But then, my blood which was already rushing through my veins due to adrenaline, also started boiling.

I narrowed my eyes. "You abandoned me!"

"I know. I'm sorry."

My voice almost shook from rage. "You said you were tired of me!"

His eyes dropped. "I just couldn't keep watching you hurt yourself...and everyone around you. Including me."

Ouch. My anger deflated. "You...you told me to fuck off."

"So did you."

Instant cringe. I guess I had. Multiple times.

"Fair," I muttered, finding the green drapes very interesting all of a sudden on my quest to avoid looking directly at Joe's eyes. Voice shaking, I added, "But I really thought you wanted to get rid of me..."

Joe lifted my chin, forcing me to look him in the eyes.

"I already told you once: you can't get rid of me even if you tried."

When I stayed silent, too close to fainting to form any coherent words, he continued. "I just need one thing from you."

Anything. "Yes?"

"Answer me this one thing—honestly; what exactly do you want from me?"

It was clear in his voice, that in his words laid a challenge. No—a dare.

He was daring me to take the lead and face whatever laid in store for me. The question was: could I? And more importantly, should I?

Thankfully I already knew the answer to that.

"All of it," I whispered, as I wasn't sure if my voice could carry anymore.

He smiled and closed the rest of the distance between us. "Then you shall have it," he breathed, so close that I could feel it tingle on my lips.

I was swept away by the rush of the biggest relief of my existence. I couldn't resist the pull of him anymore. And I realized I didn't need to. Instead, I rose on my toes, my lips meeting his halfway.

Joe pulled me closer by my waist, and I was happy to press my entire body against him. He became hungry, fast, demanding my compliance with his lips. I was glad to lose. Hell, for the longest time in a long while, I felt okay. More than okay.

We were both panting when we pulled apart to take a breather.

"Chris…I need you," Joe admitted between his sharp breaths. His eyes were closed so I couldn't see, but his slightly trembling hand that was laying on my waist and the tone of his voice told me he was—for once—being the insecure one of us.

"I need you too," I said, my voice almost as shaky as his.

Joe's eyes fluttered open and darkened almost instantly as he studied my face. I don't know what he found in my expression, but the resolution was clear in his eyes as he claimed my lips with another intense kiss.

It proved to be the end of the last doubts in my mind. I could no longer deny my feelings toward him, and I knew right away that I was done for life. My heart agreed by hammering so fast I was sure I could've fainted any minute.

Meanwhile Joe was exploring my mouth with his tongue, licking and nibbling to his heart's content. It was almost as if he was taking revenge for the time lost.

Or on me, I couldn't really tell.

But being reminded of all the time lost made me eager for more. My yearning for his closeness started burning me inside out so hot I was damn close to bursting into open flames. Before I realized it, my hands were already yanking Joe's shirt buttons open. With unnecessary force I might add, but I was desperate.

Joe caught up with what I was after instantly. Which meant we were a whole, equally busy mess for a while, heading to the bed. We pulled and tore each other's clothes practically apart in order to get naked as fast as possible…all without parting our lips once.

As soon as Joe got me naked enough, he ended the kiss by tossing me on top of the bed. My sudden longing for his lips didn't last for long though, when another sensation made me arch my back so fast I was momentarily afraid I'd snap my spine—it was Joe's mouth attacking the side of my neck. Then he moved further down with his lips and tongue, until he reached my cock. I held my breath in anticipation, or a pure need for more.

Joe provided me that "more" by swallowing most of my length. My hands gripped the sheets beneath me as I gasped. The heat of his slick mouth over my throbbing dick was a sensation powerful enough to make my toes curl involuntarily. I squeezed my eyes shut—I couldn't believe I was lucky enough to feel all these sensations.

And Joe didn't stop there.

A moan of pure bliss came out my mouth before I could stop it when Joe started working his mouth on my dick so skillfully I saw stars. Shiver after shiver ran through my whole body. Just a little bit more and I would get my release. Only a little more...

But he didn't let me come.

Every time I felt myself getting close, he stopped short. Completely ceasing all magic that he was working on me with his mouth and tongue, he would let my cock slide out of his mouth and fall flat on my stomach.

The umpteenth time it happened, my eyes snapped open. The tip of my dick glistened with saliva and pre-cum, the sight so hot I could've nutted right then and there if I wasn't so frustrated.

"What the fuck are you doing?"

Joe only smirked and said, "God I missed you," before driving me right back to insanity with his mouth back on my cock.

But by the next time he stopped right when I was about to cum, I had had it. Annoyed, I sat up, grabbed Joe's elbow, and yanked, ultimately forcing him to fall on his back right next to me. A surprised huff escaped his lips when I straddled him, his fully erect dick pressing against my bum.

"My turn," I said and attacked his chest with my lips as my ass rubbed against his boner.

A groan erupted from the depths of Joe right about then and I knew it was working. After all, it was a game for two, and I wasn't about to let history repeat itself; if there was something to regret about our last time having sex, it was that I didn't do any of the work. And I was going to make him regret the time he had been away from me.

The only problem was that I wanted more myself. Just being this close wasn't enough. I wanted him so close we'd become one. I needed him inside me. Making him suffer with my revenge wasn't enough, even though hearing his distressed groans and attempts at stopping me was highly satisfying.

I reached for the nightstand for the lube that I had hidden there for…well, lonelier nights. Even though a couple of my own fingers up my ass didn't even remotely compare to feeling all of Joe inside me.

But when Joe caught up on what I was planning when I squeezed some of the lube to my hand and started working it on his dick, a slight panic flashed in his eyes.

"Wait, you've not been prepared, it'll hurt—" he started, but the rest of it was muffled due to my hand that I pressed against his mouth.

"Shut up," I said and aligned his huge cock against my entrance.

Joe mumbled, "What about a condom?" through my hand.

Aish. I almost forgot. I reached over to the nightstand, but Joe stopped me by grabbing my arm.

"I mean…I'm clean. But…um, I kind of hate to ask this now, but did anything happen…with…um, you know. Others. I'm not judging or anything but—" He evaded my eyes.

I pressed my index finger across his lips.

"Look at me," I said, and waited for him to turn his eyes back to mine. "Never."

He let out a relieved sight. "Then I'm fine without…if you are."

I started lowering myself, ever so slowly, centimeter by centimeter. And fuck had I underestimated the pure size of Joe's rod once again.

I wasn't going to give up though. I didn't care if I was going to be sore after this. I needed it so bad it hurt more emotionally than the physical discomfort ever could. Besides, it was all worth it when his humongous dick finally reached the magic spot inside me, and my half-way softened dick once again hardened to its full strength.

When my ass cheeks finally touched Joe hips, I let out a content, relieved sigh. Glancing down at Joe, I noticed he was in some other world already, eyes shut tight. I admired him, his god-like physique and the look of absolute bliss on his face. Then marveled at the realization that I had caused that look while I waited for my ass to get used to his size. When I was done, I slowly removed my hand from on top of his mouth, ready to shut him right up if he had any protests.

He didn't have any.

"Oh my fucking god you're tight," he mumbled instead, his voice all kinds of strained.

Smiling, I raised my hips carefully, before lowering myself back down. Joe let out another grunt of pleasure, shivering under me. His hands grabbed my waist—either to slow me down or urge me forward, I couldn't really tell—so I kept my pace as it was. Which was agonizingly slow—the only pace I could manage in this position.

Soon, I was rocking back and forth in a euphoric state when the discomfort finally dissolved completely, and all I could feel was immense pleasure.

Joe became impatient, raising his hips to meet me halfway every time I was coming back down. He also dug his hands tighter against my flesh, which told me he was about to lose it any time now.

And then he did.

"Chris," he breathed, looking like he was losing it. "Fuck, I need–"

To be honest, I wasn't quite attached to reality myself.

"I'm sorry," he continued then, stopped me, and rolled us around so abruptly I was forced to get back to the present from the paradise land of pleasure momentarily, to try and keep up with him.

That brief visit to sanity got cut off right away though, as Joe buried his cock back inside me balls deep with one fast and powerful thrust. The wave of pleasure washed over me so forcefully I was sure I was about to pass out any second. Our voices which we could no longer control even as little as we had been able a moment ago, combined in a lustful symphony that filled the whole room—I could only hope the others weren't nearby or at least so deeply immersed in their own activities that they couldn't hear us. Not that I cared much; it wasn't like we were the only ones that were desperate to engage in some adult exercises from time to time.

Joe crashed on top of me, his full weight pressing me against the mattress. I held him even closer, circling my hand on his back and combed through his black, velvety hair with the other. His chest and abdomen muscles rippled and flexed against my skin in a way that I could only describe as delicious and erotic when he picked up the pace.

Truth to be told, it didn't take much more than four, five thrusts from Joe to send me screaming over the edge. Spurting countless streaks of milky white substance on my abdomen, I could only hang on for dear life while Joe started working even more to reach his own undoing.

I was thoroughly spent when he finally pummeled his cock deep inside me with a long, whiny groan escaping his lips.

Later that night, we lay in the room's hot tub. I was so goddamn happy I could've burst if I wasn't so hurt by our earlier activities. Leaning my back against Joe's broad chest, slick but warm skin to skin, was everything to me.

Unfortunately, every good thing must come to an end sooner or later. Even though I was happy and content where I was—having a nice relaxing bath with the man I wanted to spend my future with—I couldn't help but start worrying about said future. I might have started the recovery process, but I wasn't anywhere near having fully healed the mental scars I had. Let alone the physical ones. The nightmares were still a common occurrence, and I hadn't gotten rid of the sudden anxiety attacks either.

Of course, Joe noticed. What wouldn't he notice? He still had the ability to read me like a newspaper after all.

"What's wrong?" he asked, brushing my back with the tips of his fingertips in a manner that seemed kind of absentminded but still a little concerned—there was some hesitance there.

"Nothing," I replied. I wasn't going to explain the whole thing to him. Instead, I picked out the first and foremost worry from the top of my head. "I'm just not really looking forward to tomorrow's flight."

"Well, let me distract you, hmm?" he said, lathering some soap on my back.

"Mmhm," I mumbled. "I think your wandering hands are already pretty distracting but go on."

"Well...shortie, what would you do if I confessed that I just might be in love with you?"

Man, I thought we were already past the cardiac arrest bullshit Joe had been pulling on me since day one. Yet here he was, involving saying our feelings out loud and shit. Fuck. As if I wasn't in deep enough shit with him already.

"Love is a strong word, you know..."

"I know," he said and turned me around.

Last second, I pulled a straight face and met his deep, golden brown eyes. They were mesmerizing, as always. I almost couldn't breathe, let alone reply, while he laid his hand on the side of my neck and brushed his thumb along my jawline.

"I'm still saying it," he continued and took a deep breath. "I love you."

It was like I got kicked in the nuts. All air left my lungs, my stomach clenched and in my head it felt like I was as high as a kite.

"O-okay," I said and hastily turned around, the water splashing over the edges of the tub and all.

"Okay?" Joe asked, letting out a laugh. "You know, this is the part where you'd normally—I don't know—run away or something."

Well, in his defense, I did consider it for a brief second. But this time, I only shrugged instead.

"Nah, I'm too tired to move, and it's warm and nice here."

"Good," Joe replied and pulled me tighter against his chest.

Rematch

I squinted my eyes at Joe, who was sitting next to me in his own first class seat, way too relaxed for the topic at hand. As it turned out, he hadn't even tried to look for a replacement for his services as my guard—the bastard had planned everything. Thus, now he was accompanying me to Busan after a few days of "relaxation"—one might also call it having sex non-stop at my home in the mountains back in Seoul.

But none of that was what bothered me this time.

"Let me get this straight, you've never even visited a Hanok before?!" I asked, still trying to untangle this new information in my head, but not being very successful.

"Nope. Why?" he replied, totally oblivious to the fact that we were, in fact, heading to one. A *very* over-the-top traditional one at that—my childhood home. Mom still strolled on the inside yard regularly on holidays, wearing a Hanbok just for the heck of it. There wasn't a rite or tradition existing that wasn't rigorously followed in that household. It was an oddity these days, but Mom enjoyed it, always had, even though she wasn't otherwise very conservative.

"Are you even Korean?" I mumbled under my breath, right when the plane's tires hit the ground when we landed at Gimhae International Airport, Busan.

"I don't get why this is a big deal," Joe replied as the plane halted at the end of the landing strip. "It's just a house, right?

With maybe an odd floor heating system and furniture that's too low for anyone's liking."

"You do realize the walls are made of *paper*, right?"

"So? We'll just have to be quiet," Joe replied with an uncharacteristic, quirky wink. He had incorporated those into his daily expressions ever since the fan-meeting day—let's call it the "Helsinki incident." Or jealousy incident, because I wasn't 100% convinced about Joe's reasoning that he wasn't jealous, rather than just pissed at me. I liked the outcome though, so I wasn't super mad.

"No, you don't understand," I said after shaking off the lustful thoughts that momentarily took over all of my brain capacity upon remembering the Helsinki incident. "Look. Within those walls, everything gay ceases to exist. Literally."

"So your family is a bunch of homophobes?" Joe asked, frowning. "I did not expect that."

"No, not exactly," I replied, already rubbing my temples. Fuck this was going to be hard to explain. "It's just a…taboo. In the literal sense. We don't talk about these things. Ever."

"Huh?"

"Nevermind," I sighed. "Just promise me no funny business while we're there. *Please*. Pretty please."

Joe shrugged, but a smirk still played on his lips.

Shaking my head, I decided to drop the subject, for now, as we were about to arrive at the terminal. I just…had to rely on his professionalism, I guess. If there was even an ounce of it left.

The plane was already rolling towards the terminal lazily but at the same time definitely. Airports were terrifying. My disguise had failed before. It was never fun. I found myself rubbing and toying with an age old scar on my earlobe—yeah, airports could be painful.

The safety belt sign turned off. A chorus of metal clicking against metal momentarily filled the whole space, as each and every passenger on the plane opened their belts roughly at the same time. People in the back started pushing each other in their desire to get out of the metal hellhole as fast as possible—I could hear the ruckus. Thankfully first class had a tad more...well, class.

The whole ordeal of grabbing our handheld luggage from the overhead cabinets and shoving a pair of huge sunglasses on my face—thankfully it was a sunny day so it wouldn't look so suspicious—and exiting the plane was over in minutes. I pulled my cap's visor lower and followed Joe closely through the terminal.

Our goal was to get to the first class luggage drop as fast and unnoticeably as possible. Even Joe hadn't put on his regular suit to prevent looking like an obvious bodyguard. He was sporting some regular jeans and a loose button-up. Here, he didn't need to wear the earpiece either—as this was a personal trip of mine, there wasn't really a need to communicate with other guards. There were none. The world tour was on a two week break before we'd head to tour Asia, much to my relief. I wasn't still quite over almost losing my hearing due to my little breakdown.

Thankfully the first class luggage claim worked incredibly fast and we were able to move along after barely 15 minutes of waiting around. At the same time we walked through the doors that would lead us to the common area of the airport, I started hunting down my phone in order to call our ride—Hana—and tell her that we had arrived.

Joe's thoughts were somewhat in line with mine. "Now, you mentioned something about a ride...?" He glanced around the lobby full of busy people. "Or should we rent a car?"

"No, just give me a minute. I'll call her–" I said. No need to start any kind of ruckus–

"CHRIS!" someone with an awfully familiar and cheery voice, yelled directly from behind me right at that second.

The said someone hopped to strangle me from behind. Giggling.

Sigh, so much for not causing any commotion

"Finally," Hana said, dropping down to give me a proper hug.

I turned around as well, with a full grin on my face. But before I could even say a word, Joe leapt into action. He grabbed Hana's shoulder and yanked her back from me with a strong, firm fist.

I tried to yell, "Joe! I wouldn't—" Too late.

Hana's self-defense instincts kicked in and she had Joe's arm in a tight lock in a nanosecond while his whole face wrinkled up in serious pain.

I couldn't help but facepalm.

The whole airport had turned their attention directly on us now. Even the regular guards were on standstill, ready to charge towards us any time, hands already gripping the tasers that hung on the belts of their uniforms.

"Seriously," I hissed. "Both of you, calm the fuck down." When nothing happened, I whisper-yelled a bit more loudly, "*Now!*"

"Who the fuck are you?" Joe and Hana demanded from each other in unison.

I sighed once again, watching the two idiots as if they had lost their collective minds. Which, to be fair, they had. Hana was still holding Joe's whole arm in such a tight hold it honestly looked like Joe had a hard time not screaming in pain. Joe was still struggling to escape the grip, but I knew from experience that it would be impossible. I guess it was good that Joe was tough.

"Here, let me introduce you to each other. Joe, meet Hana—the sister. Hana, meet Joe—*the boyfriend.*"

They only blinked a couple of times—again in unison—as they processed the information. Meanwhile I already managed to make myself antsy and start blabbering. "Though Joe's a little bit older than me. So maybe he's more like a manfriend. Wait, is that even a thing?"

No one answered.

I came to my own conclusions. "Maybe he's my sugar daddy."

They were still just…blinking. Speechless.

"Oh wait, I'm the one with the money, so that doesn't apply either…"

I could practically see the gears turn in their heads at the exact same time. And when the realization finally hit them, they let go of each other so fast it looked like they got zapped.

"Boyfriend is fine, Chris. Focus."

"Yeah…" I replied, scratching my neck. I guess my habit of saying more than I intended, and all the wrong things, hadn't changed even though I had gotten together with Joe. Oh well. Can't get everything right at once now can I?

An awkward silence ensued while Joe stared at me with that familiar sparkle in his eyes, and Hana looked back and forth between us. I didn't know what to say.

Eventually Hana cleared her throat and glanced at me. "I see your taste in men sucks."

"Hmph, unfortunately family can't be chosen, what a shame," Joe replied to her.

Yikes, well this turned awkward fast. Was it wrong for me to presume they'd get along right away? I mean I got along with both of them, so I had assumed…nevermind. Because the girls on our left started gasping and pointing at us. I knew that look. I needed to get out of there. Fast.

Hastily, I circled behind both of them and started pushing them towards the exit. "Right, now that we've established who everyone is, can we just *please* get the hell away from here?"

Thankfully Joe got the hint as soon as the girls started squealing. I could see they were about to start following us. I did not intend to deal with them.

"Quick, where's your car?" Joe asked Hana, who looked at the scene unfolding before her eyes right before we reached the exit.

"Wow, I guess Chris really is just that famous," she said, still baffled.

"Oh, just tell us where your car is!" I whisper-yelled. "And keep it *down*."

"Mom's Fiat is in the second line, around the back," she explained, finally being somewhat quieter.

But it was too late. One of the girls screamed, "It's Chris!" to the others and they all started approaching us.

"Fuck," Joe said, a wrinkle of worry now prominent between his eyebrows. "I suggest we make a dash for it."

"I guess we have to," I said, already tightening the straps of my backpack and gripping the bag in my hand more tightly.

"Seriously? What harm can a few teenagers cause?" Hana asked, chuckling. "It's not like they're gonna defeat us or anything."

"You'd be surprised," I replied under my breath. "Trust me, *run*. For your life," I continued and charged towards the back of the parking lot full-speed, Joe following right behind me.

Hana stayed put at first, too weirded out to move I suppose. Until the crowd thickened, and flashes filled the air.

"Shit," she yelled, and dashed to catch us.

She was also surprisingly fast and caught us around the half-way through the lot. "There," she yelled, grabbing her keys to unlock the doors.

It was a somewhat old, rusty and dark blue Fiat Punto. I didn't get Mom's affection towards the car. Numerous times, I had offered to buy her a new, safer thing. But she refused every time. Anyway, the car's—if someone would call the scrap metal deathtrap a car—indicators flashed in a sign that the doors unlocked, and we all took a last spurt to reach it before the crowd reached us. Hana opened the trunk, helped us toss the luggage there in a hurry before we all dived on our seats—Hana to the drivers' seat, Joe in the back and me to the front passenger seat.

"Come on. Come on," Hana mumbled, turning the key in the ignition, praying the car would start. And boy did it take a fucking while to roar—or more like cough—into life.

Thankfully Hana then proceeded to slam the gas pedal down in order for us to escape the scene.

Still, I couldn't properly breathe, let alone relax, until we were at least a mile away. Hana was speeding as fast as the shitty old car could go on the highway, Joe was looking kind of humongous in the smallest possible backseat, and I was just wondering how the hell the car managed to stay intact at this speed.

I missed my Lambo.

"I must say I have a thing for Italian vehicles…" I admitted. "…but I think I prefer slightly newer ones. And possibly slightly more expensive ones."

Hana let out a ringing laugh. "I can imagine. So what's your ride these days?"

"2019 Lamborghini Aventador."

"You have got to be shitting me!" Hana exclaimed. "Just how rich are you, exactly?"

"Er… I'm not actually sure. I think most of my money is tied into some real estate and some shares. Anyway, I have people who take care of that at my bank."

"Fuck. I have 20 000₩ to my name before the pay day arrives finally on Wednesday."

"For the hundredth time, I can send you money."

"Nah, I get by fine."

I turned my attention to Joe. He was sporting this kind of green-ish tint on his face, holding the handle as if his life depended on it.

"I thought cops aren't supposed to go over the speeding limits," he mumbled, to which Hana only laughed.

"Oh relax. If we get caught, I'ma just bribe the officers with a few donuts and tell some celebrity news…perks of being a cop you know," Hana explained and even dared to wink at Joe.

"But with this car…"

"Hey, don't trash the Punto!"

"Hmph," Joe mumbled and fell back into total silence.

Meanwhile Hana and I started chatting about random things. Weather (sunny and way too hot), what had happened during our flight (nothing much) and how our family was doing (fine).

At some point we exited the highway and started climbing up. Then we hit the familiar narrow paths that we'd have to drive through somewhat slowly, zigzagging between the countless non-matching neighborhoods of apartment blocks, all built in different decades.

In these parts of Busan, no-one really cared about the aesthetics—there were tangled electric chords hanging here and there, some about to fall on the road. The backs of the buildings were unkempt, cars were parked wherever they fit as the narrow roads took us higher and higher.

Even I started to feel somewhat nauseous in the small old car that had such shitty suspension that we all bounced into every direction upon encountering even the slightest bump on the road—and there were plenty of those on the forgotten asphalt.

Right there at the end of one slim and badly kept street, behind a tall apartment building from the 90's, were hidden two forgotten Hanoks on each side of the road. One was my childhood home, a familiar figure making my heart warm up a degree or two—Hana bought the other one when it went on sale after the old tenants died.

Behind the traditional houses spread out a natural park, with a small portion cleared out and made into a playground. So many memories—good and bad—hit me at once when I took in the familiar scenery. Nevertheless, it felt good to be *home*.

Hana parked the car onto her side of the road and hopped out. I followed soon after. Joe—still sporting the slight green tint on his face—practically staggered out of the car. I stretched and pulled out my bags from the trunk with Hana's assistance.

Then I breathed in deep. The fresh mountain air filled my lungs much like back at my hiding place back at Seoul, but this air was even more special—it had the slightest hint of an ocean scent to it.

"Thanks for the ride," I said to Hana, who was also stretching her stiffened back beside me.

"No problem. Just tell Mom I said hi and to save me a seat at dinner."

"Sure thing," I said and smiled, before turning to face Joe who looked like he was recovering from the wild car ride inside the way too small for him Fiat. "You okay?"

"Getting there," he mumbled, rubbing the back of his neck. "Just show me the way."

"And you promise to behave?"

"Yeah, yeah. Let's go."

Hana let out one more chuckle.

"Well, good luck," she said and waved.

And while she was walking—or maybe bouncing in a way too energetic manner—Joe looked after her, a weird look on his face.

"You do realize she's crazy, right?" he mumbled when he was convinced she was no longer in the hearing range, pointing his thumb towards Hana's front door.

"Yeah, ain't she just great?"

Joe narrowed his eyes at me. I narrowed my eyes at him.

"I'm not sure if I like her," he admitted. Eventually. After a minute's worth of staring contest.

"What's there to not like?"

"She drives too fast. And she nearly broke my arm."

I rolled my eyes. I got it. His precious manliness got hurt. "You're just pissed that she managed to surprise you at the airport, aren't you?"

"Hmph. No," he mumbled, not very convincingly.

"Yeah, right. Oh well, I'm sure you can take a rematch with her anytime."

Family

Hana kicked Joe's ass.

And I don't mean like, once. I mean multiple times, over the course of three days. I would've joined them but honestly I doubted me and Joe together could've beaten Hana.

It was fun to watch them, though. Besides, all the physical exercise kept Joe's...err...*desires* for other types of exercises in check. No need to wake Mom up in the middle of the night. Especially with anything *gay*.

Speaking of Mom, she appeared through the door to the patio right then.

"They're still at it?" she asked, glancing at the two on the other side of the yard while putting the tray she was carrying down on the table in front of me.

The delicious scent of Mom's famous hand-brewed coffee momentarily dazzled me, so I almost forgot to reply. God I had missed that smell. "Mhm," I mumbled, pouring Mom a cup before filling up my own. "I bet they're going to be 'at it' for a while still."

Mom sighed and sat down on my left. "It has been a while since the house has been so lively. I miss this."

I had a hard time not growling in frustration. "Please don't start with the guilt-tripping again. I promise I'll come by more often—"

"Hmph, you don't get to whine after getting *arrested*, young man."

"*Eomma,* I already told you, *he* tried to get us *killed*—you know what? Topic change. Where's everyone? Usually they at least come by once while I'm here. We're leaving tomorrow..."

"Well, Chae-won's pregnancy has been a little difficult, so she won't be coming over this time. Truth to be told, hearing her scream and throw up at the same time makes me feel nauseous as well. Not very good company for a dinner that's for sure."

Right. I had forgotten my closest cousin got herself knocked up. What was with everyone multiplying around me lately? First Mr. Won and now Chae-won. Ugh.

"And the twins?"

Mom glanced at her wristwatch. "*Chang-nam* and *Chang-woo* should be here any minute now—" she started, making sure I got that she still hated whenever anyone referred to my brothers as only *the twins*. Which was funny because she was perfectly fine with everyone calling me Chris. Thankfully she got cut off by the sound of a motorbike revving in the distance before she could get *really* into nagging. "Well, as you can hear, they're here," she added, rolling her eyes profusely while I chuckled.

Then she started rambling, "I'm glad the promise of getting my stir-fried bulgogi still has the ability to lure them in." Her voice got louder and louder as the sound of the motorbikes rose.

Still, she continued, "'Busy with college' they say, yet they've been at it for five years. I'm never gonna see them graduate..." until the noise drowned her voice completely.

Even Joe and Hana stopped their mock-fighting and turned to look at the road. Two flaming red Ducatis appeared from behind the corner and sped past us. Leaving behind a cloud of dust, I might add.

"Show-offs," I muttered.

Joe, however, whistled after them. His eyes gleamed as he dreamily watched in the distance where the bikes had disappeared behind the house—I could've sworn he even drooled a little bit.

Interesting.

I guess he was more a motorcycle kind of guy rather than a car kind of guy.

The tires screeched against the asphalt somewhere behind the house, most likely right in front of the garage we had built and hid there a couple of years ago. I grimaced internally—they'd better not total the bikes. Even though they were technically a gift, they cost me quite the amount of money.

"Those deathtraps are going to get them killed, I swear," Mom muttered, bringing me back to the present. "You never should've bought them those."

While I tried to mumble something to my defense, Mom had already turned towards the pair that had resumed fighting. "Hey, you two!" she yelled. "Dinner in an hour."

The fighting stopped at once. "Thanks, we'll be right there!" Hana and Joe shouted at the same time, hastily bowing slightly towards Mom before resuming fighting as soon as they were done with the formalities.

The really were way too similar, weren't they?

Hana had Joe in a chokehold when I walked over them. "Maybe you should really stop and head to the shower? Mom's bulgogi is great, after all."

"I know, and I would, but this dude just doesn't give up," Hana said at ease, barely even struggling to keep her hold on Joe. She made it look like it was easy.

I sighed. "Joe, I think we've established you're no match to Hana. And guess what: it's *okay*. I've never seen anyone beat her."

"Ugh, *fine,*" he wheezed, barely able to breathe. And he finally did tap Hana's arm, surrendering. I could see how much it ate his ego that he had to admit he had met his match. Good.

Hana let go of Joe at once, who dropped to his knees.

While Joe was busy catching up his breath, coughing and wheezing on the ground, Hana couldn't resist adding a little salt to the fresh wounds on Joe's ego.

"See, the thing is…you're just a boyfriend. I will be here forever," she said, giggling.

I shot her a warning glare. No need to announce the whole town I was gay. It was dangerous around here. Especially when Mom was around.

"Oh relax, Mom can't hear us this far away," she said and rolled her eyes, before turning back to mock Joe. "No wonder a few teenagers are an issue for you if you can't even defend yourself against one woman. I wonder how you're supposed to be anyone's guard, let alone Chris's—"

"Hana, enough."

"Fine," she chirped, again being overly energetic, before skipping across the yard. "I'm heading to shower. See ya at dinner!" she hollered and disappeared through the gate.

I watched her skip over the road to her house.

Meanwhile, Joe was still picking himself up from the ground. Unsuccessfully. I had this impulse, an almost insufferably strong urge to pat his head. Or maybe even scratch behind his ear a little and say: *there-there. It's gonna be alright.*

I did manage to hold down that urge. Instead, I crouched down beside him and helped him up. Like the good boyfriend I was supposed to be. No need to fuck this up so soon after we finally sorted thing out, somewhat. At least we were back to fucking, so that was a start.

"I can't believe I can't beat her," Joe mumbled.

I had to take a deep breath to not burst laughing my ass off. "You should believe it."

"She's not human."

Okay, this time I might've rolled my eyes discreetly. "Get over it."

Thankfully right then the hurricane—also known as the collective of my two brothers—came banging through the door.

"Your brothers?" Joe asked, pointing at the disaster twins who were now jogging across the yard towards us.

"Yeah," I managed to mumble before they slammed at me, yelling their greetings and whatnot over the top of each other.

Their energetic attack on me became rather impossible to bear in seconds. I had not gotten used to it lately—they must've inherited all the energy that had ever run in our bloodline. Plus, all my energy to play nice had already run out while trying not to be an ass to Joe.

I snapped.

Despite the fact that they were much taller than me—seriously, I got all the worst genes—I had them piled up on the ground in seconds, begging for mercy. One could've thought two rather big men could defend themselves, but they were too sloppy for any of that. And they always underestimated me. Granted, they had not been trained in martial arts ever, so I guess this was to be expected. They had chosen to go to the army only after graduating from college and now they were stalling. I wondered how much longer they were going to put the whole army thing off.

"I think I'm going to hit the shower," Joe mumbled, trying to hold down a laugh based on the look he had on his face as he gazed at me. "I'm certainly not needed here."

"Yeah, see you at dinner."

"Nice to meet you," one of the twins, possibly Chang-nam, tried to mumble at Joe but I tightened my chokehold on him right then. "Geez, relax man."

"Yeah, seriously Chris. My back hurts," the other one muttered. He laid face down while I had straddled him.

"You'll behave?"

"Yes, hyung."

I rarely got such an honorific as the youngest of GriD, so I grimaced before I muttered, "Good," and let them go.

Both of them stood up, brushing their clothes, and stretching. I yawned. They were no fun as they were way too easy to beat.

"Oof, bro's gotten feisty," Chang-woo said. "Anyway, who was that?"

"Who?" I played dumb.

"The tall dude with weird eyes. Was with you when we arrived."

"Oh. That's Joe, my bodyguard."

He scrunched his eyebrows. "What happened to Mr. Won?"

I shrugged. "Marriage. Reproduction."

"Oh, right."

"I dunno. I'm getting weird vibes from this Joe," Chang-woo continued, rubbing the back of his head.

"Yeah, I mean are you sure he's just a bodyguard and nothing more?" Chang-nam added, wiggling his eyebrows.

I gritted my teeth together and glanced around, making sure Mom was still not around.

"What did I mention about behaving?"

After dinner I was so done with socializing with my crazy-ass family I just *had* to get out. My brothers had decided to stay for the night, so now Mom was anxious to clean one of the guest rooms that hadn't been used in ages—probably not after we all moved out. I did not want to be in the way of that under any circumstances.

Looked like I wasn't the only one either; I spotted Joe sitting by the gate, toying with a pack of cigarettes. He was so deep in thought too that he didn't even notice me until I sat beside him and greeted him.

"Oh hey Chris," he said, flashing me a glimpse of that half-smile I had grown attached to. But it didn't quite reach his eyes like it used to, so I became worried fast.

"You smoke?" I asked. Maybe just to start a conversation.

"No, not anymore."

"Then what's with those?" I asked, pointing at the cigarettes.

"It's a habit I guess," he shrugged. "It's fun to toy with the idea of smoking from time to time. This pack is like two years old."

He opened the pack to show me it was still full.

"Then...what's wrong?" My shoulders stiffened.

He didn't reply. Only continued to toy with the cigarette pack as if I hadn't said anything.

I continued blabbering, "Don't tell me you're still upset about losing to Hana..."

He chuckled inwardly. "No. She's surprisingly quite fun to be around. When she's not pissing me off, that is."

And, although I was relieved I got some kind of reaction out of him, I pestered on, "Then what is it?"

Joe sighed and messed with the hair on his neck. "I don't know. It's just that...it's like I'm constantly waiting for something bad to happen. And it's been so weird and nice to be here, as if the world has stopped just to give us a couple of days of breather from everything..."

"...And now we're heading back to the circus that is my life tomorrow," I finished for him. "I get it."

Joe flashed me another smile, but we still fell silent. It wasn't like I hadn't thought the exact same way today even though I tried not to.

Fortunately, I knew how to cheer him—and myself—up.

"Come on, I'll show you something," I said, yanking the cigarette pack from him and stuffing it into my own pocket.

Joe looked at me like a lost puppy for a moment but stood up as I did. In total silence, I led him around the house, all the way to the back. On the way, I hit Mom up with a quick text explaining the twins could sleep in their room as Joe would be elsewhere with me for the night.

Eventually, we reached the shack-looking thing no-one paid attention to, which was actually a modern garage in disguise. Almost giddy of anticipation, I opened up the garage doors and switched the light on…

And then watched with ultimate satisfaction as Joe's eyes lit up at the sight.

Better Remember

It didn't take much—if any—persuasion to get Joe on board for a little evening drive with the two Ducatis before the sun set. Chang-nam's jacket fit him relatively well as did his helmet, so I didn't need to worry about that either. I had my own gear stored at the garage locker—it didn't take much time for us at all to get ready to go.

Soon, we were speeding up the snaking roads that climbed up the mountain rising directly from the ocean. The narrow, curvy paths were ideal for having some fun with the motorcycles, so even Joe let loose. Frankly, I had never seen him drive that fast. Well, we were definitely not counting the one time I had lost it with the Lambo and he had had to keep up.

The pure mountain air mixed with a bit of ocean and gasoline scents smelled like heaven to me as we climbed higher and higher on the mountain road we had picked. We took turns taking the lead, though Joe waited for me at crossroads every time, since he wasn't familiar with the area. The motor purred loudly under me, the sound reaching my ears even through the thick padding of the helmet. All the negative thoughts, which I had harbored for what felt like ages now, got caught up in the wind and flew away.

There, I finally made peace with myself.

I realized that everything which truly mattered in the end had not changed for the worse—rather than for the better. We were more successful than ever with GRiD, despite all the shit that had happened. My family seemed to be doing well. I had Joe right there by my side…Or, well, currently trying to get past me with his motorcycle.

I couldn't change the past, and that's a fact. But the future…it was all mine to take and mold to my personal preferences. It was time to start living it instead of floating around without taking any responsibility for the course I was headed.

Of course, when I finally reached that point on my short but effective self-reflection period, I had almost sped past our first destination—the familiar parking lot near a view deck I had visited so many times before alone. I did manage to pull the brake lever just in time though, to slow down to an almost full stop before steering to the side. I parked the bike, hopped off and yanked my helmet off.

Joe was much more aware than me it seemed, as he pulled aside much more gracefully. That or he had more experience with motorbikes than me. I realized I still didn't know a whole lot about the guy. Then again, I now hopefully had a lot of time to get to know him.

"This thing is awesome," Joe hollered over the wind that messed up his hair as soon as he pulled off the helmet.

"I know," I shouted back, smiling, while stuffing my gloves inside my helmet.

I hung it on the mirror at the same time Joe hung his and we walked on the cliff-edge together. Such a familiar thing for us to do, except now we were watching the sun set into the horizon of the ocean, instead of the cityscape of Seoul. We both leaned against the fence, silently admiring the view.

Meanwhile bearing my new resolution in mind, I was trying to figure out the way to voice my feelings to Joe. Except

I couldn't quite find the right words. Nothing seemed to fit. And I had never been very good with words. Thus, I kept my mouth shut and tried to enjoy the moment.

Joe was the first to interrupt the peace by taking my hand in his and interlocking our fingers. Shockingly, I let him. I even let him pull me towards him so we were mere inches apart and I was mesmerized once again by his weird brown eyes that had a golden halo around the pupils.

He lifted my chin with his other hand as he pulled me even closer, our lips now mere a couple of centimeters apart. Our breaths mixed with the wind in the frustrating space between us, and I wanted nothing more than to taste his lips. Everything I was about to say left my mind and I was left standing there, somewhat brain-dead.

"Thank you," he said, pulling me out of the fantasy.

I blinked. "For what?"

"For existing..."

"Ugh, cheesy."

"...and for the ride."

Evading his eyes, I tried to not blush and mumbled something about "Anytime," but I was cut off by his lips on mine.

A warm tingle settled on my stomach and my head felt light. My toes would've curled if they weren't trapped in the tight boots. I could've stayed there forever.

I wasn't the only one affected by the kiss either, which I realized once Joe placed my hand under his jacket over his heart. It was beating fast and wild, as if it wanted to reach out to me. I leaned against him, the warmth of his body enveloping me into a blissful sense of ultimate safety and warmth.

That's where I was meant to be.

Unfortunately, all moments come to an end sooner or later, and we parted our lips. I couldn't quite bear to stay too far away from him anymore, so I stayed in his embrace. Ugh, maybe I was turning to a cheesy ball of fluff myself.

"We should head back. It's getting dark and it's a long way back," Joe stated.

"Oh, we're not going back," I said, letting a smile dance on my lips. "We're going there," I continued, pointing up ahead where there stood a house strikingly similar to mine back at Seoul, only the huge windows were facing the ocean instead of my neighborhood and the city.

Joe squinted his eyes as he followed my line of sight with his. "What is that? Chris's hiding place 2.0?"

"No, that's actually the first one. And it's not mine. It's Dad's. Granted, I did mine to resemble that one, yes."

"Oh," Joe huffed. "I thought your Dad wasn't in the picture anymore?"

"He isn't. Not really. He and his partner moved to Thailand some years ago. They run a beach-bar these days."

"Partner?"

"Yeah, he's gay."

"Oh."

"Mhm."

"Well, that explains some things."

"Yeah, I don't want to come out to Mom before she has 100% gotten over the whole thing. I'm glad you behaved."

Joe glanced at me. "There's still surprisingly a lot I don't know about you."

"Ditto," I mumbled. "Well, we could do that thing where we state our name and tell a highly disturbing fact about ourselves right after. You know, Alcoholics Anonymous style. And it has to be something we don't know already."

Joe laughed. "So we start with 'my name is...' then add a bunch of uninteresting too-much-info -stories in between before ending it with 'and I'm an alcoholic?'"

"Yeah, sounds about right. You go first."

"Whoa, why do I have to go first? This was your idea!"

"Just do it," I said. "We ain't got the whole day."

He gave me a skeptical look, which I ignored the best I could. It took him a little while, but he eventually did mutter out a "Fine," while rolling his eyes. Then it took him another while of scrunching his eyebrows as he tried to come up with something to say.

"Okay I've got something. You ready?"

"Shoot," I stated, and leaned back. This was going to be interesting.

"My name is Lee Joo-hwan. After my mandatory military service here in Korea, I served an additional year in Lebanon as a peacekeeper—that's where I got the scar on my back. Long story short; we drove right into a road-side bomb. The rest of my unit died."

I couldn't help but look at him with my eyes wide and jaw hanging open—*whoa this shit got deep and dark real fast.*

"What? You specified that it was supposed to be a highly disturbing fact. I think that qualifies."

Yeah, but, *come on.* "Right. Continue."

Joe didn't, though. Because first, he made sure I was okay. Apparently. Because I had to force my face to a deadpan before he did continue.

"I still get haunted by that incident from time to time, but it gets better. Especially now that I have this insanely stubborn brat to keep up with, who I happen to love," he added with a wink. Maybe to lighten the mood. I guess it worked a little, though I was still slightly shaken.

"I guess the bottom line is…" he continued after a while of staring me in the eyes so lovingly and sweetly I would've blushed if I wasn't so busy trying to keep my face from not showing the shock. "…that I know what you're going through with those nightmares, anxiety attacks, taking scorching hot showers to get rid of the cold… Maybe even more than you think, because I've been there. But Chris, I promise it'll get better over time. And I'm here to get you through it. I'll always be here if you let me," he concluded, touching my cheek softly with the palm of his hand.

I leaned into his touch, closing my eyes for a brief moment. I had no idea that he had gone through all that. But I guess, in retrospect, it made so much more sense why he was able to read me like an open book, and knew how to distract me from my own demons so efficiently. Someone else might've been scared off upon hearing such a dark story so randomly, but I couldn't help but admire him for getting through that. I guess we were both broken, but hopefully we could heal together.

"Oh, and I'm an alcoholic..." Joe added with a chuckle, after dropping his hand to his lap. "Though that last part isn't entirely true—your game, your rules."

"Thank you for sharing that," I replied simply. What more could I have even said to that? That I'm sorry for his loss? Pssh, yeah nope. Even inside my own head, it sounded fake and unsolicited.

"You're welcome. Now, I believe it's your turn."

Fuck. I forgot that part.

"My name is Cho Chang-ho," I started after taking a deep breath. This was it. The part where I was supposed to come clean with my feelings towards him. But I had to hide it somewhere in order to be able to say it out loud. So I started from way back.

And I mean...*way* back.

"When I was sixteen, my dad suddenly came out as gay, as you now know, resulting in our parents' divorce. Obviously. It wasn't pretty, but it is the sole reason I joined GRiD when I got scouted—to get away from that mess."

"Yes, I think we established that a moment ago."

I nodded and took a quick glance at Joe, but as I found him deep in thought, listening to my story, I gained confidence to continue. "I left everything behind. Including Hana, which I've started to regret lately. A lot. But it wasn't until I figured out that our manager had been stealing our money, before I started to have real trust issues with people. You know, because no-one believed me since I was the youngest of us. It was eventually Tae who took me seriously enough, followed shortly by the rest of the guys. We got close trying to navigate this brutal music industry and started gaining fame.

"Then there was the incident where I got this," I said and tapped the already faint scar on my earlobe, which had developed after this crazy bitch yanked my earring right off. "That was the first time the security around us was tightened, and I got into martial arts. Which eventually led us to the night when everything went downhill, I lost my shit and beat the fuck out of Min-ho."

I took a deep breath, before continuing my little speech. "The bottom line is, that my life consists of these weirdly random happenings that I have had little to no control over. And while I would've gladly not experienced some of it, I'm glad it all led me to this obnoxious, flirty douche that is nine years my senior and almost as stubborn as me, who I just so happen to have accidentally fallen in love with."

Joe took a while to process the whole thing, but when he finally did catch the most important part, I couldn't have missed it even if I tried. I could see his whole face light up.

"Wait...does this mean...?" Joe asked, eyes as wide as mine had been a while ago during his speech, though probably for an entirely different reason.

"Yeah, I love you." I mumbled, for once not wanting to let anything unclear, despite how weird it was to say it out loud.

"Wow. I kinda thought you'd never say it back," Joe said, but I did hear a slight chuckle.

"Hmph. Well, don't expect it to be a frequent thing or anything. Better remember it for a while."

"Okay, but just promise me you won't run away from me again."

"I can't promise such things. You'll just have to catch me every time I do."

"Deal."

Epilogue: Fanservice

"...the scandal ridden idol group–" Click.
  "What a year it has been for GRiD–" Click.
  "...they SOLD OUT Jamsil Olympic Stadium–" Click.
  "Will they be able to live up to their legacy–?" Click.

The random news anchors' and tv hosts' voices echoed around meeting room 4 when Minjae flipped through the channels of the 65-inch TV on the back wall. Our final meeting before our biggest concert to date, was about to start. We were supposed to go over it one more time, it was to be taking place at the Seoul Olympic Stadium after all.

We were just waiting for Jiwoo to appear.

A flashback hit me, so strong it was almost like there was a glitch in the matrix.

And Do-hyun was about to throw the pen he was toying with towards Minjae in three...two...one.

"Minjae please, just turn it off," Do-huyn huffed as the pen went flying off his hand and hit Minjae in the shoulder.

Minjae rolled his eyes.

Yes, there was definitely a glitch in the matrix.

My chair knocked over as I stood up way too fast, which in turn earned me everyone's undivided attention. Ignoring the four pairs of eyes staring me, startled as fuck, I stepped in front of the tv and shut it down from the master switch. Taking a deep breath and rubbing my already aching temple, I turned back around to face the four staring men.

"Can we please not repeat last year?"

There was a nano-second of such a total silence, I could hear them not breathe. Then Minjae lost it first and started laughing hysterically. Soon, they all joined in and even I had to let out the smallest snicker.

When everyone called down a little, Joonie wiped the corners of his eyes before pulling a semi-serious face. "No, Chris is right. I'd like to keep my memories intact for the whole of the next 365 days, thank you very much. It's not fun being brain damaged."

"Yeah, and the next sextape I make with Minjae will definitely stay private," Do-hyun added, still chuckling.

"Shut up, Do," Minjae mumbled, throwing back the pen at Do-hyun who was now roaring with laughter once again.

"I don't know guys..." Tae started, leaning back on his chair with a full smirk on his face that showed a little dimple I had never seen before. Weird. "I kinda like things a little gay., he continued, sending a wink towards Joonie, who—believe it or not—slightly blushed.

Right then, Jiwoo waltzed through the door, graciously flipping her bright red, bouncy curls on the way through the door. Another fucking flashback.

"No, not you too!" I complained slamming the palm of my hand on my forehead. I had had it with this meeting and it hadn't even begun.

"Wait, what did I miss?" A weirded out Jiwoo asked while the rest of them couldn't stop laughing once again.

"Nothing," I mumbled towards Jiwoo through the chaos. "Absolutely nothing. Let's just get this meeting over and done with."

"You're right." She shook her head a little and strolled to the front before turning her attention to the rest of GRiD. "Hey! Shut up," she yelled, at once earning their attention.

They calmed down, somewhat. Thankfully so we wouldn't have to spend the whole evening at the HQ. I had much better things to do than sit here...like spending more time with Joe, hopefully doing activities that would make me forget tomorrow's gigantic concert for a couple of hours...

"Let's get this started," Jiwoo added, cutting my daydreams short. All while slamming a pile of paper in the middle of the table.

"What is that?" I asked, while the others still collected themselves and tried to focus.

"It's the draft of the next world tour that'll take place after the award season."

"Already?!"

"Yes," Jiwoo nodded enthusiastically. "But, I've learned from my mistakes, I'm having you review it before finalizing the plans. So, if you think it's too tight or anything, let me know."

"Huh," I muttered, picking up the list.

And for a moment I was sure I was dreaming because the venues listed were, well, famous. I read Wembley, Rose Bowl, Stade de France...the list went on.

"And you're sure we can fill these?"

"Oh absolutely. Besides, we can have less concerts if we make them big enough. Meaning—more resting time in between."

I handed the papers to Tae. Sounded good enough for me.

"Wait, what about the next album? Aren't we doing this in the wrong order? I'm not sure if I can pull off an entire album in three months," Do-hyun interrupted.

"Nah, Joonie and I have been working on a little something-something. I think you could have less of a workload with this one," Tae explained absentmindedly as he was still skimming through the papers.

"Oh, then I'm fine. And I have a couple of songs drafted as well, just not too many," Do-hyun added. "Anyone else have anything?"

"I–uh, I could try with a couple of ideas I have. Err, if you don't mind," I said, scratching the back of my head. I wasn't a really great composer or anything, but the couple of songs I did last time didn't have too bad of a reception.

"Of course," Do-huyn said, nodding. "The less I have to muster up, the better."

"Is there a theme of some sort?" asked Minjae.

"Well, we were toying with acceptance…or self-empowerment. That sort of thing. Less with anything to do with leaving things to fate, and more of taking the charge of one's own life," Joonie said, snatching the papers from Tae.

I could work with that, I thought, as Minjae nodded.

"Wait, wasn't this meeting supposed to be about tomorrow's concert?" Do-hyun asked.

"Nah, I think you've got this," Jiwoo said, leaning back on her chair and throwing her feet on the desk. The longest stiletto heels I had ever seen, thumped against the wooden surface. "Let's just chill."

Tae stood up and buttoned his suit jacket. "Well, in that case, I have some news; I have finally found us a new dorm. It's perfect."

Minjae and I groaned at the same time.

Joonie threw the papers towards Do-hyun, suddenly sulking. "Oh please, you've told us the same thing the last ten times you've 'found the perfect dorm.'"

"Yeah, can't we just give up? I kinda like our new place," Do-hyun said, glancing at Minjae so sweetly even I got a toothache.

But Tae didn't give up. "I know but hear me out. We can keep the new places."

"Then what's the point?" I asked.

"Well, apart from making things a million times easier logistically speaking, we'd be together. Like we've been from day one. Plus, I guarantee this place is awesome. I'm talking about a closed community with security gates, private house at the very back of the area, the forest starting right from our backyard..."

"Ugh, fine, show it then," Minjae said.

At once Tae connected his laptop with the tv and started playing a video that had been sent to his email. Apparently it was a video tour in some kind of a mansion? A fancy, modern mansion. With a heated pool and all. And there was a lot of space, that's for sure.

I knew the exact moment Joonie was sold on the idea: when the video showed a humongous walk-in closet at one of the suites. Possibly the master suite, even. Minjae practically squealed when the video zoomed in on a giant gym at the basement floor—he definitely was thinking about turning it into a dancing studio. Do-hyun was basically in on it as soon as Minjae was.

Me, however...I wasn't convinced. It was way too big for us, too fancy. Most importantly, I couldn't see myself living in it. Not in a million years.

"What do you think?" Tae asked right after the video ended.

"Can I watch it again?"

"Sure, but we can go see it live next week as well."

"Hmph," I muttered, and Tae handed me the laptop.

Meanwhile as the rest of them started blabbering about the possibilities, I played the video again a couple of times. Still, the marble countertops at the kitchen, the humongous living area, the fully equipped gym and the bedrooms...none of it seemed right. I guess the whole place lacked the nature factor I was so fond of these days.

Until I spotted a building beside the gigantic, over the top pool. I paused the video and turned the screen towards Tae. "What's that?"

"Oh, that's the pool house. There's a guest room inside, with an en-suite bathroom and a small closet."

Perfect. "I want that."

"The tiny pool house?" he asked, blinking.

"Yeah."

"Well, suit yourself. So you're in?"

"I guess. I need to see it in person first, though."

I've never heard Tae sigh so deeply relieved. "Finally. I'll arrange the viewing as soon as possible then."

I nodded, and everyone started to gather their things. I did too. The new dorm could wait until next week—all that mattered right now was the fact I was going to spend the evening with Joe. And I couldn't wait.

"Oh, I almost forgot!" Jiwoo hollered abruptly when we were almost out the door already.

Joonie halted at the threshold, rolling his eyes at her. "What more can there possibly be?"

"About tomorrow night…" she started, stalling.

"Yes?" Minjae and I asked at the same time.

Her eyes sparkled as she glanced at each of us once. A full smile lighting her face up as she toyed with one of the curls that had escaped her loose hairdo.

"Just please, no more fanservice. I think we've had enough of that for a while."

The End

Acknowledgements

When I first started writing the first book in Minjae's point of view, I never thought it would turn into a trilogy basically on its own. Let alone that I was ever going to publish it. But here we are, and the journey has been incredible.

Therefore, I'd like to offer special thanks to my Tapas readers and my TikTok followers, for making all this possible in the first place. Without you, I wouldn't have had the opportunity or the resources to do this.

Also, extra special thanks for my online writing community—The Dumpster—for being a shoulder to cry on and for giving me all the encouragement in the world.

I hope to see you all on my next projects as well, so please check out my website for the latest news:

www.namiartopit.com

As always, enjoy…
xoxo Nami

Made in the USA
Las Vegas, NV
18 September 2022